THE GIRL IN THE BASEMENT

EOIN DEMPSEY

Storm
PUBLISHING

Ebook ISBN: 978-1-80508-689-5
Paperback ISBN: 978-1-80508-691-8

Cover design: Sara Simpson
Cover images: Shutterstock

Published by Storm Publishing.
For further information, visit:
www.stormpublishing.co

ALSO BY EOIN DEMPSEY

The Monika Ritter Series

The German Girl

The Wounded and the Lost

The Maureen Ritter Series

The American Girl

The Forger

The Secret Soldier

The Lion's Den Series

The Lion's Den

A New Dawn

The Golden Age

The Grand Illusion

The Coming Storm

The Reckoning

The Powerscourt Series

The Saint of Impossible Causes

The Garden of Ireland

White Rose, Black Forest

The Longest Echo

Finding Rebecca

The Hidden Soldier

Toward the Midnight Sun

The Bogside Boys

PROLOGUE

It's not easy opening my eyes when I'm afraid of what they'll reveal. My head is spinning, but I know I'm not drunk. This is something else—something much worse. I work up the courage to lift my eyelids, and my heart turns to ice as terror floods every cell in my body. I reach for my phone, but it's not there. I check the other pockets of my jeans, but it's gone. My money and whatever else I had are missing too. Panic spreads through me like wildfire. Fear has never been something real in my life. Until now, it was an abstract emotion, something to control while watching some stupid movie with my friends or before a test in school, but now it's all I feel. I'm paralyzed by it as I look around the dingy room, turning my head the best I can manage.

I've never been here before. It's dark, and I'm alone. It seems to be a basement of some kind—unfinished with a concrete floor. I'm in the corner on a tatty old rug with a pillow and a bottle of water beside me. I screw off the cap and drink some. The room is lined with metal shelving units, but they're mostly empty except for a few cardboard boxes. I don't know whether to call out or not because I have no idea why I'm here. The last thing I remember is leaving the party, running away from the cops, and then feeling something sinister overcome me. I have some recollection of wooziness like I'd never experienced overwhelming my senses, and then the next thing was waking up in here.

I raise myself to my feet and call out, but it comes as a whisper so low that I barely hear it myself. My voice seems to have left me, and I'm too scared to try it again. I stay quiet as I look around. It must still be night outside as the three tiny windows at the top of the wall facing me are almost opaque. I stumble over to one, but it's too high to look out. It's about two feet by one and must be eight feet off the ground. I think to look around for something to stand on but realize what I should really be trying to find is the door. I have to get out of here. This must be some kind of joke. If it is, I'm not laughing. Maybe someone stuck me down here to make sure their parents or the cops didn't find me after I passed out. I don't remember drinking *that* much, and I've never reacted to alcohol like this before, but whatever. The important thing is getting out of here.

I cross the almost empty space. It's hard to see what's on the ground in front of me, and I bump into a few cardboard boxes. I'm trying to keep calm, breathing in and out. I spot the door, a slightly darker shade of gray than the walls around it. I leap toward the door handle and turn it. It doesn't open. It's locked. Black terror infests my body like a swarm of locusts. Now it's time to use my voice, and I bang on the door, screaming for someone to open it. Part of me is embarrassed because this is probably a joke, but it's gone too far. I shout for a minute or more, all the time expecting the door to swing open and reveal a sheepish smile on one of my friends' faces while they explain that this all just got out of hand. But no one comes. I bang and smash on the door until my hands ache but to no avail. I spend the next few minutes shouting, calling out the names of anyone I think might be in on this, but still nothing. An eerie silence fills the air every time I stop.

"Get it together, Ellie," I say out loud. "This is up to you."

My eyes have adjusted to the darkness in here, and there's just enough silver light to make out the interior of the basement. I look around for something heavy to try to break the windows, a hammer or something, but after searching the shelves and boxes, I don't find anything that would fit the bill. The boxes are all full of old books and magazines. Most are from the 1960s and 70s, long before I was born.

Whoever put me down here must have fallen asleep themselves—otherwise they would have let me out by now. One of my friends has to be behind this. When I get a hold of whoever did this, I'm going to kill them, and if it's Josh, we're finished. Even if this is some kind of joke or the door got locked by accident, I'll never forgive him for this. But then I think, if this is a joke, why would they take my phone and empty my pockets? Is that part of the act too?

I pick up a book from one of the boxes and almost laugh when I notice it's *The Count of Monte Cristo*. I hurl it across the empty space. It hits one of the metal shelves and comes down with a thud on the rug I woke up on.

I don't wear a watch, and I have no idea what time it is without my phone. All I know is that it's night. I walk over to the windows again and try to peek up past the shade. It's made of hard, translucent plastic and seems to be attached to the house on the outside and leaning over the window at an angle. It seems to be in place to keep rain out of the bucket windows. I set up a pile of books to climb onto and can see some bushes outside.

I climb off the books and return to the rug. Thoughts of retribution infect my mind like a virus. If this is a joke, it's an illegal one. People go to jail for this. I imagine the door to the basement opening and seeing Josh and my other friends grinning as they stand there. I also picture myself wiping those smiles off their faces.

I walk over to the door again, taking a deep breath, trying to sound as calm as possible. It's not easy. A horrible mix of anger and fear is coursing through me. My heart is racing at a thousand miles per hour. I try to hide every emotion as I knock on the door and call out.

"Hello? Anyone? The joke's over. Enough's enough. Let me out of here now and I won't tell the cops."

No answer. Just silence. I notice a gap between the bottom of the thick wooden door and the concrete floor beneath. It's probably about three inches high. I get down onto my hands and knees and try to peer through. I see nothing but more black. The lack of breeze through the gap tells me it's not a door to the outside. It's probably stairs up to the main house.

I'm trying to stoke the anger within me. It helps distract from the paralyzing fear. I bang on the door again. I spend what must be twenty minutes calling out, but the only sound I hear is that of my own voice.

The palms of my hands are aching and my voice is hoarse. I retreat to the rug in the corner. No one's coming for me tonight. It's time to admit that. It's a horrible situation, but it's time I made the best of it. At least I have a pillow. I lie down on the rug and think about my family. My parents are probably out of their minds with worry. My only hope is that they're sleeping through the night and haven't noticed I'm not home. But Mom rarely sleeps until I'm back. It's a good bet she's at the police station or calling everyone I know.

I wish I was with her and Dad. I'd even suffer my two little brothers to be out of here right now. It's hard not to cry. I'm so scared. I know it's not doing me any good, but I can't help it. I drink some more water and close my eyes.

I wake up with a jolt. I know it's morning as dull light is leaking through the windows. I hear something—the door! I leap up and see it closing.

"Hey!" I scream. "I'm in here. I was asleep on the rug."

The door clicks shut. I throw myself at the handle, but it's too late. It's locked again. Whoever has the key is behind the door.

"Let me out! This isn't funny. Who are you?"

Silence. My breath stops when I see the tray the person has left for me. A kid's-size carton of orange juice and two slices of buttered wheat toast sit on it. I kick the door and pound on it with both fists but hear nothing from the other side. The terror is like nothing I've ever known.

"Please talk to me!" I beg. "Please!"

I hear the sound of scratching behind the door, and something appears underneath—a small chalkboard with some words written on it:

Get used to being here.

I can hardly hear the footsteps retreating upstairs over the sound of my own screams.

ONE

SIX MONTHS EARLIER

Ellie Welsh was awake before her alarm sounded. The sun was up and streaming in through the chink in the curtains above her bed, turning dust particles into gold nuggets floating through the air. She should have been tired. Her family had only arrived back from the beach the night before. Her mother had insisted on staying all day to beat the Labor Day traffic, and she'd been right—few cars had remained on the road when they'd left at eight o'clock, but it meant they hadn't reached home until almost ten. Ellie's father had protested the plan at first but knew which battles to choose after twenty years of marriage. The shore was sacred ground to his wife, and the end of summer was like a death to her. She did the same thing each year, extracting every last second on the beach before returning to their everyday lives. Ellie's mom was a teacher and had been back at work for meetings the week before, but they had all streamed down to the shore with the rest of the hordes afterward. It had been a wonderful summer, but Ellie was ready for school now. She hadn't seen most of her friends in months.

It was a bright, sunny September morning, and Ellie climbed out of bed as she heard her mother rousing her brothers next door. They were starting high school today. She shook her head at the thought of seeing them in the hallways. Her mother had made her promise to show them around and to look out for them, but they didn't need her. They never had. She could still just about remember a time before they had arrived, but only in fleeting glimpses. She recalled how her parents' dedication to her had been diluted after they were born as they'd had two babies to deal with. Two sick babies, who had been in the intensive care unit for weeks. Her mother always said that was when Ellie's independent streak had begun. She'd had little other choice. Once the boys had got out of hospital, their family changed even more. Her mother obsessed over their health even though they were completely fine. After that, Ellie got used to sharing their attention and looking after herself.

The digital clock beside her bed told her it was six forty-five. Ellie often wished school didn't start quite so early, and by the sounds of things, her mother was having a hard time getting her brothers up. Her outfit for her first day of senior year was on the chair, where she'd laid it the night before. She'd selected her favorite pair of jeans and a new crop top she'd bought with money from her job waiting tables this summer. She held the top in front of herself in the mirror, nodded, and walked into her en suite bathroom. The new phone she'd also bought herself buzzed on her nightstand, and Ellie dashed out to check it, her toothbrush hanging out of her mouth. It was her friend Lizzy.

Excited for the first day?

Ellie texted back in seconds.

Of course! Can't wait to see you!

With little time to waste now, Ellie hurried into the shower.

She wanted a little extra time to get ready today. Another text from Lizzy was waiting when she emerged in her towel.

> I hear there's a pep rally today. It should be fun.

> On the first day? It must be a special occasion.
> Gotta get ready, see you soon!

She applied a little makeup, just a touch of eyeliner and some lip gloss. The noise of her brothers play-fighting and chasing each other outside her room was intensifying, and she was glad to cover it with the sound of her hairdryer. A few minutes later, she took one last look in the mirror and gave her outfit a thumbs-up before walking downstairs for breakfast. Her father was at the table reading the newspaper and looked up with a smile as she arrived.

"What kind of a compliment can I give you?" he said smiling. "You look adorable? Cool? Great?"

"Any or all of the above are more than acceptable," Ellie said breezily. She poured herself a bowl of cereal, sat down opposite him, and started eating.

"Here we go," he said as the noise from above rolled down the stairs.

Tyler was the first to appear, with James following him. Ellie's mom always insisted they dress in different clothes, but they wanted to do things their own way, and that was what the fight had been about this morning. She hadn't been around to supervise—she'd left for work right after getting them up. She'd started out as a middle school English teacher but had progressed to special education, working exclusively with autistic kids for two years now. It wasn't easy, and sometimes she came home frazzled, but they were all proud of the work she did.

"It's our first day of high school," Tyler whined. "Is it so wrong to want to wear the same thing as my brother?"

James didn't speak as he sat down at the kitchen table, but was clearly of the same mind as his twin brother. Ellie often wondered if all identical twins were this weird.

"Isn't looking exactly alike enough for you?" her father asked as he poured bowls of Cap'n Crunch for them.

Neither answered, instead keeping their eyes on the cereal in front of them as they shoveled it into their mouths.

"Slow down, guys," Ellie's dad said. "It's not a race."

"It's always a race when he's around," James said, and punched his brother in the shoulder. Tyler reacted by doing the same, and Ellie's dad reached in to break them up before sitting down with them.

"How are you feeling about the dreaded first day?" he asked Ellie.

"Fine. Looking forward to school. There's a pep rally this afternoon too."

"Maybe the boys could sit with you during it, and you could introduce them around a little?"

"That'd be a hard no," Ellie groaned. "They have friends, and each other."

"Yeah, Dad, we don't want to sit with her," Tyler stated, and finished wolfing down his cereal.

Their father threw his hands up in faux histrionics. "Just a thought."

Ellie finished up and walked over to get her book bag, which she'd packed the night before, and slipped it onto her back. Although she was ready in seconds, Ellie waited for her brothers as they packed their bags.

Her father gave her a big hug. "Good luck today, you'll be great." He then turned to the boys to give them both a squeeze.

"I can't believe my brothers are going to be freshmen in my school," she said through gritted teeth.

He walked them to the door and Ellie turned to wave good-bye. Her brothers didn't bother as they saw one of their friends up the street and ran off with him instead. That was just fine with Ellie. She enjoyed her morning stroll to school, except in winter, on the days when icy winds cut through her and she had to struggle through the snow.

She felt a flutter of excitement as Lower Merion High School came into view. The last she saw of her brothers was them running inside with their friend. They never stopped or turned around to say goodbye. Lizzy, Maddie, Giselle, and Hope were standing outside chatting, and each greeted her with a hug. The pep rally on the first day was the talk of the school.

"I heard it's for the football team," Hope said as they walked inside. She'd been dating one of the boys on the team for a while and got all the inside knowledge from him. "It's all very hush-hush, but Ray told me they're revealing a new player who's going to take us all the way to the state championship."

Ellie wasn't a big football fan, but her school had invested a lot in the program in the last few years. And it was working. They'd gone from massive underdogs to one of the best teams in eastern Pennsylvania since she'd been there. The games were exciting, and they'd gotten to the last stages of the state championship last year before falling to one of the powerhouses from western Pennsylvania.

The long banners lining the hallways seemed to back up Hope's inside scoop. It seemed the place had gone football crazy even though the season hadn't even started yet.

"How's Nate?" Lizzy asked as they went to their new lockers. The seniors had their own lounge area, with ping-pong tables and even televisions mounted on the wall. It was somewhere Ellie had looked in on in envy for years.

She examined the lock, struggling with the combination she'd received, before turning to her friend. Nate was the boy she'd been seeing at the beach this summer. He was a lifeguard. The other girls had been jealous until they'd spoken to him and realized his personality didn't match his tan or toned abs. Ellie had dropped him after a few weeks.

"He's back in Baltimore. He was nice but more of a summer thing."

"Are you ever going to like a guy for more than two weeks at a time?"

"I was seeing Nate for almost three weeks, I'll have you know."

Lizzy smiled but kept staring at her, waiting for an answer.

"I don't know," Ellie finally said. "Not all of us want to settle down and have babies like you!"

She hoped her friend understood she was joking and was relieved when she smiled. Lizzy and her boyfriend, Tom, had been together for three years.

"I look forward to meeting the boy who could tie you down," her friend joked.

"What can I say? I get bored easily."

Her locker opened with a clunk.

A few minutes later, Ellie walked into psychology class—one of her electives that semester. It was something that had always fascinated her.

Mr. Wells was sitting at his desk and greeted her with a smile. "Back for more, eh, Miss Welsh?"

"Couldn't keep me away!" she retorted.

"We gotta keep those standards up. Don't rest on last year's achievements."

"Are you kidding me? I'm going to leave the rest of the class in the dust. When have you ever known me not to get an A?"

"Not yet, but don't get cocky, Ellie," the teacher shot back.

"Never, Mr. Wells."

She took her seat next to Claire and Ari and greeted them both as the rest of the students filed in. It felt like a reunion.

· · ·

The end of the day arrived, and the pep rally she and her
friends had been talking about finally came. The gym was
already crowded as Ellie walked in with the rest of the seniors.
She passed by the freshmen, looking for her brothers. They
jumped up as they saw her, waving as if their lives depended on
it. Surprised by how friendly they were being, Ellie waved back
with a smile before taking her seat between Lizzy and Hope,
with Maddie on the other side.

The gym was draped with flags, and someone had dressed
as a bulldog—the school mascot— to pump up the crowd. The
noise inside the gym was deafening but came to a sudden end as
the principal picked up the microphone on the stand set up in
the middle of the floor. He welcomed everyone back for the
school year before handing over to the coach of the football
team, who was met with a similar level of respect. He spoke
about the football program for a few minutes, and Ellie's mind
wandered as she scanned the crowd for kids she hadn't seen yet.

The coach introduced the football team, and they ran out to
the loudest cheers of the day. But the coach hushed the crowd
once more for the big announcement. "As you know," he said,
"we take pride in our football program, but this summer we
were lucky enough to welcome an exceptional talent to our
district. It's a great pleasure to introduce, formerly of the Media
School District, the new starting quarterback for your Lower
Merion Aces, Josh Thomas!"

Realization hit her like a fist and her blood went cold. She
stood up with everyone else as a single figure emerged through
the door and walked into the gymnasium. He wore a Lower
Merion hat and took it off to wave to the crowd. The first thing
that struck Ellie about him was how tall he was. He must have
been well over six feet, and as he came closer and looked up at
the stands, she saw his face. He had deep brown eyes, high
cheekbones, and a strong jawline. He was undeniably
handsome.

"He's gorgeous," Lizzy gushed.

"He was the one—" Maddie started.

"Whose girlfriend was murdered a few months ago," Ellie interjected grimly.

"It feels weird to cheer for him," Hope murmured, discomfort crossing her face.

"Innocent until proven guilty, girls," Maddie said above the din. "The cops cleared him."

Some of the younger kids in the crowd didn't know who he was, but Rachel Kubick's murder in Media Township was all anyone had talked about six months earlier. The killer had never been caught, but the person so many people had assumed was guilty was now their star quarterback. Ellie was sitting in the third row, only about thirty feet from where Josh was standing. The coach handed him the microphone, but he only said two words before handing it back: "Thank you."

He stood alone as the rest of the team waved to their friends. And maybe Ellie was going crazy, but she could have sworn he stopped scanning the crowd when he saw her. A shiver ran down her spine as they locked eyes, and he stood there staring at her until the rest of his team obscured him from view.

TWO

Football mania gripped the school. Posters were put up in the hallways, with the biggest reserved for the new quarterback, Josh Thomas. An image of him dressed in his football uniform was erected over the main entrance to the school so anyone who walked in could see who the place belonged to now. Ellie and her friends laughed about the new messiah who would bring their school to the promised land. It was all so ridiculous. Rumors spread like wildfire through a wheat field. Most were to do with his late girlfriend. Whoever hadn't been aware of her story during the pep rally knew all about it now. A particularly vicious piece of slander saying he'd murdered Rachel Kubick because she'd been cheating on him circulated the school. Some said he'd come here as a favor to the local police chief who'd kept him out of jail. But kids always talked, and Ellie knew better than to believe everything she heard.

Ellie remembered his eyes as she'd stared at him during the pep rally. He'd seemed unprepared for all the uproar attached to his coming here. She wondered what this boy must be thinking and if he was prepared for the pressure that all this would entail. The kids who knew football said he was the best

young quarterback in the state and that fame and a future in the
NFL awaited. The first game of the season was approaching
that weekend, and everyone was already making plans to be
there. Some of the crueler jokes making the rounds focused on
Josh killing the opposition like he'd done to his girlfriend. It was
becoming more apparent why he'd moved school districts, but it
seemed he hadn't gone far enough. The truth was there was
probably nowhere in the country he could have gone to avoid
the rumors, and moving abroad would have meant giving up his
future as a football player. Ellie could see why his parents had
chosen to move somewhere not too far away and ride out the
chatter surrounding their son.

Ellie and her friends were hanging out near their lockers just
after lunch on the second day of school. They, like everyone
else, were talking about Josh Thomas. Ellie stayed quiet for
much of the conversation.

"I don't think it's right," Giselle said in a self-righteous tone.
"The entire school is dedicated to a murderer. The poster of
him over the main door?"

"He wasn't convicted," Maddie insisted.

"Tell that to the girl's parents. What was her name?"

"Rachel Kubick," Ellie offered.

"It's disgusting," Giselle hissed. "Fawning over a killer just
because he's good at football?"

Ellie stood back and watched as her friends argued. She was
glad when the bell rang and they had to go to class. Slinging her
book bag over her right shoulder, she said goodbye to the girls
and walked down the hallway toward her English class. She
knew most of the kids already and said hello to a few before
taking a desk toward the back of the room. The teacher, Mr.
Barnes, came in and was about to begin when Josh Thomas
appeared at the door.

"Is this honors English?" he asked.

Mr. Barnes nodded and gestured for him to take a seat. The only one left was at the back beside Ellie. He walked between the desks, whispers and sideways glances following him all the way. Ellie kept her eyes down as he took the seat next to her. She didn't want to be seen staring at him like everyone else.

Ellie loved English and relished the prospect of studying *Macbeth* that semester. Mr. Barnes, with his thinning hair and glasses, played the part of English teacher well, and he had a similar passion for the subject. The class sat rapt as he spoke about what actors referred to as "the Scottish play."

Halfway through the class, Ellie heard a whisper and turned to find Josh was mouthing something to her, holding out a broken pencil.

"Do you have a spare pencil? I forgot mine," he whispered. "Rookie mistake," he added with a smile.

Momentarily frozen, Ellie nodded and reached into her bag. "Here you go," was the best she could manage.

"Thank you," he said and turned to face the front of the room again.

Ellie tried to return her focus to the lesson and had just about achieved her goal when he whispered again, "Hey, what's your name?"

She whirled her head around. "Ellie Welsh."

"Nice to meet you, Ellie Welsh. I'm Josh—"

"I know who you are," she cut in and immediately regretted it.

"I think I saw you in the crowd at the pep rally yesterday."

Ellie felt her heart quicken. "I was there... along with everyone else," she blurted.

He ran his fingers through his hair. "That was crazy. I had no idea they were doing that until the day before. I didn't know what to say when Coach gave me the mic. I made an idiot out of myself."

Surprised to hear him say that, Ellie tried to figure out if he was being sincere or not. He seemed candid. Perhaps he didn't want any of the attention being heaped upon him for being the savior of the football team. The other attention that came with the death of his girlfriend he had little choice about.

"It must have been hard. You did great," she said.

Ellie couldn't help but think about what Giselle had said just before class at their lockers. Was she staring into the eyes of a killer?

"You're a good liar, but thanks," he said with a crooked smile.

He looked up at the teacher for a few seconds before returning his eyes to her. It was hard to deny her attraction to this boy, no matter how she tried to fight it.

"I should concentrate on what Mr. Barnes is saying," she said, feeling herself blush.

"Of course, but it was nice to meet you, Ellie."

"Likewise," she replied.

She didn't say anything other than a goodbye to him at the end of class and hustled back to the lockers to tell the girls what had happened.

"You talked to him? Are you insane?" Hope said with concern etched all over her pretty face.

"He's not about to attack her in class!" Lizzy said.

"Who says he ever attacked anyone?" Ellie countered. "What happened to Rachel Kubick was a tragedy, but he was cleared of all charges. Quickly. That's why a lot of the kids in school had never heard of him when he walked into the pep rally yesterday. I recognized him because..."

She trailed off, but Lizzy filled in for her. "Because you paid attention to the case."

"Some people say Rachel's murder was the work of a serial killer," Giselle said. The others looked at her with daggers in their eyes. "I mean, if it wasn't the boyfriend, it could have been, right? It's always the boyfriend or the husband on true crime shows, isn't it?"

"Yeah," Maddie said. "It seems like the worst thing a girl can do is find a boyfriend."

"Who said it was a serial killer?" Hope asked. She looked terrified.

Giselle shrugged. "Kids in school, who do you think? Whispers in the schoolyard—the reason they spread like wildfire is there's always a grain of truth in them, then they spiral out of control."

"Tom's never tried to kill me once," Lizzy said, referring to her boyfriend of three years with a sly smile.

"You got yourself a keeper then," Maddie said.

"Maybe Josh deserves a chance," Ellie said. "He seems like a nice guy."

"That's what all the wives and girlfriends say on those shows," Giselle mused.

"What? After they're dead?" Lizzy said pointedly.

"You know what I mean!"

Ellie left her friends more confused than ever about the boy who'd sat beside her in class.

Ellie waited for her brothers after school. They were excited about the football team and wanted to walk past the practice field on the way home. Ellie thought to protest at first but then decided not to. Josh was a potential hero for the school. If the police had found him innocent of Rachel Kubick's murder, perhaps everyone else should treat him like he was.

Tyler and James ran ahead of her to the swelling crowd watching the practice. Ellie had never seen anyone watching it before, but the throng of kids and teachers standing on the sideline must have numbered a hundred or more. And they were all there to see one person.

Ellie caught up with the twins near the fifty-yard line. Mr. Barnes, her English teacher, was standing there too, and he smiled as Josh called out instructions to his teammates.

"I saw videos of this kid over the summer," Mr. Barnes told her. "He's a phenomenon."

"I spoke to him today. He seems cool."

"Smart too. Just about a straight-A student. I feel bad for everything he's been through."

The center snapped the ball back through his legs, and Josh stepped back, scanning for receivers. He dodged a tackle and rolled to the outside before launching a pass through the air. It landed perfectly in the wide receiver's grasp, and he ran it in for a touchdown. The crowd on the sideline burst into applause, and several boys watching, including her brothers, high-fived each other.

Ellie had seen enough and wanted to leave, but her brothers wouldn't have it, so she stayed with them, promising to watch a few more plays. She didn't know much about football, but it was easy to see how fast, strong, and accurate Josh was. He was a class above everyone else and seemed to glide around the field, probing for weakness. And he could run too. The coach had to tell him to stop scything through the opposing defense to avoid the risk of getting injured on contact.

It was a warm afternoon, and the boys were sweating in their heavy uniforms. One of the assistants called for a water break. Ellie felt a jolt of electricity through her body as Josh began running toward her.

"He's coming this way!" Tyler said with glee.

Josh removed his helmet and stopped a few feet short of where they were standing. He reached down for his water bottle and took a swig. Only then did he raise his eyes to the crowd, and a handsome smile crossed his face.

"Ellie!" he shouted, and she almost jumped out of her skin.

"Thanks for coming out to watch us practice. It means a lot to the team."

"Delighted to be here. These are my brothers, Tyler and James."

He gave them each a glance. "Nice to meet you, guys."

Neither could manage a word.

"They're big fans," Ellie said.

Josh laughed and put his helmet back on. "We have our first game on Friday. The play calls are a bit of a mess right now, so we'll see how it goes, but I'd love to meet up after if you're going."

"I'll be there," she said.

"Great," he answered and returned to the field.

"Time to go," Ellie said to the boys, and they didn't run ahead of her this time.

"I can't believe Josh Thomas just asked you out!" Tyler said once they were clear of the crowd.

"He did not ask me out!" Ellie replied defensively, feeling her cheeks color.

"Are you gonna marry him?" James teased her. "Are we going to be brothers with an NFL star quarterback?"

Ellie couldn't help but laugh at her brother's joke.

"You might be getting ahead of yourself a little," she replied.

She waited until they were through the school gates to text her friends.

> Josh Thomas just asked me to meet him after the game on Friday!

Lizzy was the first to respond.

> I'm not letting you out of my sight!

THREE

It took Ellie an hour to pick out her outfit for Friday's game. It seemed like the entire student body was going, and most of their parents too. It was the biggest event the school had seen in years. Her parents were bringing the twins, but she was riding with her friends and waited by the window until Maddie pulled up in her Honda. The sound of the horn was her signal to run downstairs and say goodbye to her parents. Tyler and James had both been sworn to secrecy over Josh asking to meet her. Not that there was much to tell, but she didn't want her parents to know just yet. She'd lain in bed for hours the night before thinking about Josh. He wasn't arrogant or full of himself and certainly didn't seem the type who could kill someone. But she barely knew him.

Giselle and Lizzy were already in the back of the car. "We left the front seat for the woman of the hour," Maddie said, patting the leather passenger seat beside her before Ellie sat down.

"I got his number for you," Lizzy said as Maddie started the car.

"I don't want to text him yet. I'll look like a crazy stalker,"

Ellie groaned. "I'll have a look for him after the game, just like he asked me to."

Giselle bit her lip and shook her head but kept her thoughts to herself.

Ellie was giddy with excitement as Maddie's Honda rolled into the parking lot, which overflowed with vehicles. Inside, the bleachers heaved under lively crowds hungry for the night ahead.

After several failed attempts to edge through the teeming walkways, Ellie's group resigned themselves to standing huddled along the sidelines. They were craning their necks for any glimpse of players filing out when Ellie turned to see her parents and younger brothers smiling expectantly a few feet back. She waved at her family and promised to join them once the game kicked off, hoping they didn't notice her scanning for another face in the chaos.

The bleachers erupted as the home team charged out, all sound and fury led by their furry bulldog mascot.

A girl Ellie didn't recognize stood a few yards away with her arms folded. She was alone as she booed and jeered Josh. A few of the kids around her asked her to stop, and she whirled around to face them.

"Rachel Kubick was my friend, and that animal is walking free!" she spat.

Mr. Carter, a math teacher, stood up in the bleachers and walked down to the girl. He whispered something into her ear and then escorted her from the sideline.

"Who was that?" Ellie asked.

Lizzy leaned forward. "A new girl. She's in my biology class. She keeps to herself, but on the first day, she said she moved over from Media this year."

"Josh's old school district," Maddie said.

Ellie was curious about her. "What's her name?"

Lizzy shrugged. "Julia something or other. I don't remember."

Maddie shook her head. "Yeah. Apparently, she doesn't share the police's view that Josh is innocent."

Ellie watched as Mr. Carter brought Julia down to the corner of the field. He left her there and returned to his place in the stand. She stood alone, resting her folded arms on the fence. Ellie could see the anger on her face even from forty yards away.

Josh glanced over with an uneasy look before he began warming up. The other team arrived a minute later. They had some fans in the bleachers, too, and received a rousing welcome of their own. The referees appeared, and soon the game was underway.

Josh paced the sideline, his eyes fixed on the turf while the defense battled for possession. At last, his chance came. The offense assembled, Josh barking signals before the snap. Ellie held her breath as he pivoted deftly outside the pocket, hunting an open man. But a flash of red uniforms flooded through the offensive line. Two linemen hammered Josh backward before he could unload the pass, his body crumpling to the dirt.

Ellie's stomach lurched. She wasn't the only one raging—on the fifty-yard line, an attractive couple in their forties watched in horror. The man erupted with profane fury at the referees while the woman stood paralyzed.

"I guess they're Josh's parents," Lizzy murmured.

The man continued dressing down the officials, even the surrounding fans, as medics clustered around Josh. But the star athlete rose with an affirmative nod, walking steadily to the sideline despite his father still cursing loudly enough that everyone within ten yards could hear.

"The golden goose isn't cooked yet," Maddie said with a smile.

"Surely, they're not going to let him continue?" Ellie asked anxiously.

"He's the quarterback," Lizzy's boyfriend, Tom, replied. "They'll patch him up and send him back out."

And he was right. After a few plays by the backup, Josh ran back out to the adulation and relief of the crowd. This time he was determined to avoid the fate he'd suffered on the first play and lost the defenders with a deft move of his hips, which left them floundering in his wake as they tried to bring him down. His electric pace took him through the defensive line for a gain of over thirty yards, which brought the people in the bleachers to their feet again.

Two plays later, he rifled a pass to the tight end for a touchdown, and the crowd erupted.

Julia was still standing in the corner alone with her arms folded. Ellie wondered why she'd come at all.

"He's so good!" Maddie cheered. She seemed to be changing her tune from earlier.

The opposition was no slouch, however, and the score was tied at halftime when Ellie went looking for her family. It took a few minutes to find her mom and dad in the crowd, and they greeted her with a hug.

"The pressure that boy is under must be incredible," her mom said excitedly.

"He seems to be handling it well so far," Ellie's father added with a smile. "Every great athlete has to bear it these days. Some can deal with it, and some can't."

"And with everything else that happened to him last year, with what happened to his girlfriend..." Ellie's mom trailed off.

"Are the kids in school talking about that?" Ellie's father asked her quietly.

Ellie nodded. "A lot of rumors are floating around."

Her dad spoke again. "I feel bad for him. The police cleared him almost immediately. He was home with his family when that poor girl was murdered."

"With his parents," Ellie corrected him.

Her father continued his case for the star quarterback. "But it was a solid alibi. We shouldn't even be talking about it in connection with him—it's not fair to the kid. Accusations like that could threaten his future. The colleges are on board now, but if the rumor mill ramps up, they might dump him. People might start to believe it. Who wants to come and see someone like that play? Idle talk could destroy this kid's life."

Her dad was right about the whispers in the hallways. Some kids in school, mainly the types who didn't care if the football team won the championship or lost every game, were spreading stories about him. Ellie had heard several that week. Perhaps the most outlandish was that Josh was nuts because of a bad hit he took in a game, and he killed Rachel in a fit of football-induced rage. Another was that his dad had killed her because she was too much of a distraction. A kid called Napoleon Walker, who stood six foot five and wore shorts to class every day, even in the snow, was caught spreading a rumor that Rachel was Josh's "beard" and was about to out him as gay before he killed her. Napoleon spent two days in detention when one of the teachers overheard him spinning that one.

"I'm sure he's looking forward to leaving all the chatter behind next year when college starts," Ellie's father said. "He's a special talent. Not many kids get recruited to LSU in their junior year."

They moved on to a new subject after that, until the second half began. Ellie stayed with her parents for most of the third quarter, cheering with her father as Josh threw another long touchdown pass. She didn't tell them she had spoken to Josh, and certainly not about him asking to meet her after the game. It was too early for that, and she didn't know if anything would come of it. They didn't need to know every little thing.

Ellie returned to her friends toward the end of the game. Josh directed the team through the fourth quarter, and they ran out comfortable winners in the end. The crowd cheered, and dozens of kids began chanting Josh's name.

Ellie looked for Julia, but she was gone.

Josh jogged over to his parents, and Ellie was drawn to where they were standing. She wanted Josh to see her too. The butterflies in Ellie's stomach had turned into albatrosses, and her nerves were almost at breaking point. She was close enough to Josh and his parents to hear what his father was saying.

"Lucky," his dad said. "That pass to the tight end on third and long in the fourth quarter was insane. What were you thinking?"

Josh dropped his head and his voice. "Just trying to force it, I guess."

"How many times have I told you? It's better to punt than to turn the ball over!"

He protested, "But the defense didn't make the play. I saw the man open. It wasn't as risky as it looked."

"You got away with it—this time!"

Josh shook his head but didn't make eye contact. His mother, who'd stayed silent the whole time, reached forward and hugged him before he jogged away without acknowledging Ellie.

She had no idea what to do next. It was almost nine thirty. The dark of night had extinguished the day, and the bright yellow floodlights had been illuminating the field for a little while now.

"Maybe I should just go home," she said to her friends.

Maddie tilted her head. "Is that what you want to do?"

"No. I don't know," she answered. "I'd like to see him for a little."

Tom filled the silence. "He'll be out with the rest of the team in a few minutes. Just hang out for a while."

"Are you sure about this?" Giselle asked, but the others shushed her.

Her friends waited with her as the crowd began to disperse. She promised her parents she'd be home by midnight, but a sudden feeling came over her as she watched them leave. She almost ran after them. Something inside her begged her to go home to where she knew she'd be safe. But she didn't move a muscle. Josh was worth it. The rumors weren't true. They couldn't be.

Josh appeared a few minutes later, dressed in a suit with a red school tie. Ellie felt something between exhilaration and fear. His hair was perfect, and he strode toward his parents again. Ellie tried not to watch as he greeted his father with a handshake. But his dad still didn't seem happy and berated him for his mistakes during the game. Several people tried to congratulate Josh, but his father turned them away. His mother stood with her arms crossed— she wasn't celebrating the win either and had discontentment written all over her face.

As the crowd dissipated, Josh's parents turned away from him as the coach came over. He was the only person they seemed to deem important enough to greet.

"He's waving to us!" Lizzy whispered.

Ellie turned around to see Josh jogging over.

"Thanks for coming out," he said with a smile.

"Great game," Lizzy said.

"Thanks," he accepted sheepishly and looked back at Ellie.

"You want to hang out for a bit?" Josh asked.

"Sure," Ellie replied. She was doing this. Something about him gave her confidence. He had a presence about him that, despite the rumors, suggested he had a good heart.

"We'd better get out of here," Giselle said.

"Call me if you need a ride," Maddie said. "I'll keep my phone in my hand."

"I have a car," Josh said. "It's not exactly a Bugatti, but it goes. I can take her."

"Ellie, are you sure?" Maddie said. She might have defended Josh before, but it seemed she still had her reservations when it came to her friends.

"She's positive," Lizzy said, taking her worried friend by the hand.

Josh shrugged with a handsome smile, and Ellie knew she was in trouble, but not the kind Maddie was thinking of.

A couple of people stopped to congratulate Josh. He shook their hands before turning to Ellie.

"Do you like football?"

"Sure, but I prefer... other things."

"We can talk about them. I'm good with that."

Josh's face changed at the sound of his father calling him over. "Gimme a second. I'd introduce you, but my parents aren't easy, especially when they're not happy with how I played."

"But the team won. You were great."

"Thanks," he said with a grin. "Back in a few seconds."

Ellie tried to avert her eyes to give him some privacy as he spoke to his parents, but his father's raised voice grabbed her attention.

A moment later, Josh's parents were gone and, suddenly, Ellie was alone with Josh. The bleachers were empty of all but a few people cleaning up after the crowd.

"They'll turn off the lights in a few minutes. Do you want to get a coffee somewhere?"

"Sure," she said.

His car was one of the last in the lot. He opened the door for her, and she sat inside his old white Ford. The inside was clean. Not like most of the interiors of boys' cars she'd been in.

"I worked bussing tables for two summers to buy this beauty," Josh said with a smile.

"Where? At the shore?"

Ellie had waited tables three evenings a week in a restaurant in Stone Harbor that past summer.

"No. My parents don't like the beach much. At least, my old man doesn't. Do you have a place down there?"

"Yeah, we've been going every summer since I was a kid."

"What do you think of my ride? There's a good chance it might even get us to the café."

"Pretty sweet," she said. "The rust on the outside is particularly striking."

"You like that, huh? Makes the car go faster too. It's not just for show."

The car started with a splutter, and they started off toward her favorite coffee shop in town. It was a place just off Main Street that she went to with her mother most Sunday mornings. It had become their special time to talk, and she cherished this place because of it.

They found a round high-top table near the back, just far enough away from the live music that they could hear each other speak. Most tables were taken and several people were standing in front of the stage with drinks in their hands. She ordered coffee while he chose a hot chocolate.

"You getting used to the new school?" she asked. "It must be weird seeing your face six feet high on those posters every time you walk in."

"It is, but you'd be surprised how quickly you get used to it. It was the same deal in my last school."

She needed to know one way or the other. Ellie took a deep breath before she asked, "Why did you leave the old school? It seems like a strange move for the big stud quarterback."

"The 'big stud quarterback'?" he repeated back to her, his eyes cast down in embarrassment.

"Yeah," she said. "Should I refer to you as something else?" She took a sip of her coffee. It was delicious and she felt her nerves settle.

"No, I'm thinking of changing my name to 'big stud quarter-back,' so I should probably start getting used to it. I already asked them to change the name on the back of my jersey, but they haven't done it yet. Can't think why."

He kept eye contact with her a second longer than normal before turning around for a second to glance at the musician. She was in her early twenties with long blonde hair. The Bob Dylan cover she was singing reminded Ellie of something her father would play in the car.

Josh took a sip of his drink. "I wasn't kicked out if that's what you're thinking," he said softly.

"I wasn't thinking that at all," she replied, locking eyes with his.

"We just needed a new start. My dad didn't want to leave his job, so we couldn't go too far. My mom was the one who found the house. She wanted to move the most." He looked again at the woman playing acoustic guitar onstage and then back at Ellie. "Sometimes I wish I was good at something like that."

"At singing?"

"I don't know. I swear my dad hasn't actually enjoyed one of my games since I was about twelve. He gets so worked up."

"I saw how he was talking to you."

"That's nothing compared to how he reams me out at home."

"What does your mom say?"

"Not a lot," he answered. "She suffers his behavior like I do. She wants the best for me, I know that, but she doesn't say much."

Ellie was fascinated. This boy wasn't who she'd expected him to be at all. She thought he'd be brash and arrogant. She reached across the table and took his hand. It felt like the right thing to do.

"They fight all the time. It never used to be this way, but the last few years, it's been crazy."

"Was that part of the reason you moved?"

"Most of it, I'd say. Mom doesn't talk to me about things like that, but I think she wanted to get away from that house as if it was cursed or something. I don't know. I feel like I'm talking about myself all the time. What about your life? What are your parents like?"

"Happy. Pretty boring, really. My brothers are a pain, but I can live with them."

"Boring, eh? Sounds nice."

"I suppose it is."

"My dad didn't let me watch kids' TV when I was little."

"What?"

"All the shows you probably watched—*Sesame Street*? The one with the purple dinosaur?"

"I used to love Barney."

"And the one with the guys dressed up in colored suits in the field? The weird one?"

"I was never a *Teletubbies* girl. Too out there for me. You didn't watch any TV?"

"Sure I did, but all the stuff my dad prescribed for me. Old VHS tapes mainly. Joe Montana, Steve Young, John Elway, and Dan Marino were my teachers. My father would stick old games on the TV and wouldn't let me watch anything else. No matter what day of the week, or whether it was football season or not. Just football. All the time."

Josh picked up his cup, but it was already empty. He put it back down, his eyes never wavering from hers.

"From what age?"

"As early as I can remember. Two, maybe three."

She was amazed. "But you couldn't even play at that age."

He shrugged. "I am what I was bred to be. We'd read *Sports Illustrated* at night in bed."

"Was your mom okay with this?" Ellie was curious.

"She didn't have much of a say. My dad was the starting quarterback for Penn State in seventy-eight until... until the accident."

"The accident?"

"He was out with some buddies. He never said it, but they were probably drinking and crashed the car. One was killed. My dad broke both his legs. Never played again. His dad was a football player too. I guess he figured I inherited what they had."

The musician at the microphone was packing up her guitar when Josh said, "I know what the kids are saying about me."

"What?" she asked. She figured it was best to feign ignorance.

"About Rachel. I know they all assume I killed her."

"No," Ellie said. Her heart burned in her chest. "Some idiots are talking, of course, but who cares what they say? Do you have any idea who might have done it?"

"None." He sighed. "One minute she was with us, and the next she was gone."

"What was she like?"

"Great, but I don't think I'd still be with her now. We were just about to break up... when it happened. It's weird, but because she was murdered, I still think about her all the time. If she was still alive, I probably never would. I just feel bad for her parents and what they've gone through."

"Did she know that you were about to break up with her?"

"No. I hadn't told her or anyone else yet. So the newspapers portrayed us as this perfect couple. I didn't say anything. Her family was upset enough already without adding that to the mix." He looked at his watch. "It's time I got you home. I don't want your dad beating me up," he joked.

They stood up and walked to his car. His hand grazed hers as he opened the door for her, and her heart quickened.

It was a short drive to her house, and after Ellie gave him directions, they fell into silence listening to the radio while Josh rested his free hand tenderly over hers.

"Here we are," he said as he pulled up outside her house. The air in the car seemed to be thicker all of a sudden, and she drew heavy breaths in and out of her lungs.

A thousand thoughts flowed through Ellie's mind in the second after he turned to her, but there was one she couldn't resist. Without waiting for him, she leaned over and kissed him and felt his hand behind her neck. The touch of his lips on hers was unlike anything else she'd ever known, and she lost her breath as she pulled away from him.

She was just about to lean in again when the light came on in the foyer of Ellie's house. "I should go," she blurted.

He agreed with a smile. His eyes were on fire. "Give me your number. I'll text you tomorrow."

Ellie did as he asked. Her heart was thumping so hard in her chest she felt like it would break the skin, but she kept her cool somehow. "And I'll see you in school on Monday."

She got out of the car and he waited until she reached the front door before he drove away.

FOUR

The skepticism surrounding Josh melted over the following weeks. The rumors that had greeted his arrival persisted, but only in the background. Those who got to know him were taken by his humility and charm. The kids at school still spoke about Rachel Kubick, but the tone of their conversations had changed since the beginning of the school year. The facts were clear. Josh hadn't been at the party when Rachel had disappeared. His overzealous father couldn't handle him being out late and had come to pick him up. Some said he'd almost dragged him out, and Josh said himself how embarrassed he'd been, but looking back, it was the best protection his father could have offered him. Everyone recognized Josh was innocent, and the few who did talk to him about Rachel only did so in offering their condolences. And his talent was undeniable. The football team had never been this good and had the best record in the region. Aces' pride had taken over, and every game was the major social event of the week.

So it came as a surprise one Tuesday morning when Ellie saw the word "murderer" daubed on Josh's locker in red paint.

"What the—?" Josh yelled in shock.

"Looks like I'm not the only one who wants you out of this school," a voice from behind them uttered. Julia Leonard stood alone with an aggressive, defiant look on her face.

"I should have known who was behind this," Josh said, anger flaring in his eyes.

A crowd of students shuffling from one class to the next began to gather around the locker. Some reacted with shock, their hands over their mouths. Others laughed nervously.

"Don't look at me," Julia said. "But get the message. We won't stand for killers in this school!"

Incensed, Ellie was first to react. "Julia, you're out of your mind. Leave him—"

Josh stopped her with a gentle hand on her arm. "I don't need you to fight this battle for me." He turned to Julia, who had a smirk on her face.

"When are you going to let this go?" Josh pleaded. "I didn't kill Rachel. I don't know who did. But you have to stop this." His voice was weaker than she'd ever heard it. He sounded like a little boy.

"I'll stop when you admit what you did!" Julia shouted, bringing her face right up close to Josh's.

The crowd opened up, and Mr. Edwards, a social studies teacher, barreled through. "What on earth is going on here?" He pointed to the word on the locker. "Who did that?" He turned to Julia. "Miss Leonard, do you have anything to tell me?"

She held up her clean palms as proof. "Look at my hands."

Mr. Edwards didn't fall for her excuse and led her to the principal's office.

Josh turned to Ellie and, despite all the kids watching, fell into her arms. She held him for a few seconds before Mrs. Gates, the school counselor, pried Josh's arms from around Ellie's shoulder.

"Come on, Josh. Let's go talk."

He nodded and kissed Ellie on the cheek as a goodbye. She stood watching as he walked beside Mrs. Gates with his head down. Josh was a regular with Mrs. Gates, though he didn't talk about their sessions much.

A kid beside them whispered something about Josh getting what he deserved. Ellie resisted the temptation to snap back at him. She had to be the better person.

The paint and gloves Julia had used were stashed in her locker, and she was suspended for a week. She would have been expelled if not for her well-documented family problems. She'd been spiraling downward ever since Rachel's death. The consensus seemed to be that the school wasn't going to give up on her.

Ellie saw her in the hallway the morning she came back.

"I'm sorry for what I did," she said to Ellie. "I was upset about my friend. It's so hard to take," she muttered with little eye contact.

Ellie took a deep breath. She felt a twinge of sorrow for this fragile girl standing in front of her who'd lost her best friend in the most brutal way possible. "I understand this is painful for you, but you have to stop blaming Josh." Maybe she could end this. "Julia, if you ever want to talk, I'm always here."

Julia began to walk away but looked back at her for a second before replying. "Maybe. See you later."

Josh's open and friendly nature shone through in every situation, and her brothers adored him. He'd come to the house a few times, including for dinner with her parents, and had played football in the backyard with Tyler and James, giving them tips on finding receivers. Now they wanted to play football too. Her new boyfriend was their new hero, and their respect for her had gone through the roof because of it. Her parents approved, but one hurdle still remained—his parents.

She hadn't been to his house yet. It was November, and they'd been seeing each other for nearly two months. His parents were at every game but seemed increasingly agitated by any mistakes he made as the season progressed. He was the best player in their division and probably eastern Pennsylvania too, but nothing he did seemed to be good enough.

Josh didn't talk about them much but didn't hide the fact that things at home were difficult. It had been her idea to come over. He seemed happy that she'd insisted on meeting them, and that was enough to convince her it was the right thing to do. She'd never met a boyfriend's parents before, but she'd also never felt this way about a boy before. It was all new.

Saturday came. Soccer practice in the morning and lunch with her family served to distract her for a while, but when Ellie arrived home there didn't seem like anything else to think about. She was in her room changing when her phone buzzed. The nerves coursing through her caused her hands to shake as she picked it up and read the text from Josh.

Are you ready for this?

Ellie took a breath before responding.

As ready as I'll ever be.

Don't worry. They'll love you just as much as I do.

Her heart jumped as she read the text. It was the first time either of them had used that word—love. But she felt it. Everything was different now. She thought about him all the time, and she knew she'd never be the same again. Her friends were amazed. The girl who never committed to any boys was head over heels with the quarterback stud. Ellie laughed to herself and put the phone down with fresh confidence surging through her.

"This is something I have to do," she said as she applied some eyeliner.

A knock on the door interrupted her thoughts, and her mom popped her head around.

"How are you feeling, sweetie?" she asked in a soothingly familiar tone.

"Good," Ellie lied.

"They're just people. I'm sure they must be good ones, too, if they raised Josh. I can't help but admire his dedication to his schoolwork as well as football. A kid who can do so well under that much pressure must have a good head on his shoulders. And that didn't come from nowhere."

"Thanks, Mom."

"And how could they not love my girl?" her mother said softly, giving Ellie a hug before leaving the room.

Temporarily comforted by what her mother had said, Ellie finished her makeup and took one last look at herself in the mirror.

"Let's do this," she said and walked out.

On the ride across town, her dad wasted no time grilling her about Josh.

"Does Josh talk about college next year much?" he asked in the car.

"Sometimes, yeah. Baton Rouge is a long way away, but he's excited. They have one of the best football programs in the country."

"Oh, I'm well aware of that. What about you two? He'll be all the way down in Louisiana."

"We'll see, Dad," Ellie said, trying to play it off like it didn't matter to her. But her father didn't seem to buy her act.

"Whatever happens with Josh, you need to keep your head down and not get distracted." His voice carried an air of gentle authority. "You have your own plans whether they take you to Rutgers or Temple or even Penn. You need to focus on your future. Not just his."

"Yeah, I hear you."

"I know that everything seems like it's the most important thing you'll ever experience right now. I remember being seventeen."

"You remember the 1920s?" she said.

His smile didn't stop his train of thought. "I just need you to make sure you focus on what's really important—your future. A lot of people are going to drift in and out of your life. And it's going to be hard to stay with someone in college over a thousand miles away. I had a girlfriend when I was a senior in high school."

"You never told me."

"Clare O'Reilly. She was cute, and I thought we'd be together forever. We promised to stay together when I went to Penn and she headed to Rutgers, but it didn't last. It wasn't anyone's fault. We just grew in different directions. And she was only over in Jersey."

"Where's she now?"

"Last I heard, Clare was living in Cincinnati with a husband and three girls. Married a politician, I believe. But what I'm saying is you've got your whole life in front of you. Don't rush into anything," he said kindly.

"I'm more focused on getting through dinner right now," she replied nervously.

"How did I know you'd say that? Just be yourself, sweetheart. They'll love you."

"Thanks, Dad."

They pulled up outside a white, two-story house on a suburban street much like their own. Ellie had texted Josh when they were a few minutes away, and he was waiting at the window as she'd insisted. Seeing him comforted her raging nerves, and she got out of the car. Her father wished her luck.

"See you later," she said to him and shut the door.

An old tree with massive bare branches stood guard outside the house, and the front yard was clean and well tended. Many of the other yards on the street were covered in brown and yellow leaves, but the Thomas's was immaculate. Ellie knew it was one of Josh's chores.

She walked up to the front porch, where Josh was waiting, wearing a shirt and slacks. He kissed her on the cheek and took her hands with a nervous-looking smile. She wanted to ask him what he had to be anxious about but was interrupted by his father's voice. Mr. Thomas stepped out with a broad smile she'd never seen him wear before, and Josh moved aside.

"Hello, Mr. Thomas," Ellie greeted him.

"Ellie," Mr. Thomas said. "Welcome to our home, and please call me Gary." He was over six foot—the same height as Josh—but his eyes were darker. His brown hair was thinning at the front, but he was still handsome. It was easy to see where Josh had gotten his looks from.

He offered a massive hand to Ellie, and she shook it. Josh's mother, tall and blonde with green eyes, appeared at the screen door seconds later.

"I'm so sorry, Ellie. Josh only told me you were coming over yesterday," she said. Her voice was limp and dull, and as Ellie looked at her, she noticed her eyes were the same.

"This is my mother, Linda," Josh said.

Josh's mother didn't step forward to shake her hand, offering a nod as a greeting instead.

"Come in," Linda said and held the screen door open. "Please excuse the state of the house. I've been cleaning all day."

"You didn't need to do that for me," Ellie said and stepped inside. The foyer was spotless. The mirror by the door shone in the evening light, and there wasn't a speck of dust or dirt to be seen anywhere. She held in her gasp as she saw the wall in the family room. A bookshelf full of trophies and medals sat below a wall of dozens of framed photographs of Josh playing football. Ellie walked over wide-eyed. The photos went all the way back to when he was a baby. Ellie stared at what seemed like Josh's christening. His cake was in the shape of a football. The only other pictures were of the family posing in church with a preacher, and of Mr. Thomas handing out food at what seemed to be a homeless shelter.

"Oh, you've seen the wall!" Mr. Thomas said with a smile, and Ellie offered one in return as he approached her. Josh stood back.

"You know who that is?" Josh's father asked. He pointed to a man with receding blond hair in a red uniform. Josh was about four in the picture. Ellie shook her head. "That's Joe Montana." He pointed to another picture of Josh with someone else she didn't know. "And Brett Favre." And then another. "This is John Elway with my boy."

"Amazing," Ellie said, as if she had any idea of how much having pictures of them with Josh meant to his father. She stood back. The pictures covered the entire wall. It was a shrine.

Josh seemed bashful in front of her. "Would you like a lemonade?"

"Yes, please," Ellie answered.

Josh's mother disappeared into the kitchen, and Josh and Ellie sat side by side on the couch, his father opposite them.

"You like football, Ellie?" Josh's father asked.

"Yeah, I enjoy it. It's great to see the school team winning."

"Josh isn't having his best season. Too many mistakes. I just hope the scouts from LSU haven't been paying attention to the last few games."

Josh's face dropped, but he didn't say a word.

"My son has a God-given talent, a gift to share with the entire town and whatever team he ends up with in college and then the NFL. I knew from the first moment he picked up a ball that he was special."

"Dad, she doesn't want to hear this," Josh moaned.

"She needs to know who you are, son, and how special you are."

Ellie had no idea what to say.

Josh tried to change the subject. "I don't think—"

"No, Josh. If she wants to be around you, even for a little while, she needs to understand what your life is about. What it's for."

What his life is for?

His mother came back in with a tray of lemonade. "We don't drink alcohol in this house," Mr. Thomas said as he accepted the glass from his wife. "It slows the body and mind."

Ellie nodded and managed a smile. She and Josh had shared some beers the previous weekend with some friends. Josh didn't drink to excess but he certainly didn't share his father's views. Ellie looked at her boyfriend to see why he hadn't told her about his parents being teetotalers, particularly after the earlier story about the drunken car crash in college, but he shrugged and stayed quiet.

"I played in college myself. I was good but didn't have Josh's talent. He got that from my father, God rest his soul. Sometimes that can skip a generation," he said ruefully. "We have a few minutes, how about we show your girl the backyard and what we do?" Mr. Thomas said.

"Dinner's nearly ready. We should stay inside," Josh protested.

"Come on. Let's go. She needs to see who you are. If she can't accept that, what's the point of any of this?"

Ellie was puzzled—she'd watched Josh play countless times over the last couple of months.

"Right now." Mr. Thomas's tone commanded authority, and Josh followed him through the kitchen to the back door.

His mother was by the stove and barely looked up as they passed her. It was dark outside, but neither man hesitated. Ellie stepped out into the black as Mr. Thomas flipped a switch, and the backyard was instantly bathed in light. The lawn, about thirty yards long, was cut short and lined like a football field. Mr. Thomas went to a small shed and emerged with some footballs.

"What's going on?" Ellie whispered to Josh.

"Let's just get this over with," he answered wearily.

His father tossed him some footballs. "Ellie, can you help us out? His mother usually does this, but she's busy with dinner."

"Sure."

He handed her a long pole with a number on a screen at the top. "You know what this is?" She shook her head. "It's a down indicator. We use it in games to show what down we're on."

"I've seen that, now that you mention it."

"Okay. Walk down to the end of the yard and hold it up."

She did as she was told and then stopped about twenty-five yards from where Josh was standing. Mr. Thomas gave her the thumbs-up. "Josh has to hit that down indicator. When he does, flip it to the next number. When it gets to four, we stop. If he misses, we go back to one."

"Got it."

He walked over to Josh, practically breathing down his neck. "When you're ready, son."

Josh let fly and hit the down indicator.

"Right on the money," Ellie said with a smile and flicked the switch to display the number one. She wondered how many times Josh's mother had done this.

Josh repeated the trick, and she switched it to two.

"Two to go," she said reassuringly.

Mr. Thomas seemed unimpressed. He paced in frustration then returned to stand beside him. His son picked up another ball. "You're no good!" Mr. Thomas shouted and pushed him. "You're never going to make it to the NFL. You're too slow, too weak. That's a man's league and you're just a little boy."

Ellie was about to say something when Josh, ignoring his father, threw the ball again. It hit the down marker. Ellie changed the number but wasn't smiling now. The abuse continued as Josh picked up another ball.

"Too easy," his father said. "How about a little heat."

Mr. Thomas walked three yards away and then ran at his son. He connected with Josh's chest as the ball left his hand. Josh hit the dirt, and the ball fell five yards short.

Josh's father stood up and shouted at the supine figure of his son on the ground. "You think the NFL is some playground? Those monsters will eat you alive! You can't take me chasing you down? A middle-aged guy like me? Let's go again." He walked over to the shed, grabbed more balls, and tossed one to his son.

Ellie couldn't see Josh's face, but he hadn't said a word. He threw another ball. It struck the down indicator. The abuse started after the second throw. Josh missed, and Ellie reset the count.

Josh's mother appeared at the door. "Dinner's ready."

"We're busy," Mr. Thomas shouted. "We'll be in as soon as Josh gets this."

Ellie was trapped at the end of the yard. She stood still, holding the pole. Josh hit the first and second time but missed the third. His father pushed him. He didn't react. The cycle began once more. They did it another time when Josh missed again.

"Is right now the time for this? We're supposed to be having dinner."

"There's always going to be something else going on," his father replied. "If you can't clear your mind and play your best while the rest of the world is going crazy, you'll never make it." He motioned for Josh to throw the balls.

"I'm sorry, Ellie," he said and threw the first. It struck. A few moments later the down indicator read three, but Mr. Thomas lined up to rush his son again. Josh picked up the ball as his father ran at him. Josh jinked and threw the ball a millisecond before his father hit him. It struck the down indicator. Ellie couldn't help the cheer that came out of her mouth. It was as much relief as joy.

Mr. Thomas picked himself up and dusted himself off. Josh ran down to Ellie. "I'm sorry about that. He's a dog with a bone when it comes to his drills. I think he wanted to show off."

"That's okay." Ellie wondered where this peculiar night would take her next. Josh was worth it, but this was already a lot.

They walked back inside, and he led her through to the dining room, where his mother had laid out steaks and baked potatoes.

"This looks wonderful, thank you," Ellie said as she took her seat. Josh echoed her sentiments, but his father stayed quiet.

More framed photos of Josh playing football hung from the walls. The china plates and silver-plated knives and forks added to the sense of occasion. A single candle was burning in an ornate silver holder in the middle of the table. The delicious aroma of the food filled the air around them.

Josh's father waited until his wife was seated and then reached out. He took Linda's and Josh's hands and bowed his head to say grace. Ellie wasn't used to it but took her boyfriend's hand and did as her hosts were doing.

"Thank you, Lord, for this food which you have provided for us and for the gifts you have bestowed upon our son. Also, thank you for bringing the beautiful Ellie to our house tonight."

Josh's mother flicked angry eyes at her husband. He didn't seem to notice.

Ellie did her best to ignore his reference to her and made sure to say "amen" in unison with them before beginning to eat.

"You know what I was trying to do out there, Ellie?" Mr. Thomas said to her.

Break your son down into little pieces? Ellie chose her words carefully. "Build his character? Make him stronger?"

Mr. Thomas looked surprised at her answer. "If he can't take abuse from his own father, how's he going to react to opposition fans in college and the NFL?"

Josh's father looked around the table for a few awkward seconds. No one seemed to know what to say. Ellie was glad when he began speaking again.

"It doesn't give me any pleasure to treat my son like that— quite the opposite, it breaks my heart—but I do it for him. Josh showed huge potential at such a young age. It is my responsibility, my duty, to raise him to be the best he can be. Anything less would be failing him, and I won't do that."

He reached over and took his wife's hand. "You must think I'm crazy when you see me at the games."

Ellie felt everyone's eyes on her. She didn't know how to answer. "No…"

"Thank you for saying that," he said with a warmth she hadn't seen from him yet.

"Everyone at the games thinks you're crazy," Mrs. Thomas murmured with an eye roll.

Her husband laughed. "They're probably right!"

The atmosphere lightened. It was as if a massive weight had

been lifted, and Ellie began to relax. Her mother had been right —Josh got his good work ethic and decency from somewhere. Perhaps there was a side to his parents few people experienced.

Mr. Thomas continued. "Those games are the culmination of years of sacrifice. Thousands of hours Josh has put in on the training field and in the gym. And they're so important. Everything's on the line right now. His entire future could turn on a blown call or a bad tackle." He looked at his wife. "We have nightmares about our boy getting hurt."

"It's such a dangerous game," Mrs. Thomas said. "Sometimes I want to pull him off the field and stop those monsters running at him, but we know how much he loves the game."

"We'd never do that to Josh."

"I do love it," Josh said. "I don't know who I'd be without football."

"We've always tried to instill more than just football in Josh. He helps us in the homeless shelter and with our work in the church."

"Football's not the only thing in life," Linda said.

"One day, you will stop playing," Gary said to Josh. "And whether you make the NFL or not, the education you'll get in a great school like LSU or wherever you end up will benefit you for the rest of your life." He turned his focus to Ellie. "I know I'm hard on him and seem crazy, but Josh is my only child, and I won't let him down."

"I understand," Ellie said. She looked at Josh and smiled, and he nodded at her as if relieved that she finally understood.

"So, what are you doing next year, Ellie?" Mr. Thomas asked while he cut his steak.

"I'm thinking about studying teaching. Maybe in Drexel or Temple."

"From what Josh tells us, you'll make a wonderful teacher. I just hope you're not thinking about being a high school teacher. You're far too pretty to stand in front of a group of teenage boys.

I'm sure you had a horde of them following you around before Josh snagged you," Gary said with a smile.

I'll ignore that, Ellie thought to herself. She took a deep breath in through her nostrils and steered the conversation back to something acceptable. "I think I'd like to try elementary."

"Josh will be far away. Too far to stay in touch if you're staying in this area," Mr. Thomas asserted.

"I don't know about that," Josh argued.

"I know what you're thinking right now, but believe me, it's too far. You'll both find someone else. It's not fair to put that much pressure on yourselves." Josh's father's tone was unequivocal.

"We'll see what happens. It's Louisiana, not the moon," Josh answered.

His father ignored him and moved on. "College is a wonderful experience. I played football at Penn State. It was the best years of my life."

Ellie asked a question to move the conversation along. Perhaps she could make enough of an impression tonight to change his father's mind so that he might support her and Josh staying together. "Is that where you met Mrs. Thomas?"

"No, that was after," he responded. "She and I worked together in our first jobs out of school. Linda was the most beautiful thing I'd ever seen. I wanted to marry her after the first time we went out."

He reached across and took his wife's hand again. She afforded him a brief glance before returning to her food.

"Josh tells me you're in pharmaceutical sales," Ellie said to Mr. Thomas.

"Yeah, someone has to bring the bacon home around here," he said with a grin. "I'm away a lot. Sometimes, I only just make it home in time for Josh's games on a Friday night. The rest of the time I'm gone."

"Where do you travel?" Ellie asked.

"All over," he replied vaguely. He finished his steak and started in on his baked potato.

"The food is great," Ellie stated, breaking another awkward silence. Why did she have to be the one to do that?

"Yeah, thanks, Mom," Josh said.

"You're welcome," Linda said. "I'm glad you're enjoying it."

Her voice was soft and uneven. It was almost as if it hurt her to speak.

His father began talking about football again as Linda went to fetch dessert. She brought back chocolate brownies smothered in vanilla ice cream. The food was terrific, and Ellie tried to take refuge in it.

A few minutes later, Linda excused herself. Her husband followed her into the kitchen, leaving Ellie and Josh alone.

"How are you doing?" Josh asked in a whisper.

She knew better than to tell the unvarnished truth. "They're not who I expected. I'm enjoying myself now. The game in the backyard was a little intense."

"You're doing incredibly. We'll get out of here soon. I just have to go to the bathroom. I think my dad's in the garage, and Mom will be in the kitchen cleaning up for a while. I'll be back in a minute."

Ellie nodded and looked forward as he walked out. She sat alone for a minute, checking her phone. A few of the girls had texted. It was hard to know where to begin telling them about Josh's parents. She was just about to respond when Mr. Thomas walked back in. She felt him lingering behind her before sitting down in his chair. Ellie kept staring at the screen of her phone but knew his eyes were on her.

"Josh left you all alone?" he said. She finally looked up from her phone. "If you were my girl, I'd never leave your side," he said with a grin. "I'm glad you're here because I wanted to talk to you."

He stood up, walked around behind her and crouched

down. She froze as she felt his breath on her neck. "I'm glad you're aware of how important it is for Josh to avoid all distractions," he said, putting his hands on her shoulders.

Her body tensed. Whatever he was doing, this wasn't right. *Where is Josh? When's he coming back?*

He moved his hands in so they were touching the bare skin of her neck, and his face was inches from hers now.

"Because it'd be a crime for him to waste his talent for some girl."

He moved his hands again to cover the front of her neck. He hesitated for a few seconds. She was shaking now, unable to speak. He let his hands drop across her breasts before he stood up.

"There's nothing more important to me than my son's future. He's everything to me and his mother," he said and returned to his seat just as Josh walked in.

Not wanting to make a scene, Ellie stood up and excused herself as her boyfriend sat down.

"Everything okay?" he said.

Ellie felt the blood rush to her face. Her body felt like it was on fire. "Of course. I just need to use the bathroom."

"I don't think the food agreed with her," Mr. Thomas said as she left.

Ellie shut the bathroom door behind her and faced her reflection in the mirror. She gasped as a tear broke from her eye and rolled down her cheek. She felt betrayed, fooled. Ellie's brain was racing at a thousand miles an hour. Why had he touched her like that? What had he expected to gain? Perhaps all he wanted was to drive her away. Had he tried to do the same thing to Rachel and gone further? Was her life in danger now too? She felt a cold chill as fear gripped her. Perhaps Mr. Thomas would stop at nothing in pursuit of his dream. One thing was patently clear: no matter what Gary's motivations were, he was a disgusting creep.

He'd seemed so sincere at dinner, but apparently, the man at the games was the authentic version of who he was.

Next year Josh would be away from him. But could she hang in that long? Josh was protective of her and would want to know what his father had done, but how could she tell him? His relationship with his parents was tenuous enough, and running away from home or getting kicked out of the house might jeopardize his scholarship. She would figure out when to tell him but it couldn't be now. The important thing was to get out of the house. The thought of going back out there filled her with dread. But she had no choice.

"Time to be brave," she said to her reflection and took a deep breath to steady her nerves.

She cleaned herself up and returned to the dining room, where Josh and his father were still discussing football.

"I'm so sorry," she said, "but I just got a text from home. My mom's sick, and my dad had to go out. I need to get back and watch the boys."

"I thought they were freshmen?" Josh's father asked, his eyes narrowing. "They need you to babysit them?"

"Yeah, they're a little needy," she said, trying to still her shaky voice. "Josh, do you mind taking me?"

"It's so early," Mr. Thomas said. "Linda and I were just getting to know you." He was smirking at her.

"I'm sorry. It's a bit of an emergency."

"Well, we'll be sorry to see you leave, but look forward to having you for dinner again," Gary said and stood up.

He walked around the table and wrapped his arms around her. Ellie cringed and tensed as he pressed his body against hers, his breath on her neck once more. She drew back, looking anywhere but into Josh's father's eyes. Josh didn't seem to notice and led her into the kitchen, where Linda was doing the dishes.

"It was nice to meet you," Ellie said.

"Goodbye," Josh's mother replied with a brief glance and focused back on the soapy water in the sink.

Ellie felt like she was breaking the surface of a swimming pool and coming up for air as she stepped out of the house. She desperately wanted to tell Josh what his father had done but her instincts told her she had to wait.

"Are you all right?" Josh asked, a frown creasing his forehead. "You don't look—"

"Let's just get in the car," she said, avoiding his gaze.

He held the door for her, and she climbed into the passenger seat. "That was hard," she said once they'd pulled out.

"Yeah, I'm sorry. They're crazy. The way my dad treats my mom makes me so mad. We've fought about it hundreds of times. But you've met them now. You don't need to come over again. Once I leave next year, I'm never coming back." He paused for a few seconds before continuing. "Now you know why I'm going all the way to Louisiana when Penn State came calling too. I just have to get my mom out too."

"Is that what you talk to the school counselor about?"

It took him a few seconds to answer. She kept quiet, knew he had to be the next person to speak.

"Yeah, that and the pressure. I had some panic attacks after Rachel died. After I was arrested, and the backlash from her family. I have them less frequently now."

Ellie's heart sank like a stone. "I had no idea."

"That's because I didn't tell you," he said quietly.

She reached across and put her hand in his. "You want your mom to leave your dad?"

"She'd be safer without him," he said, but then seemed to catch himself. "Better off, I mean."

Ellie didn't know what to say. She let the silence build between them, hoping he'd elaborate. She didn't want to push him. After all, what business was it of hers? But that word "safer" seemed to be playing on repeat in her brain as Josh drove.

"What did you mean when you said your mom would be safer?" she decided to ask as he stopped outside her house.

"I said that?" he said with a perplexed look. "I don't know what I meant. I just used the wrong word, I guess. My mom just needs to get away. They'd both be better off."

Ellie wasn't convinced but decided to leave it. She reached across to Josh and kissed him.

"I'll see you in school," he said.

She got out and ran up to her house, wondering if Josh's mom would be safer away from his father, would Ellie be safer away from Josh?

Her parents were in the living room. She tried to get past them but they shouted after her.

They asked how dinner was.

"Fine," she responded and carried on up the stairs.

Ellie shut her bedroom door behind her and slumped on her bed. Her phone buzzed and she glanced at the screen. Her heart almost burst as she read the message from the unknown number.

> It's Julia Leonard. Can we talk about Josh? I sincerely believe he's dangerous, and I have to leave town. How about tonight?

FIVE

Ellie stared at the text for several seconds. What did Julia have to tell her that she didn't already know? Was this a trap? She took a deep breath to calm herself and tried to reason out the situation. But what if Julia was right about Josh and his father and wanted to protect her? Another text came through.

> My best friend is dead. I don't want the same thing to happen to you

Before Ellie had a chance to process how she'd respond, another one came through.

> I'll meet you wherever. In the most public place you can think of. But make it tonight.

And another.

> You don't have to meet me, but Josh is dangerous.

The last words knocked the breath out of Ellie's body. She had to meet this person. His previous girlfriend was dead, and even if Josh had an alibi, the killer was still out there.

How about outside the police station on Main
Street in 20 minutes?

I'll see you then.

Ellie shut her phone. She'd be safe at the police station—no one would try to get to her there.

She changed into jeans and a sweater. Her hands were shaking as she opened her door. Ellie wanted to tell her parents but knew they'd demand she stop seeing Josh, and that would make things worse for everyone. Especially him.

Her friends would think she was crazy if they knew what she was about to do. Maybe she was, but her curiosity was too much to ignore. It was hard to admit, but it was true—she didn't really know Josh. He'd talked about Rachel in flashes, but not a lot. She hadn't been the love of his young life, just a high school girl he'd been seeing for a while. But they didn't discuss her much. He'd been cleared, so they'd only be dredging up the past.

It was just before 10 o'clock—late to go out. She'd have to avoid questions. "I'm going out for a little bit," she called out to her parents as she walked out the door. Before her parents had time to react, she was gone. As she walked down the driveway, Ellie noticed a car idling on the other side of the street. It started moving as she walked away. Before she could react, it pulled up beside her.

"Ellie," Mr. Thomas sang from the driver's seat. He was alone. "I was just about to call into your house to speak to you when I saw you leave."

"What do you want?" Ellie spat. No one else was around. Her house was only a few yards away, but she was terrified of this man.

"Just to talk," he answered casually. "I don't think we got off on the right foot tonight. We don't want that to affect Josh's performance on the field, do we?"

"That has nothing to do with me."

"I'd like to believe that. Has he said anything to you?"

"About what?"

"About why he's been playing so badly?"

Other than how you treat his mom like something you dug out of your ear, and maybe like a punching bag?

"No. We don't talk about football much."

He stared at her for a few seconds too long.

"I need to go now," she said curtly.

"This year is vital, Ellie." His voice was low and menacing. "Too important to mess up because of some fling."

"I'm meeting someone."

"I think it might be best if you find someone else. A beautiful girl like you shouldn't have any problems attracting boys."

"I have to go now," she said again. She was tempted to run home but knew she'd be safe at the police station. "Don't follow me, or I'll go home and tell my father you're stalking me."

"Stalking you?" Mr. Thomas said. "Don't be ridiculous."

"You've made yourself clear," Ellie said. "Leave me alone."

"I just wanted to talk to you, Ellie. You and Josh are no good for each other."

"Do I need to scream, Mr. Thomas?"

His eyes seemed to be crawling all over her like slugs.

"Just stay away from Josh."

With that, he started the car and drove away. She ran home, taking a moment to breathe after bursting through the front door. Her parents were still in the family room watching TV, and her brothers were in the basement playing video games. The thought to tell her mom and dad what had just happened crossed her mind, but she dismissed it in seconds. She had no idea what they'd do if they knew what his father was truly like. She was going to have to negotiate this alone. First thing was to get to the police station, but she wasn't walking after what had just happened.

Her father looked up as she walked into the family room.

"Can I borrow the car for a few minutes?"

"Where are you off to?" he answered.

"Just to meet some friends. I have to pick something up. I won't be long. Just call me if you need me back."

"I thought you were going to walk," her mother responded.

"I need to go to Lizzy's house."

"Okay. But don't be long," her father said, giving her the keys.

She reached the police station a few minutes early. Taking a seat on the steps, she nodded to an officer walking inside.

Ellie waited on the steps and checked the text again but after twenty minutes she stood up to leave. Just as she did so, she saw a figure walking toward her in the dark wearing a base-ball cap. As they came closer, she saw who it was. Julia.

"Ellie?" she said nervously. "I'm glad you came. We have so much to talk about."

She was several inches taller than Ellie, with broad shoulders. She had a pretty oval face and dark eyes which burned below jet-black hair. The streetlight behind her cast ethereal white light down, framing her like a ghost in the night. She was dressed in a sweater and jeans, the same as Ellie, but hers were worn and tattered. She stepped out of the light, an earnest, determined look on her face.

"I know you know I used to go to school with Rachel, that she was my best friend before..." Her voice trailed off and her head dropped. "Before everything happened. I knew Josh. I moved over from Media this year too, after my mom died."

"I'm sorry."

Julia didn't answer. She stopped a few feet short of where Ellie was standing and glanced up at the police station. "You weren't taking any chances, were you? Meeting me here?"

Ellie almost laughed. "Are you kidding? After what you did to Josh's locker? And all the rumors you've spread? I have no idea what you're capable of."

"You don't need to be scared of me. I just wanted to let you know who you were dating."

"Why didn't you come to me in school?"

"Because I'm leaving. My uncle and aunt are moving house. I've lived with them since Mom passed. I wanted to talk to you before I left."

"You're leaving? You've only been in school a few months." Ellie felt sorry for her. Moving around so much must have been hard—particularly after her mother died.

"I don't have any choice. And they sprang it on me. They're tough to live with."

Ellie didn't have time for this. She cut to the chase. "Josh was cleared of Rachel's murder. The police said so. He was at home—"

"With his father?" Julia interrupted her. "Was that what you were going to say—that he was at home with his dad?"

"That's what the police report said," Ellie replied.

"Convenient that his father was his alibi, isn't it? Josh's DNA was all over her when they found her body."

"He was her boyfriend. They were together earlier that evening," Ellie said, parroting the points Josh had made to her when she'd asked him about it.

"And he went home early? Is that what he told you?"

"You have evidence to the contrary?" Ellie said.

Julia looked around. "Can we talk somewhere else?"

"Absolutely not!"

"Okay, I understand. You must be a little nervous, but I'm here for you. I have nothing to gain from this."

Ellie ran her hand through her hair and pushed out a breath. "By spreading slander about my boyfriend? There are plenty of jealous little idiots in school saying the same things you are. Why am I even wasting my time listening to you?" She was pacing up and down now. Her head began to ache.

"Because you could be next!"

Julia's words and the earnest look in her eyes stopped Ellie in her tracks. Her legs seemed to weaken and she sat back down on the steps behind her. Julia moved closer but remained standing. "They never found anyone else's DNA on Rachel."

"The police said the killer must have been wearing gloves."

"I was at the party at Joe McCullough's house that night. I spoke to Rachel not long before she died. She was my best friend," Julia choked. Ellie could see the tears forming in her eyes. "She told me that Josh had hit her the week before and told her he'd kill her if she ever tried to leave him."

"No!" Ellie gasped. "No... no... no that can't be true. Josh wanted to break up with Rachel."

"He told you that?" Julia said. "He was obsessed with her, jealous of anyone she spoke to. He almost started a fistfight the night she died when she spoke to a male friend of hers at the party."

Ellie shook her head defiantly. "He's not like that. I know him."

"That's the way he started out with Rachel. The perfect gentleman. He's just like his father. All he wants is control."

Ellie's head was spinning. A police car pulled up and two officers got out. Julia stopped talking as they walked past.

"You okay, girls?" one of them asked.

"Fine," Ellie said with the best smile she could muster.

The cops disappeared through the front door, and Julia began again.

"You're buying into Josh's story, just like everyone else did."

"And you know better? Better than the police who investigated the case?" Ellie said.

"Rachel was the sweetest, kindest person I ever knew," Julia said. "Her funeral was the saddest day of my life besides my mom dying. And Josh was there, at the back, in his suit. I wanted to claw his eyes out. I couldn't believe the nerve he had to show up."

"What does Rachel's family say about her death?"

"The exact same things I do. Her parents are just as mad today as the night the cops found her in the woods."

Ellie took a moment, trying to rationalize what Julia was telling her. Everything she'd said was the exact opposite of what she'd heard from Josh. Ellie rubbed her eyes, feeling like her head was about to explode. Ultimately the police had found Josh not guilty—that had to count for something.

"I'm doing this for your safety, Ellie. I don't want to read about you in the newspaper again in a few months," Julia said gently.

"But Josh wasn't there. He couldn't have killed her. His dad came and picked him up from the party. Rachel died after that." Ellie's voice was breathless, as if she was trying to convince herself.

"What time did the cops say Rachel was strangled? Just after midnight, wasn't it? And Josh's dad said he picked him up from the party alone at about eleven thirty. I was there, watching Josh that night. I knew he was no good. I'd been begging Rachel to break up with him for weeks, even before he hit her."

"Are you sure?"

"She showed me the bruise!"

"Did you tell the police that during the investigation?"

"Of course," Julia said. Her eyes were wild, and she was spitting words out at a rapid rate now. "They wrote down what I said, but nothing ever came of it. They didn't want to pin it on the big football star, the best prospect in the state."

"That seems hard to believe."

"They had their narrative. Josh's dad said he picked him up

before Rachel left and that he was normal, sober, and calm in the car on the way home. Case closed."

"Exactly."

"But that wasn't the truth. I was with Rachel until about eleven fifteen. I went to the bathroom and then she was gone. I looked around for her and Josh but couldn't find either. Then about midnight, I noticed Josh in the yard by himself, and then his dad came."

"Not at eleven thirty?"

"No. And if the pathologist got the time of Rachel's death wrong by a few minutes, then that means they were both missing at the same time, and she was never seen alive again."

"But—"

"Are you gonna say that he was calm and sober when his father picked him up? Have you seen Josh's dad at his games? He's obsessed. He'd do anything to help his son make it to the NFL like he never could. He's a pathetic loser, living through his kid. He gave Josh the alibi he needed to beat the charges, and with the cops' help, the big football star walked free while my best friend is rotting in the ground!"

Julia's face was contorted with hatred. Ellie had no idea if she was right or wrong but couldn't deny the girl's belief in her own convictions. As far as Julia was concerned, Josh had killed her best friend, and his father had helped him cover it up. Ellie's head was spinning. She didn't know what to believe. Josh was so loving and sincere—nothing like the monster Julia was portraying him as. If she'd been describing Mr. Thomas, she might have believed her more readily.

"So, why don't you walk inside the police station right now and tell them all this?" Ellie challenged her, pointing up to the door. "I'm sure they'd want to solve Rachel's murder."

"I already have!" Julia spat. "Don't you think I told them this story? All I want is justice for Rachel and to see that monster get the punishment he deserves."

"I'm sorry about your friend," Ellie said, shaking her head. "I truly am, but that doesn't sound like the person I know."

"Ellie," Julia said and took her hand. "This is a lot to take on board. I get that. Everyone in school worships the ground he walks on, but he's sick. He's evil and twisted, just like his father. You need to get away from him before something terrible happens."

Ellie pulled her hand away. Images of Rachel—the pictures that had been in the newspapers—entered her mind. What if this girl was telling the truth and Josh was a killer? Was it so unbelievable that his father would lie for him? Josh making it to the NFL seemed to be the only thing he cared about. He certainly didn't have any concern for his wife. She was probably little more than a possession to him—just like Rachel had been to Josh in Julia's story.

"I need to go," Ellie said.

"Just promise me you'll break up with Josh. I can't see the same thing happen to you as Rachel."

"I appreciate you telling me this. I need to think for a while."

"Text me if you want to talk," Julia said. "I'm always here for you."

Ellie nodded and tried to smile.

"Just promise me you'll be careful. If Josh Thomas wasn't a big football star, he'd be behind bars now. He killed my friend. I had to tell you before I left."

Ellie nodded to her. She supposed she should have thanked her, but it was the best she could manage. Ellie walked to her father's car and backed out, her mind swirling. What if everything Julia had said was true? What if Josh killed Rachel? Was she next? *No. No.* She shook her head. Josh wasn't a killer. She knew him. How could he have hidden that side of himself so completely from her? She wanted nothing more than to drive to Josh's house, to have him shoot down everything Julia had said, and be safe in the knowledge her boyfriend was the person she thought he was. But Josh's father was there. She couldn't risk that. And she had to get away from Julia. She was halfway home when she pulled over to the side of the road. After checking to see if Mr. Thomas had followed her, she reached into her pocket for her phone and texted Josh.

> What are you doing? I need to see you. Now.

She sent the text, hoping for a fast response. It came back seconds later.

> I'm at home. Dad's in a mood. Said I had to be fresh for practice in the morning. I'd have to sneak out.

Ellie typed quickly.

> Can I pick you up around the corner from your house in ten minutes?

> I'll be there.

Ellie started the car again. Dark thoughts filtered through her mind as she drove. What if Julia was telling the truth and the cops were more interested in protecting the narrative they'd established with Mr. Thomas being Josh's alibi? What if he had killed Rachel Kubick? Was she driving to see a killer?

"Stop," she said out loud. "That girl is crazy or too blind with grief to see that Josh could never do something like that. It isn't in him. And the cops would never cover up the truth because someone was good at football."

But still, the dissenting voices inside her echoed Julia's words. She had been his girlfriend, and he'd been at the party with her that night. What if even some of what Julia had said was true? No one else had any motive to kill Rachel. Maybe he'd got angry when she'd tried to break up with him. Ellie had no doubt that Josh's father would do whatever it took to protect his football career. What if she got in the way?

Her hands were shaking on the steering wheel as she pulled up around the corner from Josh's house. She found some tissues in the glove compartment and wiped the sweat off her forehead. The street was dark and empty. It was completely quiet. Everything Julia had said flooded back into her mind. She imagined Josh, different from the person she knew, hitting Rachel, his face twisted in hate, and then saw him grab her throat, forcing her to the ground as she fought for her life, kicking and thrashing in the dirt like an animal.

A knock on the window startled her. She almost screamed until she saw Josh's face through the glass. The thought of driving away and not letting him in the car flashed through her consciousness, but no, that was ridiculous. She knew Josh. She loved him. Ellie unlocked the door and he got in the passenger seat.

He reached across to kiss her, but she offered only a cheek.

"What's wrong?"

Ellie wished she could say nothing but she needed answers.

"I was just at the police station," she said, and immediately realized how misleading her statement was.

"What?" he asked in a worried tone. "Is everything okay?"

She looked into his eyes, trying to see the truth in them. He'd always seemed so genuine before tonight, but she couldn't get rid of the niggling doubt inside. Was being with this boy worth risking her life?

"I spoke to someone there."

His face was different now. He almost looked suspicious. He put his arm up on the headrest and turned to her. "Ellie, what's going on? You're making me nervous."

"I got a text earlier, from someone you used to go to school with. She knew Rachel."

Josh's face hardened. "Who was it?"

"They wanted to meet up, told me I needed to hear the truth about Rachel."

His face tightened. "And you went? I already told you the truth, Ellie. You know exactly what happened the night she died. Who was it?"

"I can't tell you that."

"Was it Janie Lee, or Maggie Fitzgerald, or Tina Morris?"

Ellie shook her head. She'd had no idea how this would go but she'd hoped for better than this.

"Was it Julia Leonard?"

Ellie didn't say a word, but Josh's face changed.

"It was Julia, wasn't it? Did she tell you anything about her life, and who she is?"

"I just need to ask you some questions, Josh. Anyone would do the same. Your last girlfriend was murdered."

"Like what?" he snarled. "I can't believe you went behind my back. I don't want to sit here and relive the worst night of my life over and over. We've been through this."

"Did you ever hit Rachel?"

"What?" he said, his eyes bulging. "Hit her? Who told you that? Julia said that?"

"Did you ever hit her?" Ellie repeated.

"No. I never hit Rachel. I'd never hit any woman. I've seen what..." He stopped himself before continuing again. "I'd never lower myself to that. I can't believe you'd think I might do that. Who do you think I am, Ellie?"

"I had to ask," she answered. "One of Rachel's friends—"

"And you think I'm going to do the same thing to you? You're my next victim, is that it? Is that what Julia told you? Well, let me tell you a few things about her. She's completely nuts. Known for it. The poor girl didn't have a dad, and her mother committed suicide six months ago."

Ellie was shocked. "I never knew."

"No one does. The only reason I do is I was in school with her last year. She had to move in with her aunt and uncle, but she couldn't let her old prejudices go. I went easy on her, even after all the things she said about me, because she's had such a hard time. But this is too much."

"You've been so patient with her. Why didn't you tell me?"

Josh ignored her question and kept on. "She hated me from the get-go and filled Rachel's mind with these horrible rumors about me. And it looks like she's still doing it. What else did she say?"

"That you and Rachel left the party together about eleven fifteen and that you were the last person to see her alive."

Josh punched the glove compartment. "That's a lie!" he roared. "I was waiting outside for my dad when Rachel left. I have no idea why she left the house. She might have been alone or with the killer, but I don't know. I had nothing to do with it. And let me guess what else she said—my dad covered for me, right?"

Ellie nodded.

"The old classic. My father let me get away with murder—literally—so it wouldn't interfere with my football career. Yeah, right. The worst part is that you believed all this, Ellie."

"I never said I believed it to you or to her. All I said is that I had to talk to you about it. If someone came to you and told you I did some terrible thing, would you talk to me about it or just ignore it?"

He held up his hands in frustration. "But we've been over this before."

"I was within my rights to ask you again. You know that." Her strong tone surprised him a little.

He seemed to calm down, staring out the window for a few seconds before speaking again. "I didn't kill Rachel."

"I know that," Ellie replied. "I just needed to hear your side of the story, that's all."

She thought to tell him about his father approaching her but deemed that too much. She would have to keep that to herself for now.

"All this stuff about Rachel..." Tears began to roll down his cheeks. "It's awful. It's going to follow me forever."

She reached over to embrace him, holding his head to her chest.

But still, even after everything he'd said, the doubts inside Ellie lingered. Perhaps he was nothing more than a convincing liar. Her heart urged her to believe him, but her mind told her something very different. It would be up to her to find the truth out for herself.

SIX

Ellie couldn't escape the thoughts plaguing her. She didn't bring her doubts up in front of Josh again and did her best to pretend everything was normal, but the truth was that his mind was elsewhere too. They didn't see each other much between classes, and he had practice every evening. Neither of them made the effort to see the other the way they usually would have. Julia Leonard's warnings haunted her. She didn't tell any of her friends. She couldn't. They would have never let her speak to Josh again. And maybe they would have been right. Her parents noticed the change in her, and so it wasn't a hard sell on Friday when she told her mom she was sick and couldn't go to school.

Ellie lay in bed long after her parents had left for work. Josh's old school was only a thirty-minute drive away, but with her parents both out at work, she didn't have a car. She considered calling Maddie to borrow hers but knew how she'd react. The last thing Ellie needed was to be buried beneath an avalanche of panic, so she called a taxi instead. It dropped her off outside Josh's old school ten minutes before the final bell. Ellie leaned against the wall and waited.

A line of parents in cars had already formed to pick up kids as the freshmen and sophomores emerged first.

Ellie approached a girl with long auburn hair and glasses. "Do you know where Tina Morris is?"

"She's gone over to soccer practice."

"Where's that?"

The girl pointed around the side of the school. Ellie thanked her and ran, slaloming through kids with bags over their shoulders as she went.

Ellie caught who she hoped was Tina walking into the changing rooms. "Tina?" she asked, but the soccer player kept going. Ellie touched her on the arm. "Do you know Tina Morris?"

"She's inside."

"Can you get her for me, please?"

"Sure," the girl replied.

Ellie couldn't believe she was doing this. What would Josh do if he found out?

She waited outside for a nerve-shredding two minutes before a small girl with two long braids in her brown hair walked out.

"Devon told me you were looking for me?"

Ellie forced a smile, hating the sneaking around but desperate for anything to prove Julia wrong. "I heard you know Josh Thomas. And Rachel Kubick, too."

Tina glanced toward the locker room, on guard. "Yeah, I knew him and Rachel. Why?"

Guilt swirled in Ellie's gut, knowing she was betraying Josh's trust. But she plunged ahead. "I wanted to ask you about the night Rachel... the night she died."

Tina looked at her for a long second and turned to walk back inside.

"Please," Ellie said. "I heard you might know. I spoke to Julia Leonard. She wanted to warn me."

The girl stopped and turned back apprehensively.

"Can we talk? Please? I don't know anyone else to go to. The cops just accepted his version of what happened with Rachel Kubick, and then Julia came to me. Now I don't know what to think."

"I have to be on the field soon." She looked around anxiously.

"I came all the way here to find you. Can we please talk for just a minute?"

"Okay, come on," Tina said, scanning around them cautiously. "Let's get away from here."

She walked toward an open field at the end of the changing rooms. They were by the corner flag when Tina turned to her.

"Who are you?"

"Josh's girlfriend. I heard about what happened with Rachel. It was all anybody talked about when Josh first came to school, but the more I got to know him, the more I saw a different side of him. We all did. The football team's unbeaten. Everything was great until Julia texted me out of nowhere. I feel like such an idiot."

"What did she say?"

"That Josh killed Rachel."

Just saying those words felt like stabbing Josh in the back. Just dredging that up in front of someone who knew him felt like a betrayal.

Tina's face tightened. "I wouldn't believe everything Julia says. She's crazy. Seemed to have it in for Josh."

"How well did you know him?"

"Not as well as I knew Rachel and Julia. But I knew him. He and Rachel were happy for a while, but then..." Tina's eyes glistened. "Julia told you Josh killed her?"

"What do you think?"

"I was there that night. At Joe McCullough's house. I don't know. I really don't. I saw Rachel talking to Julia, and then she left. I don't know exactly what time that was. I was having a fight with my boyfriend. I had my own drama to deal with." She shook her head with a rueful smile.

"Do you think Josh is the type of person who could kill his girlfriend? He mentioned your name as someone he used to know."

"I didn't think he was aggressive, and he treated Rachel well, except..." Tina paused nervously, "toward the end. They were fighting that night at the party."

A dozen questions formed in Ellie's mind. "How badly?"

"Not screaming the place down, but they weren't getting on. Anyone could see that."

"You said he treated her badly at the end? What did you mean by that?"

Tina shrugged. "They fought a lot. It was weird. They seemed to fight about his dad all the time."

Ellie didn't find that weird at all.

A few girls had run onto the field behind them. Ellie knew she didn't have long now. She wanted to scream, to reach into Tina's mind and pull out the information she seemed so determined to hold on to.

"Do you have any idea what the fight was about on the night of the party?"

"I dunno. There was a horrible rumor that it was about his dad. I didn't hear them, but I heard from somebody that Josh was angry about her spending time with him."

"With his dad? Rachel was spending time with Josh's dad?"

"It's crazy, I know. Some people said they were seeing each other behind Josh's back." Tina held her hand up. "But I don't know. It's all unsubstantiated. Not a shred of proof."

Ellie digested that for a second before she began again. "Did Josh leave before Rachel died? Did you see him go into the woods with her?"

"No, I left early too. I saw Josh outside waiting, but I didn't check the time."

"How'd he seem?"

"I didn't notice. I'd been drinking, and I was upset. Josh was sitting on the sidewalk alone outside Joe's house. I didn't see his face. But there might have been something else."

"What?"

"I walked home. It took me a while. I stopped to cry. I was alone. It was stupid, I know."

A ball flew in their direction. Tina stopped to control it and kicked it back. A few of the other girls called for her to come join them but Tina turned back to Ellie.

"I know you have to go but tell me, what did you see?"

Tina shook her head. "It was dark, and I was drunk and upset. I was sitting on the side of the road, and I looked up. A car passed me. I looked up for some reason and I thought I saw Josh's dad, alone in the car. I don't know, though. I couldn't be sure." She looked down at her feet, twiddling her fingers in front of her. "Whoever it was drove past me, back in the direction of Joe McCullough's house."

"But Josh's dad picked him up from the party."

Tina's lip tightened. "No. He left with Josh twenty minutes before that. I saw him come back after that. *Alone.*"

Ellie's insides constricted, and her breath caught in her lungs. "But you think it was Mr. Thomas?"

"Come on, Tina, we're waiting for you!" one of the other soccer players said.

"And Josh wasn't in the car with him? You're sure he was alone?"

"He was alone. Unless Josh was hiding in the passenger seat." She shook her head. "I don't even know if it was him. I barely saw whoever it was."

"Did you tell the police this?"

"Not at first."

"You didn't?" Ellie said, not trying to hide her incredulity.

"I didn't get a good look at whoever it was, and I wasn't even meant to be out that night. I would have been kicked off the soccer team if I'd been caught drinking. I thought the police would deal with it, that they didn't need me. A few months passed and it didn't seem like they were going to solve it. I called up and spoke to a detective but nothing ever came of it."

"They didn't follow up with you?"

Tina shook her head. "That's all I know. I'm sorry. Rachel was one of my best friends. I miss her every day. I wish to God I knew who killed her. I wish I'd never had a stupid fight with my boyfriend and left. I wish I'd stayed with her." A single tear ran down her cheek.

Ellie reached out and touched her shoulder but Tina shrugged her off.

"That's all I know. I've told you more than anyone. Please leave me alone."

"Is there anyone else I can speak to? Anyone who was there or who knows Josh?"

"No one knows anything I don't. I've spoken to all the other kids who were at Joe's house that night. It's all we talked about for months."

"Then why didn't you tell the other kids you saw Josh's father? Didn't Julia know?"

"I don't know. I was scared. I didn't think anything of it. I have no idea where he was going or even if it was Mr. Thomas." Rivulets of tears were running down her face now.

A woman in her late twenties wearing a sweat suit strode over. "Tina, are you okay? Is this girl bothering you?"

"We were just talking," Ellie said hurriedly.

"Who are you?" the coach said, eyeing her up and down. "I think it's time you left."

Ellie looked at Tina, but she offered no words to defend her. Ellie turned away, more confused than ever. The clarity she'd been seeking wasn't here. She began the walk back toward the school and took out her phone to call a taxi.

Her mind kicked into overdrive as she left the soccer field. Her breath caught in her lungs, and she had to stop to regain it. A massive pressure seemed to be building in her chest. A voice in her mind tried to convince her that everything she'd heard was unsubstantiated and Josh's dad hadn't killed Rachel, but every path her thoughts led her down brought her back to the same place.

But some things made no sense. How would Mr. Thomas have met up with her in the woods? He wasn't at the party. He couldn't exactly stroll inside and leave with Rachel without being noticed. It was full of teenagers. They would have scattered at the sight of a man in his forties walking into the house. Most of them had too much to lose, and those that didn't might have presumed he was a cop. Ellie knew what kids did at those parties. Did he just meet Rachel in the woods by chance? She shook her head. No one would have gone in there alone at night, particularly a girl. If Mr. Thomas did it, how did he know she'd be there? Did she go there thinking she was meeting Josh? Did Josh text her to meet him and then have his father return? Did he have his father do what he couldn't?

Her hands were shaking so much that she dropped her phone on the grass. She reached down to pick it up. Her voice was trembling as she called a taxi. Ellie's head ached. Her heart felt like it was torn in half. She loved Josh. She'd never met anyone like him, but how could she stay with someone who might endanger her life? If her family knew what she'd learned, they'd ban her from seeing Josh forever, and perhaps they'd be right. Ellie sat on the curb on the side of the road and let her head fall into her hands. The tears came in seconds. The pain was too much to bear. Their relationship had to end. She knew that now.

SEVEN

Ellie was lying on her bed at when her father came into her room. The bed creaked as he sat down, but she didn't turn to face him. She longed to tell him, to unburden herself, but how could she? With all the digging she'd done, she hadn't unearthed any concrete evidence. It was all hearsay and guesswork. The only things she was sure of were her feelings for Josh. Her dad pulled up the covers to tuck her in just as he used to when she was a little girl.

"How are you doing, kiddo?" he asked softly.

"Okay, I guess," she answered without turning toward him.

"You get some good rest today?"

"Yeah," she muttered flatly.

"I heard some scouts from Penn State and Texas Tech are coming to check out Josh tonight—to try and poach him out from under LSU's noses! I think he'd want you there if you're up to it."

Josh had already agreed to go to LSU but hadn't signed anything yet. He could still change his mind. It was up to him. He was being courted by some of the biggest colleges in the country. Perhaps if he played well tonight, his father might finally let up. She couldn't break up with him yet. Josh's father might come for her if she put him off his game in front of the coaches. She was trapped. Maybe until the season ended. Then she'd be free to break up with Josh and send him on his way to college. It would just be a matter of keeping up appearances until then.

Ellie finally faced her father. "I think I'll be able to go," she said. "I know Josh'll be looking for me."

"It's an important night for him. And the school. He needs you there."

Ellie knew her father wasn't trying to heap pressure on her, but she still felt it. As if on cue, her phone buzzed on the bedside table. It was from Josh.

"I'll give you some time to get ready. Game's in an hour. Dinner's on the table downstairs when you're ready."

"Thanks, Dad," she said and sat up in the bed.

She waited until her father closed the door behind him before checking the message.

> Where were you today? You okay? Sorry I've been MIA lately. I've had a lot on my mind. I'll be a better boyfriend from now on. Scout's honor.

His words only added to her consternation. A deep cloud of confusion enveloped her. She was what Josh needed. He didn't kill Rachel. He couldn't have. She stared at the screen for a few seconds before typing her reply.

> Just felt a little sick. I'm fine now. I'll be at the game tonight, cheering you on. You must be nervous about the scouts coming.

> No more so than I am every week. My dad told me to go out and enjoy myself, and that's what I'm going to do.

Ellie set the phone down and shook her head. His father told him to go and enjoy himself? While he was screaming curse words at him from the sideline? Perhaps it was another of his mind games to build his son's character. Sometimes it was hard to know exactly what Josh thought of his father. Every assertion Josh had ever made about him had been subtle, as if some hidden meaning was lurking behind his words. It was almost like he didn't know himself. Everyone saw how Mr. Thomas treated him on the sideline and after the games, and it was no wonder that Josh wanted to go far away for college next year, but he'd never said he hated him.

Ellie felt better after a shower but still dabbed concealer over the bags under her eyes. She stood in front of the mirror once she'd finished. She looked presentable, and that would have to do for tonight. She sat on her bed for a few minutes, aimlessly texting her friends about subjects she no longer cared about and skimming through the replies she received. Her mom called her down for an early dinner before the game, and she sat at the table poking at her chicken pot pie, speaking little.

"Is there something wrong?" her mom asked halfway through.

Ellie smiled. "Just nervous for Josh, I suppose."

Her mother looked at her dad for a long second but nodded to Ellie in reply.

Ellie wanted nothing more than to tell her parents everything, but she couldn't. Not yet.

She was silent in the car. Her brothers didn't try to contain their excitement and sang several songs they'd made up about Josh and the Lower Merion football team on the way to the game. It was at home again, then the team would be on the road for the next two weeks.

"Will you stand with us for a while?" Ellie's mom said as they pulled into the parking lot.

"Sure," Ellie replied with the best smile she could muster. She texted her friends and told them she'd join them after the first quarter.

Once in the stands, she took her place with her family. Lizzy, Maddie, Giselle, Hope, and about six or seven others were near the fifty-yard line, and ten yards beyond them stood Mr. and Mrs. Thomas. A huge roar greeted the team as they ran out onto the field. Ellie felt excluded from the joy and excitement gripping the rest of the crowd. It was almost as if she were here against her will. Josh ran out onto the field, and Ellie felt her stomach twist into knots. He scanned the crowd for her as he always did. She raised her hand as part of the charade. Everyone expected it. Him. Her family. His father. She had no choice. He smiled back at her, pumping his helmet in the air a couple of times.

He began warming up. Several middle-aged men had gathered near where Josh's father stood. Each was wearing the different colors of some of the top football schools in the country: Penn State, Texas Tech, Ohio State, Michigan, and, of course, LSU.

"Seems all the scouts have come the same night," Ellie's dad said. "I hope our boy brings his A game."

"I'm sure he will," Ellie murmured.

Ellie's mom grabbed her hand. "Are you sure you're okay? Do you need me to take you home?"

"No, I'm fine," she said without looking at her.

The game began. Lower Merion won the toss and chose to receive the kickoff. Josh's first pass was a completion for fifteen yards. The crowd cheered, but Mr. Thomas didn't seem happy.

He stood with his arms crossed, glowering at the scouts, who were chatting amiably among themselves.

"I hope they don't get into Josh's head," Ellie's dad said, pointing up at the scouts. "They understand that one game doesn't define anyone. Josh has been on each of their radars for years."

Ellie didn't reply. She might have had more riding on that game than Josh himself. If the star quarterback performed well in front of the scouts, they might cement their offers there and then. If he didn't play well, his father might just come looking for someone to blame. She turned to watch her boyfriend throw an interception. She winced as Mr. Thomas yelled. The scouts looked on in stony silence. Josh and the rest of the offense trotted off the field, defeated for the time being, at least.

The other team had the ball for most of the rest of the first quarter, and when Josh got it back in his hands, the Aces were 7-0 down. A stifled rush by the running back followed by an incomplete pass the wide receiver should have caught left the Lower Merion offense facing a daunting third and long.

The crowd held their collective breath as Josh dropped back into the pocket. His wide receiver, the same one who'd dropped the ball on the last play, was open, but Josh hesitated, looking for someone else. The offensive line collapsed, and a massive defensive end crashed into Josh. The ball flew out of his grasp. One of the opposing linebackers picked it up and ran it the length of the field for a touchdown. Ellie stared on in disbelief. It was like a flaming dagger in her chest.

"Oh no," her dad said, barely audible over the sound of the groaning crowd.

Josh got up, covered in mud, and took his helmet off. He scanned the crowd again before running off the field.

"Ellie, go on up to stand with your friends. I could swear Josh is looking for you in the crowd. He could do with seeing a friendly face right now."

She did as her father suggested and joined her friends near the fifty-yard line. Kids in the stands whispered and pointed to her as she walked. Apparently, she was a part of this game too. Even if she didn't want to be.

"What's going on with Josh?" Maddie asked as she arrived beside her friends.

"I don't know," she answered. "I haven't spoken to him much this week."

The urge to tell them what she knew was almost too much to bear, but his parents were standing ten yards away, and between her and them stood the scouts who could decide Josh's future. Being near Mr. and Mrs. Thomas was like standing next to a volcano, but Gary was calm—for now. His wife stood right beside him but seemed far off, staring into the distance. What did she know? What was going on behind those blue eyes? Perhaps she was in the same position as Ellie, afraid to break up with one of the Thomas men for fear of what would happen if she did. Ellie suddenly felt close to her, even though she didn't know her at all.

Ellie could hear the conversation from where she was standing.

"Maybe you came the wrong night!" Josh's father said in the general direction of the scouts.

"One bad game doesn't make a bad player," the representative from Michigan said.

"Form is temporary, Gary," the man from LSU asserted. "Class is permanent."

The score was 14-14 at halftime, and while Lower Merion had fought their way back, it had more to do with the defense and the running game. Josh was having his worst game of the season. Ellie looked around. The pressure in her chest was building again. Mr. Thomas was in conversation with the scout from LSU, whose jovial expression stood in stark contrast to

Josh's father's. His wife stood alone, quiet, and staring out onto the empty field.

Ellie checked her pockets for her phone and realized she'd left it in her car. She walked down to her parents to get the keys, and the crowd faded as she made her way into the parking lot. Her father's car was a short walk away. Night had come in earnest, and the parking lot was dark. Being alone there made her feel like a child again and she fumbled for the keys and unlocked the door. Sure enough, her phone was on the back seat where she'd left it. She slipped it into her pocket and turned around. She almost jumped when she saw Mr. Thomas standing a few feet behind her.

"Ellie, what are you doing here?"

Alarm bells rang inside her mind. Her entire body tensed with fear. "I left something in the car," she said.

She began to walk back but he was standing between her and the field. She tried to brush past him, but he took her wrist.

"I'm glad I ran into you. I wanted to clear the air."

His face was a foot from hers. The floodlights behind him illuminated his silhouette but rendered the middle of his face a menacing shadow.

"I really need to go," she pleaded.

"I wanted to apologize for my behavior," he said.

"It's fine," Ellie answered, but his grip remained. It wasn't tight, but it wasn't loose enough for her to shrug off without enough effort to formalize that he was keeping her there against her will.

"I get so worked up sometimes about Josh. I just... I want the best for him, like any father would. I'm sure you understand."

"I do, but I also need to get back."

"Let's hit the reset button. I know how keen Josh is on you. Maybe it's better you stay together. He might need that stability."

He released his grip.

"I know we got off to a rough start, but we're on the same team, Ellie." He put his hand on her shoulder. It felt like a dead fish. "We should be friends."

"I gotta get back," she said and rushed away.

"I want to ask you something," he called after her, but she kept going, walking as quickly as she could until she reached the bleachers. She thought she might vomit and took a few long breaths to try and compose herself.

"What took you so long?" her father asked as she handed him back the keys.

"I... er... nothing," she mumbled.

The sound of the players running back onto the field saved her from further questions, and Ellie drifted over to her friends. Mr. Thomas wasn't back yet but arrived in time for the second half kickoff.

"You okay, Ellie?" Maddie asked her with a look of concern.

She brushed off the question with a forced smile. "I'm fine, just a bit tired," she lied, hoping they couldn't see through her facade. *If only they knew the truth*, she thought, her mind reeling from the events of the evening. The memory of Mr. Thomas's unwanted advances made her skin crawl, and she couldn't shake the feeling of his hands on her. She longed to confide in her friends, to unburden herself of this terrible secret, but fear kept the words locked inside. What would they think of her? Would they even believe her? Ellie felt trapped, alone, and desperate for a way out.

She peered over at the other sideline, where the teams were watching from. Josh was sitting with some of the other players. Telling him what had just happened would add yet another string to what was already a gigantic tangle. She knew how he'd react and didn't want to layer even more pressure on him.

Mr. Thomas was sharing a joke with two of the scouts. He

was on his best behavior tonight. The three men laughed as Josh and the offense ran back onto the field. Mr. Thomas's smile turned sour as Josh got the ball in his hands again. A dropped pass led to a three-and-out, and the offense trotted back off the field again. The game went back and forth. Neither quarterback seemed to be able to move the ball much until the other team scored with a minute remaining in the fourth quarter. Ellie tried not to look at Josh's father, but her eyes were drawn to him like magnets. He muttered something to his wife but received no answer.

"Let's see what our boy does now!" the scout from LSU said out loud.

"Just you wait," Mr. Thomas stated with a confident grin.

Ellie turned away and was staring across the field when Lizzy nudged her in the side. "Look who's coming your way," she whispered.

Mr. Thomas smiled at her friends before stopping beside her. "Ellie, can we talk for a moment? I wanted to ask you something before."

Her friends were all staring at them. With no other choice, she nodded her head.

"Will you come and stand with me and Josh's mom for their last possession? I think it'd do him a world of good to see us standing together—putting up a united front for his sake."

"I don't know," Ellie said. The thought of being close to him made her skin crawl, but saying no to him terrified her even more.

"Please?" he said. "For Josh?"

Ellie looked down at her parents a few yards away. Her mother waved back.

"Okay," she replied.

It felt like she was being led away to her execution. "Hello, Mrs. Thomas," she said as they reached Josh's mother.

"Hello, Ellie. Don't you look pretty." Her voice was dull and distant, delicate like an injured baby bird.

"Here they come," Mr. Thomas said as the offense jogged out again.

Josh was last. He took a few seconds to fasten his helmet and joined the rest of the team in the huddle.

"This is the ultimate test," Mr. Thomas whispered to Ellie so the scouts couldn't hear. "They know he can play, but can he lead? Can he bring them back to win? This is about heart," he said and struck his chest.

Ellie wondered why he was talking to her and not his wife but kept her thoughts to herself.

"You want to see what my boy's made of?" he said out loud to the scouts. "Watch this."

They smiled back, but it seemed like they were tolerating him rather than enjoying his banter. Ellie had heard about the lengths they'd go to in order to secure a top prospect's signature. New cars for the parents. Cash gifts. Mortgages paid off. They were investments for the college. A hot quarterback who could win games and draw eyeballs would bring enormous revenue.

The Aces were on their own twenty-yard line. They needed a touchdown to tie. A two-point conversion after would win it. Ellie looked around. Several people had their heads in their hands. Tension gripped the fans like a giant bear trap.

Mr. Thomas bent down to whisper to her. "Before I call to him, stand a little closer. Let me put my arm around you."

"What?" She looked at Mrs. Thomas for some reprieve, but none came.

"Come on. This is the most important game of his life."

He slithered an arm over her shoulder and called out, "Hey, Josh!" His son looked over. "Look who I got here with me! We're together. Both here for you!"

Ellie waved. It felt pathetic, but she didn't know what else to do. A violent, angry look that Ellie didn't recognize crossed her boyfriend's face. Ellie shrugged off Mr. Thomas but Josh was already running onto the field.

"Were you trying to rile him up?" she asked, but Mr. Thomas turned away with a smug look on his face.

EIGHT

The text from Josh didn't come until much later that night. She knew he'd be too busy with the scouts after the game to talk to her. She'd gone out with her friends after to celebrate the win but her heart hadn't been in it. Now, alone in her room, her thoughts drifted to Rachel. Had she stood with Josh's dad at games last year like Ellie had? Ellie wanted to reach out to Rachel's family, but they'd moved away a few months before. Someone told her they were living in California now, trying to rebuild their lives by the ocean.

She picked up her phone. It was almost eleven o'clock.

> What a game! I saw you standing with my dad at the end. Thanks for that. It meant so much.

His text didn't move her the way it should have. All she could think of was Rachel, a girl she'd never met, who would never graduate high school or go to college. She'd never get married or have children. Everything she'd ever hoped for or dreamed about had been stolen from her that night.

Ellie needed to see Josh.

> Can we meet? Are you free now?

The reply came back seconds later.

> I can be over at your house in ten minutes. Can you get out?

> If you don't tell my parents, I won't.

She wondered about the wisdom of going out alone with Josh without anyone else knowing but dismissed her thoughts as ridiculous. *He isn't a killer.* She waited by the window until she saw his car outside. Her mother and brothers were already in bed, and her dad was in the basement playing pool with one of the neighbors. She could hear them laughing as she snuck out the front door. Josh greeted her with a kiss. It felt better than she wanted it to.

"Where d'you wanna go?" he asked, his face buried in her hair.

"Anywhere. I just want to talk," she said, knowing her voice sounded distant.

"Sounds ominous," Josh said, turning the keys in the ignition.

Ellie wanted to tell him not to worry, but she had no idea what she would say herself. She knew what she wanted to happen and what she wished was true, but her reality was different. She tried to smile, but the muscles in her face seemed frozen. He pulled out, and suddenly, she felt paralyzed by fear, as if this was the last thing Rachel had seen before she died.

"Are you okay?" he said when they pulled to a stop at a red light. He reached over and put a hand on hers.

"No," she responded. "I feel like everything's getting on top of me." She looked into his eyes.

"Is this about Rachel?" he asked.

She nodded, and he pressed his forehead into the steering wheel. His eyes were burning as he brought his head back up.

"I'm never going to escape this, am I?" He turned to her. "I'm sorry for her and her family, but I didn't kill Rachel. I wasn't even there when she died. I don't know how many times I need to explain that to you."

Ellie pressed on. "Why did you get angry when your father put his arm around me? I didn't want to do that. I only did it because he said it would benefit you."

He gripped the steering wheel as if he was trying to crush it. "No reason."

"No? You were angrier than I've ever seen you."

"Dad tries to push my buttons to make me win. He says I play better angry."

"Why would that make you so mad?"

"Because he knows I'm protective of you, all right? He used to stand with Rachel at the games like that."

The stoplight turned green, and the car behind them beeped. Josh drove on. The silence in the vehicle swirled around them. Ellie didn't know what to say next. Everything was damning and, once alleged, could never be taken back. He turned on the radio. This should have been a moment of triumph. He should have been telling her about the colleges courting him, about the bright, shining future that sparkled before his eyes. But this felt like an ending. Something beautiful was about to die. It wasn't fair. She loved him. Neither of them had ever said it out loud, but she knew he felt it too. Perhaps one day, the truth would come to light. Mr. Thomas or whoever killed Rachel would be brought to justice.

They didn't speak until he pulled up to the wooded area they sometimes visited together. A creek swirled past below them, and through a gap in the trees, a trail led to a playground, abandoned and eerie in the moonlight.

"This okay?" Josh said.

The mood was markedly different than it usually was when they came here. He sat back in the seat and exhaled deeply. "I spoke to all the scouts tonight. They came and sat with me and my parents one by one, offering us the world," he said with a tired smile.

Ellie was puzzled. He should have been happier.

"Did you decide anything?"

"Not yet. I'm still leaning toward LSU. I like the coach and the program, and I think I could get into the team pretty quickly. My dad wants to hold out—to start a bidding war. He wants to cash in."

"He's been waiting for this for a long time," Ellie said.

She was staring through the gap in the trees at the empty playground. It was somewhere she'd spent a lot of time as a child.

"Yeah, but somehow I don't think that's what you want to talk to me about."

Now was the time to voice her concerns, but how could she confront him with her theory that his father had killed Rachel?

"It's just been a lot lately," she began.

"I understand," he replied before she had a chance to continue. "Don't get me wrong—I'm lucky, but I wish my dad would give me a break sometimes. I can't remember the last time we talked about something other than football or my grades. And the only reason he's interested in them is coz I can't play if they drop."

"Do you want this, Josh? What do you want?"

"What do you mean?"

"Do you want to play for LSU and in the NFL?"

He looked shocked at the question. "Of course I do."

"Sometimes I wonder if you wouldn't be happier as just a normal guy."

He gripped the steering wheel. "Of course I want to be a

quarterback. Who wouldn't? This is what my whole life's been about."

"It doesn't have to be. There are other things."

Josh shook his head. "I love football. I love being so good at it. I know I'm good."

"But is this what you want?"

"I've never known anything but football. It's my way out of this town. It's how I get away from my dad and secure my mom's future as well as my own."

"What?"

"That's part of the deal with LSU. They're going to put my mom up in her own apartment on campus and give her a job in the bookstore or something with an inflated salary. I haven't told anyone else. My dad doesn't know. I hatched the plan with her last year when the colleges first started calling."

Ellie's heart froze in her chest. "You never told me. I knew you wanted to get here away from him—"

"Only a few people know. My dad would go nuts if he found out."

"I'm so glad for her." Ellie was impressed. Josh was doing this for his mom more than anything else.

"I owe her. She's stuck with the old man for years for my sake. It's not easy when someone gives up their own happiness so you can play better football. It's a lot of pressure. They've been fighting my whole life."

He paused for a moment then continued. "I think he had an affair when I was little. I remember the epic fights back then, but my mom just stopped fighting a few years ago. It was as if all the screaming matches wore her out, and she just shut down. So football is our escape. It's our salvation. I'm my father's dream. I owe my career to him, but how can I share it with him after how he's treated my mom all these years?"

She reached over and held him.

"Did he treat Rachel well?" she asked.

Josh paused a second before answering as if the question had taken him by surprise. "That's what I can't understand. He loved Rachel and she liked him too. He gave her rides home from my house, and she was happy to go alone with him. I don't think you'd be willing to do that."

"No, I wouldn't," she said. "What about your mom? Did she get along with Rachel?"

"Not much. She and my dad fought a little over her."

"They fought over your girlfriend?" The alarms that went along with those words started sounding in Ellie's mind.

"Yeah. Dumb, isn't it? Well, as much as my mom fights with anyone. I heard them once, though. She was annoyed at the way he looked at her. She was pretty, not like you, but she was good-looking. It was so stupid. I don't know how Mom got that into her head."

"Yeah, that's crazy," Ellie said, nodding, but her internal voices were screaming. She turned to Josh. He looked so hand-some in the half-light. She wanted to reach out to him but knew she couldn't. Frustration coursed through her. All she wanted was to be with this boy. But that wasn't possible.

"Did you ever suspect she liked him too?"

"What?" he looked startled. "That my girlfriend liked my dad?"

"I don't know... He's been weird with me." The words escaped her mouth before she could stop them.

"How?" Josh bristled.

"When you left the room at dinner. He leaned over me. Inches away..." She trailed off, unable to see the point in hurting Josh by telling him.

Josh's face contorted in anger. "What did he do?"

Ellie didn't want to complicate the situation even more with the whole truth. "He got close—too close."

"Did he touch you?"

Ellie closed her eyes, backed into a corner. She was starting to wish she'd never brought it up. Riling Mr. Thomas wasn't a good policy. She shook her head.

"Then what? Did he say something to you?"

"Just that..."

"What?"

"He told me not to distract you."

"But he scared you? I noticed you were off. Why didn't you tell me?" He almost seemed angrier at her than his father.

"It was a difficult situation."

"I could murder him sometimes."

"And at the game, I met him in the parking lot when I went to get my phone."

His ire seemed to fade to resigned frustration. "He told me about that. He said he just ran into you, that he went to his car to get something too, but wanted to talk to you." Josh reached across and took her hand. It felt good. "I know he's crazy, and I hate the way he treats my mom. I can't stand him for that..."

"How does he treat your mom?"

Josh didn't answer. She could sense him clamming up. Ellie asked the question again.

"I don't want to talk about that," he replied sharply.

"I'm scared, Josh. The way he is with me, and then you tell me he and Rachel were close..."

"What are you getting at?"

"I don't know," she said, her voice raw. "Your last girlfriend was murdered, and they never found who did it."

"It wasn't me, and my dad is many things, but a murderer is not one of them." Josh looked wild-eyed.

"I know you didn't," Ellie said. "But it's not as simple as that. I'm getting to the point where I'm fearing for my safety. I can't live like that. I love you, but nothing is worth that."

"You love me?" he said.

She shifted in her seat and looked away. "Yes, but that doesn't make any difference. I can't put my life in danger."

"You think your life's in danger because you're with me?" he asked grimly.

She tried to stay calm but could feel her voice rising. "Yes! Whoever killed Rachel could come after me next."

Josh hit the steering wheel with an open hand. "I love you too, Ellie, and next year—"

"Is nine months and over a thousand miles away," Ellie interrupted. "I understand why you want to get away—"

"I can't wait. And..." He paused before turning toward her. "Mom will be safe, too. She can have the life she deserves after dealing with my dad for so many years."

Ellie forced a smile but the mention of Josh moving away hit her like a punch to the gut. She genuinely wanted Josh's mom to be happy and for Josh to be everything he could be, but the thought of losing him was too painful to think about. She blinked rapidly, trying to push down the welling emotions.

"So, um," she began, her voice slightly unsteady. She cleared her throat and tried again.

"Did the police interview your dad about the night of the party?"

Josh shook his head. Ellie knew he didn't want to talk about this, but she didn't care.

"Where's all this coming from?" he asked.

"You know where," she said. "I'm trying to see if I can stay with you. If it's safe."

Josh nodded. "Okay, I get it. It's just hard talking about it."

"Try," she demanded.

He leaned back against the head rest and stared out into the darkness.

"Of course they did. I was the prime suspect until they realized I didn't do it. My dad picked me up before she died."

"I know that part, but what did you do when you got home? What did he do?"

"He sent me to bed."

"What about him?"

He seemed to cringe as he spoke. "He and my mom had a fight. Well, he started in on her. I told him to lay off, and for once, he listened. He often went out driving to cool down. It's something that happens way too often in our house."

"Where did he go?"

"I have no idea, but the police interviewed him. He said he drove around for an hour and came home. I don't know where he is half the time. He's always out working, at all hours of the day and night."

"Did you see him when he came back in?"

"No, I was asleep. I know where you're going with this. Why would my dad kill Rachel? And if he did, why didn't the cops figure it out? Dad's no killer."

"I'm just trying to work this through in my mind. I'm sure the cops didn't charge him because they didn't have enough evidence, but they must have thought it was a possibility."

"Well, according to them, he didn't do it," he said, his voice bristling with anger once more. "The case is still ongoing. I wake up every day hoping they'll find whoever killed Rachel. I can't imagine the pain her family must be feeling. But the cops haven't come up with anything."

Ellie tried to process everything Josh had said, attempting to mix it up and come to the conclusion she wanted to—that Josh's father hadn't killed Rachel, and she could be with his son. But no matter how she tried, she couldn't escape the gnawing feeling inside her.

"I don't think we can be together anymore," Ellie said, a tear rolling down her cheek.

Josh went pale. He shook his head but didn't answer for a few seconds. He put his hands to his face.

"No! I didn't kill her, but everyone thinks I'm guilty. I wish I'd never met Rachel Kubick. Maybe she would never have gone to that party if I hadn't asked her. She might still be alive. I have her death on my conscience all the time and now you're breaking up with me because of it. I love you, Ellie. All this will be a bad memory this time next year."

"When you're all the way down in Louisiana?"

"I could go to Penn State, only three hours away."

"And what about your mom?"

"They might do the same deal as LSU."

"No. I don't want you to base that level of decision on me. It's not just your future. It's your mom's too. Go where you need to."

"This is all because of my dad? You think he killed Rachel. You think he drove back out to Joe McCullough's house after he dropped me off and found her somehow. Why would he do that?"

"Maybe he thought she was a distraction and wanted to eliminate her. Or there might have been more to their relationship than you thought."

"You're being crazy," he said, and immediately looked like he regretted saying it.

She could feel the anger coiling inside her. "A girl died, Josh. Your last girlfriend before me. I think I have the right to—"

"Yes, of course, you do. I'm sorry. It just seems so nuts to me that my dad could have murdered Rachel. How would he have gotten her away from the other kids at the party? It's not like he wouldn't have stuck out. He was twenty-five years older than everyone else there."

"I don't know. Maybe they'd arranged to meet or he happened to see her."

"I don't buy it."

"Could he have texted her?"

"They never found Rachel's phone. Whoever killed her must have taken it. And they checked mine and his. They went through every text and call we both made and never found anything incriminating. It doesn't add up." He reached over and took her hand. "If I can convince you my dad didn't do it, will you give us another chance?"

Ellie knew he wouldn't let her go without a fight. Just as he'd shown in the game earlier that evening, he wasn't one to quit easily.

"How do you figure we could do that when the police couldn't?"

"I'm not saying we could catch the killer, but maybe we could find enough to rule out my dad. That's the most important thing for us, isn't it?"

"I guess."

"I understand your reasoning, Ellie. I'm sorry I said you were crazy. But you're wrong. And if we can prove that, then we'll have nothing in our way. I don't want to lose you. Give us that chance."

Ellie looked into his eyes. He was a hard person to say no to.

"I don't see how—"

"I have a few ideas. People we can talk to, places we can search. I've already talked to a lot of people but I kept on expecting the cops to find the killer. Now, I'm thinking we might have to do their work for them. I knew Rachel. If we work together, I'm confident we can do this. You're the smartest person I know."

"Let me think about it," she said. "But I'm not coming within a country mile of your dad if we do try and figure this out."

"I'll keep him away. Scout's honor."

"I need some sleep," she said, her eyes feeling bleary. "I'll let you know in the morning."

Josh nodded and started the car. The ride home was quiet, the silence heavy with unspoken words. As Josh pulled up to her house, Ellie felt a twinge of disappointment when he didn't lean in for a kiss, but a part of her was relieved.

"I'll respect your decision, whatever it is," he promised, his voice soft and sincere.

Ellie managed a small smile, her heart aching with the weight of the choice she knew she had to make.

She slipped inside, the muffled clack of pool balls drifting up from the basement, where her father was still playing. Ellie carefully eased the door shut, wincing at the faint click that seemed to echo in the stillness. Her hand trembled slightly as she gripped the banister, and she kept to the edge of the stairs, her footsteps light on the worn carpet. Each step felt like a mountain to climb, her legs heavy with exhaustion and the burden of the night's events. All she wanted was to retreat to the safety of her room, to curl up under the covers and forget, just for a little while, the turmoil that churned inside her.

Ellie woke from an indecipherable dream with her heart thumping. The clock beside her bed told her it was almost four. She rolled over and picked up her phone. She moved onto her back and stared up at the ceiling. A single glow-in-the-dark star remained as a hangover from her childhood. It offered her comfort as she lay alone in the darkness.

She was still awake as the birds began their song, and she reached for her phone again as the first rays of the sun illuminated the edges of the blinds over her windows. She drew a sharp breath, hesitating only a moment before she typed the reply.

> Okay, let's give it a try.

Ellie set down her phone, a tiny shiver running through her.

NINE

Josh came to pick her up at eleven later that morning. Her brothers greeted him with bright smiles and high fives so loud they reverberated through the kitchen. They were in awe of Josh Thomas and weren't afraid to show it. Her father shook his hand enthusiastically, blissfully unaware of what was beneath the surface. "Great game last night."

"It was a close one, especially with the scouts from all the colleges there."

"I'm sure they were all as impressed as we were."

"Thanks."

"Ellie told me you're still on the fence with where you're going to end up next year."

"Just stringing them along," he said with a sly smile Ellie's father seemed to love. "We'll see what they're willing to do to get me to sign."

Her father laughed and shook his head. "I'm jealous of you, man. If you need a roommate, give me a call."

"Eh, what about your family?" Ellie gently teased her dad.

"Okay, maybe just for one semester," her dad said with a wink.

The minutes ticked by as Josh fielded question after question about the game, his college prospects, and every football topic her dad and brothers could think of. He leaned against the kitchen island, his easy smile and friendly demeanor never faltering, even as Ellie stood silently by his side. She couldn't bring herself to join the conversation, her mind still reeling from the yesterday's events. Instead, she watched as her father and brothers hung on Josh's every word, their faces lit up with excitement and admiration.

Josh finally made his excuses for him and Ellie to leave. Ellie's brothers clamored for hugs, and he obliged with a grin, wrapping his arms around each of them in turn. Ellie's heart clenched at the sight, a bittersweet mix of affection and sorrow washing over her.

With a final wave and a promise to see them soon, Josh headed for the door, Ellie trailing behind him. She could feel her family's eyes on her back, their expectant smiles and hopeful glances burning into her skin. But as the door closed behind them and they stepped out into the sunshine, Ellie knew that things could never be the same. The truth of what had happened, the ugly reality that lurked beneath the surface of their seemingly perfect relationship, had changed everything. And now she had to find the strength to face it head-on, no matter how much it hurt.

"You're good to them," Ellie said as they walked to his car.

He held the door for her. "It's fun for me too."

"Is this a new thing?" she said with a smile as she got in. "Don't get me wrong, I like it."

"Just trying to keep my girl happy."

Ellie let him pull out of the driveway before she asked where they were going. "So, where does the investigation begin?"

"Back to my old school. You talked to Julia Leonard. I want

to even things out a little. She's about the worst character witness I could ever call on."

"Why does she have it in for you so much?"

"I honestly don't know. We used to be friends when we were little. I remember playing with her at the park when we were about five or six. A few times. I had the football with me. My dad never let me leave the house without it."

"But she hates you now. When did that start?"

"I don't know, probably when I got together with Rachel. I didn't pay much attention to her in middle school, and then before I knew it, she started spreading rumors about me."

"What kind of rumors?"

"I can't remember exactly..."

"There's got to be some reason she was fixated on you," Ellie said. "A crush, maybe?"

"Not even close. She never treated me with anything but contempt. Then her mother killed herself. Poor girl. I feel bad for her, but I think it does explain a lot about her behavior."

Josh drove her out to his old neighborhood. They called into a house near where he used to live, and he introduced her to a girl named Kate Bonner, who had been expecting them. She was blonde with striking blue eyes, and welcomed them in with a smile. It was unseasonably warm for November, and they went out to her backyard and sat overlooking a covered pool.

Kate spent the first five minutes telling Ellie how a kind person like Josh could never kill anyone, let alone someone he cared about, like his girlfriend. Josh sat in silence as she spoke.

Ellie turned to him. "Can you take a walk around the block for a few minutes?"

"Sure," he said and got up.

Ellie waited until he was gone to start. "How well did you know Rachel?"

"Pretty well. She was fun and sweet. Lots of girls were

vying for Josh's attention. Sparks flew when he chose her. There was a lot of jealousy."

"Enough to want to take it out on her?"

Kate glanced around her nervously. "I don't think so. All the girls I know seemed to move on."

"Does he keep in touch with you all? It's funny I've never met you before."

"Not much." She shrugged. "He said he needed to leave his old life behind after everything that happened. It's a shame, but I get that. We miss him."

"He's made plenty of friends at our school."

"And I'm sure he will next year wherever he ends up. You want a cup of coffee?" Kate asked, trying to change the conversation.

"No, thanks."

"A soda? I can get you whatever you want!"

Ellie tried to give her most reassuring smile. "I just want to talk."

Kate's paranoia seemed to be contagious, and Ellie looked around to ensure no one was listening before asking the next question.

"What about Josh's dad? Did you know him?"

"Gary?" she asked with wide eyes, visibly shuddering. "Yeah, we all knew him. He's a total creep."

"How so?"

"He was so inappropriate. Always telling us how good we looked and how if he was twenty years younger... I mean, yuck."

"Did Rachel talk to him much? That must have been a lot for her to deal with."

"She never mentioned it. She knew Gary's reputation, but as far as I know, he never bothered her."

"Did he...?" Kate trailed off as if the next few words were too sordid to even utter.

Ellie sat forward. "Did he what?"

"Ever bother you?"

Ellie wondered how she should answer Kate's question. Perhaps telling her the truth might gain her confidence and make her open up more.

"The creep thing fits. I've seen that too," Ellie said.

Kate nodded knowingly. "Can't say I'm surprised. I've heard a few things about him."

Ellie could tell Kate wanted to open up to her now. "Other women?"

Kate shook her head, her lips tight. "No. Nothing. I shouldn't say anything I can't prove."

"Please tell me, Kate," she encouraged her.

"It just feels wrong..."

"What does?" Ellie asked anxiously.

Kate looked around. Her movements quickened, and she let out a deep sigh before continuing. "There were rumors."

"About Gary Thomas?"

"Yeah."

"What kind of rumors?"

"A few things. You know the way kids talk. Stuff about him seeing other women behind his wife's back. No one would have paid so much attention if he wasn't Josh's dad. His stardom put the whole family under the microscope. I think that's a lot of the reason they moved—along with what happened to Rachel, of course."

"Do you know how any of these rumors started?"

"Who knows? I swear this town should be renamed Whispers Down the Lane. Everyone talks all the time. Someone probably saw him out with a woman sometime. It might have been someone he works with. I have no idea."

"What do you believe?" Ellie could feel anxiety rising in her chest.

"I don't know what goes on in that house, but I think there's a reason Josh wants to get away next year. Maybe his dad cheats. Maybe he doesn't, but something's up with him and his wife. I'm sure you've seen the way they interact."

Ellie wanted to tell her about Josh's plan to take his mom with him to college next year but knew she couldn't.

"Have you ever talked to her about it?" Ellie asked.

"Are you kidding? You think she'd talk to me about her marital problems?"

"No, of course not, but did you ever speak to her about anything? I've been with Josh a couple of months now and I've barely said fifty words to her."

"She was different when we were little kids. A lot happier. Something changed."

Kate looked up as if someone had just caught her with her hand in the cookie jar. Ellie turned to see Josh coming toward them. He was smiling.

"You guys have a chance to talk?"

"Yeah, we had a nice chat," Ellie answered as he leaned in to kiss her cheek.

They sat in Kate's backyard for another hour. The fog in Ellie's mind began to clear—about Josh at least. As for his father, the murk had only deepened.

TEN

It was a late Tuesday night in early December when Ellie's phone buzzed on her nightstand. She put down the book she was reading and picked it up. Josh's name flashed on the screen. She wondered why he was calling so late. It was almost eleven o'clock.

She barely had a chance to speak before he was blurting words down the line.

"Ellie, it's my parents." His voice was raw and strained like elastic stretched to its furthest extent.

Ellie sat up. "What happened? Is your mom okay?"

"They had a fight. I don't even know what it was about. But they're gone. They drove off in his car. My mom's car is here, but I couldn't find her keys. She must have them. Mine's in the shop again. That's why I'm calling you. Can you come over?"

Taking the car was risky, but Josh needed her.

"Okay, I'll be over as soon as I can. I just need to throw on some clothes and grab my mom's keys. I'll be right there."

She threw on a sweater and a pair of jeans before finding her sneakers. She tiptoed down the stairs, making sure not to wake her already sleeping parents.

Her mother's keys were in her bag, and she plucked them out, knowing the trouble she'd be in if she got caught. She paused at the front door.

I'll stay in the car. Just drive Josh to where he needs to go. If anything develops, I'll get out of there.

She ignored the alarms blaring in her mind and carried on. Pushing the front door open seemed like making a decision that would change her life, but she ignored the urge to run back inside. Ellie jumped into her mom's car and took one last look at the house before turning the keys in the ignition and driving off.

Her heart was thumping like a jackhammer as she pulled up outside Josh's house. He was waiting for her. They didn't kiss. His eyes were wild, and his hands were cold to the touch.

"Did you hear from them? Did they call?"

He shook his head. "Nothing. I must have called them ten times each."

"And you have no idea what the fight was about?"

"I went upstairs and put on my headphones, but I heard something smashing and ran downstairs. The kitchen was a wreck but they were both gone. I sprinted to the front door and saw my dad throw Mom in the car. I tried shouting something, but I don't think he heard me."

"He threw her in the car?"

"I'll kill him. If he lays one finger on her, I'll kill him." Josh's face darkened. Ellie knew not to push him any further.

"What about where they might have gone? Where should we go?"

Josh directed her to a bar his father frequented, in a desperate hope they'd gone for a drink to sort things out, but they weren't there. Nobody had seen his father that night. They tried another place down the road and got a similar result. Josh tried each of their phones again and again, almost snapping his cell in half with frustration. He called family friends, his mother's sister and brother. But no one had heard from her.

Two hours had passed, but they were still none the wiser as to his parents' whereabouts. Josh's mood had changed. He was pale and fidgeting with his phone. His threats to get even with his father had waned, but only in the last few minutes.

"Let's try your house again," Ellie said gently. "They've probably realized how stupid they were being and driven home."

The power was gone from his voice now. "My mom wasn't being stupid. Dad dragged her to the car. She wasn't there voluntarily."

They arrived back at the house a few minutes later. The BMW that LSU had given his father was still missing. His mother's car was still in the driveway.

"We should try the house," Ellie said. "And I think it's time to call the police too."

She didn't want to go in there. Who knew how his father would react to seeing her at this time of the morning after fighting with Mrs. Thomas? But she couldn't desert Josh now. Her hands were shaking on the steering wheel. Her knuckles were bright white.

"And say what? Two adults in their forties went for a drive after eleven o'clock?" His bewilderment was obvious.

"No. We tell them your father forced your mom into the car and took her against her will," Ellie responded as calmly as she could.

Josh got out of the car and walked up to the door. He called out for his parents but received no answer. Ellie followed him in. The foyer and living room were in their usual immaculate condition, but the kitchen was covered in broken plates. Several pots and pans were strewn on the floor, and Josh bent down to examine some drops of blood left in the wake of their fight.

His voice was filled with pain and remorse. "She must have snapped. I guess she could only take so much."

"Josh, we need to call the cops."

He did as he was ordered, but just as he said, the advice he received was to sit tight and wait until they got home. It was too early to send out a search party for a married couple having a spat. Josh hung up the phone. "They must hear this all the time."

"You want to keep looking?"

Josh was already walking back to the car. "Maybe they went to our old neighborhood? I don't know."

"We can look wherever you want."

Ellie picked up her phone. It was almost two in the morning. She considered calling her parents before deciding against it, and she followed Josh to the car. It felt wrong, but Josh didn't deserve any of this. Without her, he had no one. It was about twenty minutes to Josh's old neighborhood, and Ellie expected nothing from the trip.

"I think we should go home after this. You can stay in my house. I'm sure my parents wouldn't mind," Ellie said gently.

"They're out there somewhere. My mom needs me. I let her down." A tear streaked down his cheek, glinting silver in the moonlight.

He was silent for a few minutes, frantically checking his phone for calls and messages that didn't come. They came to a small bridge over the river about two miles from his house when she saw the broken fence.

"Josh," she said.

He looked up in horror as Ellie stopped the car. The light above the gap in the fence shone gold down into the dark void below. Josh got out and ran to the edge. Ellie was beside him seconds later. Tire tracks led down the hill into the river. Nothing was moving. The only sound was the gentle breeze.

Josh started down the incline. Ellie tried to grab him but knew it was useless. She was already dialing 911 as he reached the water's edge.

"Where is it?" he shouted.

"Just wait until the police get here," Ellie replied frantically.

But Josh was already wading up to his waist in the freezing water.

"No, Josh, don't!"

But Josh didn't have any interest in her advice. He disappeared into the icy-cold river, re-emerging seconds later, shivering. "I can see the car."

"Come back out. There's nothing we can do. It's too late."

"I can get them," he said, his teeth chattering as tears rolled down his cheeks. "We don't know how long they've been in there."

Ellie followed him down to the water's edge and picked up the coat he'd thrown off.

"Josh! Josh!" she cried.

He either didn't hear or didn't care and dove into the frigid water again. Ellie watched in horror. Powerless. She thought to follow him in but knew she needed to be here in case he got in trouble. Several seconds passed before he surfaced again.

"I can see her. She's in the car." His face was a horrible fusion of grief and pain, his lips almost blue. "The door's open. I couldn't see my dad. I couldn't see him," Josh repeated.

He stumbled into Ellie's arms. His whole body shook with the cold that had seeped into his bones. "My father's around here somewhere. He might be hurt."

"Just wait a minute."

Ellie ran back to the car and got an old towel her mother kept in the trunk. All thoughts of getting in trouble with her parents had long since faded away. She ran back and dried him off as best she could, and he seemed to get some energy back.

He slipped on his coat and began searching the riverbank for any sign of his dad. Ellie wanted him to dry off and rest but knew trying to dissuade him was futile. He trudged up and down the riverbank but found nothing. The sound of him sobbing was clearly audible in the silence of the night.

"I... I... I couldn't save her." His voice was tiny. Almost inaudible.

She steeled herself for him. "This isn't your fault."

"My plan. So much for my plan. He got to her first."

Ellie called her parents while they sat waiting for a few minutes. She left a message on her mom's phone, then sent a text, before the police arrived and a detective in plain clothes stepped out. He was older, in his late forties, and balding. "I'm Detective Harris. Can you tell me what happened here, son?" he said, taking in the sight of Josh, and then he turned to Ellie. "Who are you?"

"I'm his girlfriend, Ellie Welsh."

Harris turned back to Josh.

He was shaking as he spoke but he found the words. "I was home a few hours ago. My parents were downstairs. I was up in my room and slipped on my headphones to drown out the fight they were having. But then I heard the sound of plates smashing. When I went downstairs, I saw my dad throw my mom in the car. They left before I had a chance to try to stop them."

"How did you know where to find them?"

He shrugged. Tears glistened in his eyes from the lights of the police cars. "Dumb luck. I tried a few places with Ellie before we figured they might be driving back to my old house for some reason."

"Why would they do that? At this time of night?"

"I dunno. To see something. Maybe my dad was trying to prove a point."

"What were they fighting about?"

Josh hesitated and turned away. The detective wasn't going to back down, however. "Come on. This is important."

His voice shook as he spoke. "I think it was another woman. I might have heard something about that."

Ellie's heart dropped. *Why didn't Josh tell me that before? Does he not trust me? Is he still trying to protect his dad?* Or maybe it was something different—maybe he was trying to keep her out of it, and not drive her away.

"I'm sorry to ask you this, but did your dad have a history of... that kind of thing?"

Josh stared at the ground like a little kid. "In the past. I didn't think he did it anymore."

"Is there anything else you can tell us?"

He shook his head. "That's it."

"Do you have somewhere you can stay tonight? Any family around here?"

"My aunt lives in Pittsburgh."

"He can stay at my house," Ellie said.

"You should go there now," Harris said. "If you do go back to your own house, please try not to disturb anything. I'm afraid we're going to have to treat it as a crime scene."

Right on cue, Ellie's mother pulled up. She got out and ran over, hugging Ellie first before putting her hand on Josh's arm. "I'm so sorry," she said in a tender voice Ellie knew well.

Josh looked at her with tears in his eyes. "Thanks."

He held on to Ellie's hand like a life raft on a raging sea.

"Mom, can Josh stay at ours tonight?"

"Of course."

"I don't want to leave my mom."

"It'll be hours until we can get the divers out here or pull the car up. And believe me, you don't want to see that, kid," Harris said.

"Come on," Ellie's mom coaxed.

"We have two cars," Ellie said. "I can drive Josh home."

Her mother glared at her.

"I'm sorry for taking it, but it was an emergency."

"You should have told me, but I understand."

Ellie led Josh over to the car. He walked as if he was in a trance, and she opened the door for him. He still had the blanket from the ambulance wrapped around him.

"Should I give it back?" he asked numbly.

"I'm sure it's okay if you keep that," Ellie replied.

She started the car, knowing she had to be strong for him. Every plan he'd ever made was destroyed, but thoughts like those could come tomorrow. Tonight was all about getting through.

"Can we stop off at my house on the way?" Josh asked when they were on the road. "I want to pick some things up."

"Of course."

Josh didn't talk, and Ellie had no idea what to say. They rode in silence all the way to his house.

He unfastened his seat belt as soon as she pulled up. "Just give me a minute."

"I should probably come in."

"No. Stay here. I'll only be a minute."

"Just remember what the detective said about not touching anything."

"I heard him."

Ellie watched him run up to the house, slide his key into the front door, and push it open. She let the emotion out as he disappeared inside. Tears streaming down her face. She dabbed her face as best she could. He couldn't see her like this. She had to be strong for him. His mother was dead, and his father was missing. What would the charges be when they brought him in? Involuntary manslaughter? If the cops could prove he'd hit her, or forced her into the car, he would surely go to prison. And there was only one witness to those things.

She stared at the front door, waiting for it to open again.

Time crawled. Josh took much longer than she'd expected. She was just about to get out of the car to check on him when the door opened and he ran out with a sports bag on his shoulder.

"Sorry," he said. "I had to get my stuff for practice tomorrow."

"I don't think anyone will expect you to go to practice for a while."

"It's all I have now. Besides you."

Ellie reached over and hugged him tightly. He seemed so vulnerable. So alone. Most kids thought they'd give anything to switch places with him, but the truth was he was the one who wanted to switch with them.

She drove home. Her parents were waiting when they arrived, and the spare bed was already made. It was almost four o'clock in the morning. Josh's whole world had fallen apart in the last six hours.

"You should get to bed, dear," Ellie's mom whispered.

"What if the police call with news about my dad?" Josh asked, his voice etched with fear.

"They'll wait to resume the search in the morning. No point in the dark. You need to get some sleep. I know that's not going to be easy, but you have to try."

Josh nodded. "Okay."

She led him upstairs with Ellie behind.

"Thank you for letting me stay."

"As long as you need," Ellie's mom responded.

Josh shut the door behind him.

"I'm sorry, Mom," Ellie said, hugging her mother.

"It's okay. Get off to bed now. He's going to need you tomorrow. This is more than any seventeen-year-old can bear alone."

Ellie was in bed ten minutes later, but sleep didn't come easily. Questions abounded in her mind. What prompted the fight? Why did Gary Thomas flee the scene? What took Josh so long when he went into his house? The minutes on her alarm clock seemed to go like seconds, and before she knew it, the time read 5:30. A sound from Josh's room next door stole her attention. He was probably awake too. She needed to see him.

The house was deathly quiet. This interminable night was still upon her. Her door creaked as she opened it, but she was beyond caring about trivialities like getting caught sneaking out of her room. In a world where Josh's mother was dead and his father was missing, things like that didn't seem to matter anymore.

His door was closed, but she turned the handle and pushed it open, expecting to see him sitting up in bed staring out the window, but he was asleep. She stood watching him for a few seconds, her heart breaking. No one deserved this, especially not him. None of this was his fault. Not his mother's death, not Rachel's. It was all his father, and soon that monster would be brought to justice. Maybe for Rachel Kubick's death too.

She was just about to leave when a piece of paper jutting from Josh's jeans pocket caught her eye. Ellie looked at Josh again. He was fast asleep. She didn't remember seeing the letter in his pants earlier that night. She turned to leave but stopped herself.

I shouldn't, she thought as she stared at the letter. *This is for my safety.* She tiptoed across to his clothes and reached down. After checking once more that he was still asleep, Ellie reached for the letter. It was important; she knew it. Her hand was on it when she heard Josh's voice scything through the silence in the room.

"What are you doing?"

Ellie snapped her hand back, not knowing how to answer his question. "I was just checking on you. I heard something."

"So, you thought you'd wait until I was asleep and then go through my pockets? Was that your plan?"

She'd never heard that tone in his voice or seen that aggressive look in his eyes.

"There's no plan, Josh. I need to get some sleep. It's been a terrible night. I'm sorry."

She turned around and went to the door, expecting him to tell her to stop or to ask to talk about it, but he said nothing, and she left without another word.

ELEVEN

Josh was still asleep when the police came at eleven the next morning. Ellie went upstairs to wake him. The letter was gone from the back pocket of his jeans. Questions about the letter and where it was now bounded around inside her mind. Resisting the temptation to look for the letter, she sat on the bed, trying to rouse him with a gentle whisper. His eyes opened with a jolt and she could see they were full of pain.

"The police are here."

He sat up in bed. "Now?"

"They want to speak to you."

The twins were in school, and Ellie's dad had gone to work as usual. Only her mother had stayed home. She had called the high school on both Ellie's and Josh's behalf, excusing their absence.

"I'll be down in a second," he said and got out of bed.

Ellie gave him a moment, waiting at the top of the stairs. He was pale and drawn when he emerged, his eyes bloodshot. Grief seemed to be choking him from the inside, but he still hugged her before they descended together. She held his hand. She wanted nothing more than to be there for him but had no idea how. This seemed like too much. His aunt was coming later that afternoon, and he would leave then, but Ellie didn't want him to. She didn't want to let him go when he was like this. She'd written off his reaction to her trying to take the letter from his pocket as an instinct. She had been the one in the wrong after all, even if his reaction had been a little harsh.

Detective Harris was in the living room. He looked like he hadn't slept more than an hour or two. He stood up as Josh walked in and shook his hand.

"Sorry to meet you in circumstances like these."

"Likewise," Josh answered and sat down. Ellie went to join her mother in the kitchen, but Josh reached out to stop her. "Do you mind if my girlfriend stays?"

"Not if you don't," the detective said.

"Can I get you something? Coffee or a glass of water?" Ellie offered.

"No, thanks. We should sit."

All three did as he said.

Harris cleared his throat before he began. "First thing, Josh, I'm sorry but we confirmed that it was your mom in the car last night."

Josh's face contorted in grief, and tears rolled down his cheeks. Ellie put her arms around him, and he rested his head against hers. It was hard to grasp the depth of what Josh was going through. Ellie could hardly imagine it. The policeman gave them a few moments before he spoke again.

"The divers brought her body out of the water. She's being taken care of. You don't need to worry about that."

His voice was tender, his movements slow and even.

"She was wearing her seat belt when we recovered her, but she had bruises and cuts on her face that she might have sustained before the car went into the water. We haven't found your father yet. Do you know anything about what might have caused those injuries?"

Josh wiped the tears from his face. Ellie wanted to tell Harris to leave him alone and find a better time but knew he was only doing his job.

"It must have been during the crash."

Harris clasped his hands together. "I understand you're trying to protect him. I really do. My father wasn't the best guy, but he was still my dad. But think of your mom. We need to get to the bottom of how she died. Don't you think she deserves that much?"

Josh nodded.

"Was your dad ever violent toward your mom?"

He nodded again, unable to keep his sobs in. He stood up and went to the window, hiding his face. The detective didn't move, giving him the space he needed.

"There were no skid marks before the barrier. Whoever was driving that car didn't brake before it plowed into the river."

Josh turned around. "That doesn't make any sense. Why would he drive into the water? He could have killed himself too."

The detective didn't answer his question. "We need to speak to your father. Do you have any idea where he might have gone? Any friends of his? A holiday home?"

"I have no idea. We don't have anything like that. Have you searched the woods for him? How do you know he's not out there lying in a ditch waiting for help to arrive?"

"He cleared out his bank account about an hour ago. We missed him. Someone is examining the cameras in the bank as we speak. One of the houses near the river reported a stolen car last night too."

Ellie's brain was buzzing. Josh was right. None of it made any sense. Had Gary just snapped and crashed the car in a rage?

"Do you think your dad wanted to hurt your mom?" Harris asked.

"Kill her?"

The detective didn't answer.

"Mom wanted to get away from him. I was going to bring her to LSU with me next year. They set up a job and an apartment for her."

"Is there a chance your dad found out?"

"I don't know... maybe," he said. "I went back to my house last night, just to stop in and get some things. I found something."

Harris sat forward. "What?"

"Give me a minute." He walked upstairs and returned with the letter Ellie had wanted to read so much. It was crumpled and torn, and he flattened it out on the coffee table. He handed it to the detective, who took a few seconds to read it.

"Where did you find this?"

"In the kitchen, crumpled on the floor."

"What does it say?" Ellie asked, unable to contain her curiosity.

Josh looked at Ellie, hesitating for a few seconds before speaking. "It says, 'Can't wait to see you again. I'll be waiting for you. At midnight.'"

Harris drew a plastic bag from his jacket pocket and slipped the note in. "Do you know who sent this?"

"No clue."

Harris gave Josh his card. "You call me if you think of anything and especially if your dad contacts you. We just want to ask him a few questions. If this was an accident, we want to clear it up. In the meantime, you should get some rest."

"I have a game tonight," Josh said with a watery smile.

"I'll talk to your coach if you need," the cop said and stood up. "I'll let you know as soon as I have news about your dad."

"He's going to jail, isn't he?"

"We're not making any judgments yet, just trying to piece together what happened."

Josh and Ellie walked him to the door.

"I'm sorry about your mom. Get some rest," Harris said.

"When can I see her?" Josh asked quietly.

"I'll let you know." He walked out to his car.

Ellie led Josh back to the family room; he could barely stand.

"Is there anything you didn't tell him?" Ellie asked as they sat on the couch together. "Anything you kept back to protect your father?"

"No. I just wish he'd come back. It must have been an accident. Who would kill someone that way? He could have just as easily done it to himself. And in his brand-new car? He loved that thing. And why would he let her find that letter? I can accept that he had other women, but not that he'd be so dumb as to get caught like that."

"Why did you take it last night?"

"Some misguided loyalty to my dad, I suppose, but my mom's the one who deserves that, not him."

"You think he'll come back when this all dies down?"

"I have no idea what'll happen next. My head is spinning."

Ellie held him again as he began to cry. His body shook as the grief he'd been holding in poured out of him.

Josh's Aunt Maureen, a woman in her forties wearing a fur coat and too much makeup, arrived a few hours later. Ellie answered the door to her.

"You must be Ellie," Maureen said and threw her arms around her. The smell of her perfume filled the room like water. "Where is he?" she said. "My poor little nephew. He had the world at his feet. And my sister…" Her mascara ran down her cheek. A tissue from her bag served to clean up the black marks. "Give me a minute," she said. "I don't want him to see me like this."

Ellie showed her to the bathroom.

"How is he?" Maureen asked.

"As bad as you'd expect."

Josh appeared at the top of the stairs as she emerged.

Ellie wondered what Josh's aunt knew about her sister's relationship with Gary, but Maureen whisked him away in minutes, and Ellie was left standing at the door. Josh waved to her through the open window and shouted that he'd call her later before his aunt backed her car out of the driveway and drove off.

It was almost dinnertime when his name appeared on the screen of her phone. She'd been talking to her friends for most of the afternoon, dealing with their questions—most of which she either didn't know the answer to or wasn't prepared to talk about.

"Josh?" she said as she answered.

"The cops called," he said. Each word he said was dripping with pain. "Someone tampered with the brakes."

"What?"

"They pulled up the car. The brakes didn't work. That's why my dad crashed into the river."

Ellie's heart was thumping in her chest. "Who?"

"They have no idea. They're going to start interviewing my neighbors to check if anyone saw something, but I have no clue. My dad didn't kill my mom. I knew it. But then, why would he run?"

Ellie longed to answer his question. To ease his pain. "I don't know."

"I gotta go. I'll talk to you later."

The line went dead.

TWELVE

Days passed with little word from Josh. His father hadn't returned, and rumors abounded. Some said he'd gone to Canada. Others swore Mexico. One kid told a story about seeing him behind a gas station just outside town. The rumors didn't change the facts. They just gave bored kids in school something to talk about. The same question whirled around in her mind: why had he fled? People said it was because he'd hit her so many times, she was a bloody mess, and he'd let her die in the car. He'd saved himself and got out of there. Maybe he hadn't realized the brakes had failed and thought he was responsible. Or perhaps he'd had something else to take care of. Something the cops would stand in the way of. Perhaps whoever had written that note had been the one to cut his brakes. It seemed Gary's philandering had come back to haunt him, and he'd chosen the wrong woman.

She felt little pity for him. She hadn't forgotten about Rachel Kubick, even if most others had. Josh's dad was reaping what he'd sown. Perhaps one of Rachel's friends had even planted the note to lure him out and exact revenge. It seemed insane that his wife would catch him with a written letter after all this time. Ellie had little doubt that he'd been cheating for years. Men like Gary Thomas took what they wanted without regard for others.

It didn't seem there were any answers, just more and more questions.

Josh didn't come to class, or even to practice. The semi-finals of the state championships had happened on Friday, but Josh had missed the game. The team had dedicated their perfor-mance to him and squeaked through in rainy conditions in a low-scoring, defensive battle. Josh had wanted to come, but his aunt had forbidden it, saying he wasn't ready yet. She was with him at his house. Her kids were all in their teens and able to fend for themselves for a little while, but it wouldn't be forever. Talk that Josh might be leaving school and moving to Pittsburgh spread through the halls as quickly as the other rumors, but when Ellie asked him about it, he just said he didn't know. She didn't push him. Everything was uncertain. He was drowning and didn't need her to heap any more pressure on him.

The day of Linda Thomas's funeral came with still no word of where her husband might have disappeared to. It had been a week since she'd died. Ellie hadn't seen Josh since he'd left her house and had only spoken to him on the phone a handful of times. His aunt's family had come from Pittsburgh. With Christmas coming up, they'd decided to spend the holidays in Philadelphia with Josh, waiting for news of his father. Decisions about the future could wait until the new year, but Ellie was increasingly afraid that they might involve taking him away from her. It didn't seem like there was any other choice. His aunt and uncle weren't going to let him live alone. But Ellie had let her own concerns take a back seat. Josh was the one in pain.

Her family came with her to the church. Her father found a space at the edge of the packed parking lot and led them inside. They were ten minutes early but could only find seats at the back. The boys from the team and the coaches were sitting as a group, dressed in matching gray suits. They took up four rows. A united front. The head scout from LSU sat at the edge of the third row.

Ellie hesitated as the rest of her family sat down. "I'll be back soon."

Her mother tried to argue, but Ellie walked up the aisle of the large church. The casket was on the altar, covered in flowers. Linda's family was gathered behind Josh. He was sitting in the front row with his aunts and one of his uncles. His face was red and streaked with tears as Ellie came to him. He stood up and hugged her, lingering for several seconds.

"I need to talk to you," he whispered.

"Now?"

"It can wait. I'll see you at the luncheon after."

She nodded and returned to her seat. Dozens of her classmates and the entire football team had their eyes on her as she walked. She kept her head high and strode on.

Josh's uncle took to the lectern during the ceremony. Ellie was glad Josh had decided not to speak. He had more than enough pressure on him. He took the condolences of the crowd with grace and poise, waiting at the church door to greet each person who'd come out.

Ellie waited until the luncheon was almost finished to search him out. She had to wait her turn. His offensive coach was talking to him as she waited. Everyone wanted to support him, to show him they cared. He managed a smile as she finally made it to him. His aunt and uncle looked up at her.

"This is Uncle Carl, and you met Aunt Maureen," Josh said.

Carl wore glasses and had thick brown eyebrows that contrasted with his bald head. Ellie wondered how he'd snagged someone as pretty as his wife. They shook her hand.

"We meet at last," Carl said. "Josh has told me all about you."

Ellie smiled. "It's a pleasure to meet you too. I'm so sorry for your loss."

They thanked her and for a few minutes she made small talk with them about school and what she wanted to do next year, waiting for her chance to get Josh alone. He stood up to excuse himself when a suitable break in the conversation arrived.

They walked away from the table together and stepped outside. A light snow was falling.

"How are you?" she asked him, taking in his gray pallor and the dark circles under his eyes. "I'm sorry. That's such a dumb question."

"No, I'm terrible, but it's fine to ask," he replied.

She kissed him tenderly, putting both hands on his cheeks. His skin was cold.

"I have something important to tell you." The urgency in his voice startled her.

"What is it?"

He took a breath before telling her. "My father called me."

Ellie's hand flew to her mouth, muffling an involuntary gasp. "From where? Didn't the police say they've been trying to track his phone but it's been off?"

"Yeah. I got a text from an unknown number telling me to pick up, and the call came through a few minutes later. I didn't know it was him at first. I couldn't believe it." Heavy breaths came with each word he spoke.

"When?"

"This morning."

"What did he say?"

Josh shrugged, his hands working as he talked. "He told me he was sorry, but that he hadn't killed Mom on purpose. He said the brakes hadn't worked, and they crashed into the river. He got out of there the best he could and ran."

"Why?"

"Because of the fight he'd had with Mom. He admitted to hitting her but knew how it'd look. He wanted to get away to figure out his story."

"If he was telling the truth, he wouldn't have to figure things out. Running just makes him look guilty."

Josh shook his head. "I don't know. I think he's ashamed. He blames himself for Mom's death."

"What do you think?"

Josh tugged awkwardly at his suit jacket. "I just want him to come back. I know he hit Mom. I just don't understand why he didn't try to save her. She was wearing her seat belt when the cops found her."

Ellie wasn't sure she should vocalize her thoughts but took the risk. "You ever think he left her in that seat on purpose?"

"That he let her die?"

"Maybe he saw his opportunity to be rid of her and then realized what he'd done afterward?"

Anger flared in his eyes. "You think he deliberately let Mom drown in that car?"

"I don't know what happened. I'm just trying to make sense of it all."

Josh stammered, tripping on his words as if his brain was trying to prevent him from delivering them. "Someone killed my mom. It wasn't my dad. Whoever cut those brake lines in his car was trying to kill him, but Mom ended up dead instead. He wouldn't leave her behind like that. He must have realized she was already dead. He isn't much of a swimmer. It's dangerous in that water."

"I know that, but wouldn't you go back? You went in for her yourself."

"He was probably scared or hurt, for all we know. The cops are fumbling this whole case just like they did with Rachel. If they'd found her killer, I wouldn't have had to deal with half of what's been thrown at me this past year."

"Do they have any leads on who tampered with the brakes?"

"Nothing. No one saw anything. The real killer is out there."

"The same person who typed that note."

"Exactly."

"You ever think he might be with her?"

"Who?"

"The woman who wrote the note?"

The pained expression on his face deepened. "I really don't know."

"How long did you talk to him for?"

"Maybe thirty seconds. When I called back the number was already disconnected. It must have been a burner phone. The last thing he said to me was to keep my head down and win the state championship. Then he hung up."

"Have you told the cops yet?"

"No. I only took the call a couple of hours before the funeral. I haven't had a chance."

"Are you going to?"

"Um, yeah, of course," he said quietly.

Ellie didn't ask him again, but doubts about whether he'd call the police niggled at her for the rest of the afternoon.

THIRTEEN

The principal organized a guard of honor when Josh came back to school the following Monday. The forty-five players from the football team lined the hallway just inside the main door, along with hundreds more students just beyond them. Ellie wondered if any kid would have gotten this treatment or just one who could win the state championship. Ellie stood just after the football players with Maddie, Lizzy, and the rest of her friends. A huge banner reading "We love you, Josh" hung from the rafters, and the kids applauded as he made his return. His story was all over the papers—the star quarterback whose mom had died under mysterious circumstances and whose dad was still missing. Ellie had noticed some reporters hanging around outside the school grounds to get a photo of Josh coming back. It was a surreal glimpse into his future as a star.

Josh took the attention with poise and grace, stopping to shake hands with some and hug others before ending up where Ellie was standing.

"I can't believe this," he said to her with tears in his eyes.

"We're all here for you."

Maddie reached forward to put a hand on his shoulder. He

thanked her and the rest of the crowd before continuing on. The principal, Mr. Bell, and several teachers shook his hand, offering their condolences. But the welcome party disbanded two minutes after it had begun. Ellie went to him, squeezing through several football players surrounding him. She waited until they left to take him aside, and only when she was sure they were alone did she ask him the question on her mind.

"Did you hear from your dad?"

He looked away and shook his head. "Not since the morning of the funeral."

"I can't believe everything that happened."

His voice faltered as he spoke. "I know. I just want to talk to him. I'm in this weird limbo right now. I'm going to have to go to Pittsburgh to finish out the school year if he doesn't come back."

"What about LSU?"

"They've been in touch. The coach came up to visit at the weekend. He was great. Really understanding and kind."

"You're still planning on signing for them?"

"As of right now. The deal with my mom was what got them over the line with me in the first place, but they've been so great since she died."

She moved toward him and clasped his shoulders. "You need to focus on your future. It's what your mom would have wanted."

They both clammed up as Principal Bell walked over and shook Josh's hand again. "You ready for this?"

"I think so."

"You still coming to practice after school?"

"Yeah. I'm itching to get back, and I need to be ready for the state championship game on Saturday."

"Good man. I'm proud to have you back. I know we can rely on you."

The principal patted him on the shoulder and walked away just as the bell rang for first period.

"I gotta get to English." Josh sighed.

"I'll see you later," Ellie replied.

Josh tried to smile, but it came out crooked and sad. His heartbreak was hard to witness. He walked down the hall and faded into the crowd.

The week carried on in a similar fashion, and come Saturday, Ellie's brothers were bouncing off the walls. Both were dressed in football jerseys, and Tyler had made a flag with Josh's face set against the school's colors. Everyone had been talking about the state championship game for days. Josh was back at practice and playing well. He needed to. The team they were up against from Mechanicsburg was a fearsome match, and Josh would have to be at the top of his game if they were to have any chance.

Several reporters from the big papers in Philly had been seen at practice that week, and the coaches had had to hide Josh to protect him from them. Ellie had spoken to him every day leading up to the game. She knew how much he was hurting—putting on a brave front to play but consumed by grief. The searches for Gary Thomas and whoever had severed the brake lines in his car had both come to dead ends. Detective Harris hadn't called in days. Linda Thomas's death still hadn't been ruled accidental, and Ellie surmised that the police still wanted to charge Gary with something, but only they knew what. It was clear that he knew he was in trouble and had probably gone to shack up with whoever had written the letter, or maybe even to avenge the sabotage of his car and death of his wife.

Josh could only put the questions aside and try to focus on the biggest game of his life. The scouts from LSU were coming. His contract wasn't signed yet, and certain kids said they might renege on the agreement. Signing him would be a significant investment. A star quarterback would bring eyes, TV contracts, and large ticket receipts. A flop, still trying to recover from personal problems, could lose them millions. It seemed like everything had been thrown back into flux with the death of his mother. Josh was determined to prove himself in the championship. Ellie had been over to his house the night before. He'd seemed nervous but confident. The pain, though, still permeated his body, coloring every movement, every word. She'd held him for hours, wishing she could reach inside him and extract it somehow.

They'd spoken about their future. Ellie had her own to look forward to. Sometimes, she had to remind herself that Josh's dreams weren't hers. Perhaps wanting to be a teacher seemed less exciting in comparison to his ambitions of playing in the NFL, but it was her focus. Her grades were still excellent, and she was confident of getting several college offers. Her relationship with Josh had recovered since his father went missing. Many of her doubts had been dispelled by his father's behavior. It was obvious he was the guilty one, and without him breathing down their necks, she and Josh were able to be together. But even if she wanted to, how could she break up with him now? He was dealing with so much, and she was determined not to add to his already considerable burden.

He still intended to go to LSU and wanted to be with her. As for the new year and next semester in school, who knew? His uncle had returned to Pittsburgh with Josh's cousins a few days before, promising to come back to watch him in the championship game. But his aunt missed her family. It seemed like Josh might have little choice but to move with her. Ellie realized there was little she could do. The best thing was to make the most of whatever time they had left and then see what the future held for them.

. . .

The championship game was in Hershey, about an hour and a half from where they lived outside Philadelphia. The team bus left at noon after a pep rally at the school. From there, all the kids returned home to organize themselves and travel out later that afternoon.

Ellie's dad's excitement level was only slightly below that of his sons, and he ran around, herding Ellie and the rest of the family into the car for the trip ahead.

"How's Josh feeling?" he asked when they were on the road.

"I think he's okay. He just wants to play football."

"What he's best at," Tyler added from the seat beside her.

She shot her little brother a look and paused a second before continuing. "It's been so hard for him. And the pressure from everyone in school isn't helping."

"It's been awful. The poor kid," Ellie's mom said, shaking her head sadly.

"And the father disappearing like that? I can't imagine him missing the championship game too. He's obsessed with Josh's career. I mean, I didn't know the man, but I saw him at the games along with everyone else. It's all so strange."

"Kids in school are saying he's coming to the game today. They're going to be looking for someone in disguise," James chipped in.

"Maybe the cops will be too," her father commented.

Ellie sat with her friends among the 15,000 spectators. Her family was a few rows below them. She knew scouring the stands for any sign of Gary Thomas was ridiculous, but she did it anyway. Everyone did. Josh hadn't heard from his father since that one call. The police had tried to trace the phone it had come from, but it was a disposable cell, no doubt destroyed after he'd used it. They'd come up with nothing. Gary Thomas had vanished into thin air.

Ellie and her schoolmates rose to their feet as Lower Merion took to the field. Josh turned to the stand, his helmet in hand, pumping it back and forth to get the crowd going. Their side of the stadium erupted. Flags flew, and drinks were thrown. Josh returned to his teammates, but not before stopping to pick Ellie out in the stands.

The game started a few minutes later.

"Even with Josh, Mechanicsburg is still the strong favorite here," Maddie said.

Ellie frowned. "Since when are you such a football expert?"

"Since we got good."

Mechanicsburg won the toss and received the kickoff. They marched down the field in five minutes, chewing up the turf with a hard-hitting running game before punching into the endzone for the opening score.

Josh and the offense ran out after the kickoff to try to answer. The crowd cheered as Josh completed two passes in a row, but after a foiled running play, he tried to throw deep and was picked off. Ellie and her friends groaned. Mechanicsburg took the ball and moved downfield again, scoring seven points off the turnover.

Lower Merion's offense couldn't move the ball again. Josh seemed off, missing targets he usually would have hit with ease.

Ellie made her way down to her family at halftime. Her father's miserable face told the story of how they were all feeling. "Josh is miles off today," he said. "Poor kid. I can't imagine dealing with what he's gone through these last few weeks. And then all this?"

"I just hope it doesn't affect his scholarship," Ellie's mom said.

Ellie looked down at the scouts on the sideline and silently agreed.

The second half started a few minutes later. Josh had the ball in his hands after the kickoff. He completed a few passes, but the attack sputtered out again in the face of the ferocious Mechanicsburg defense. Josh was sacked, and he fumbled the ball for another turnover. He trudged off the field with the rest of his downcast teammates. He was only on the sidelines for two minutes before Mechanicsburg scored again.

Ellie looked around at her friends, but no one spoke. The excitement of earlier had dissipated, and this had turned into an ordeal.

Josh ran in a touchdown in the fourth quarter, but it was only a consolation, and the game ended in a 35-7 loss. The Mechanicsburg players and fans exploded into rapture as the clock reached zero. Ellie's brothers were crying, and they weren't the only ones. Ellie walked down to the sidelines. Josh was on his knees, his teammates all around him. As she got closer, she realized he was crying. He stood up and hugged a massive boy called Jeremy Davis, who played center on the team. Josh turned to Ellie and threw his arms around her.

"I let everyone down," he sobbed. "All my buddies on the team, the school, and my mom."

"No. No, you didn't. The team never would have gotten this far without you." She drew back from him, taking his face in her hands as she stared at him. "This isn't on you. You've done so much."

"It's my fault. All of it."

Several other players heard what he said and walked over to dispute it. He embraced each one before his aunt and uncle arrived with his cousins.

"I'm so sorry, Josh," Maureen said gently, tears welling in her eyes.

"I feel like I let Mom down," he choked.

"No. She's proud of you today," Maureen said fiercely, pulling Josh into a big hug.

"I gotta go get changed. But there's a party at Jeremy Davis's house tonight. You know where it is?"

"Yeah. I know him. I was at a pool party there a few years ago."

"Great, I'll see you there in a few hours. The whole team's going."

He retreated to the dressing room with the rest of the players. The scout from LSU was gone. Ellie was confident they'd honor their offer. Everyone knew what had happened to Josh, from the dejected kids in the stands to the journalists scribbling on their notepads. No one could have blamed him for playing badly under those circumstances.

Ellie found her family in the stands and they followed the crowd toward the parking lot. She texted her friends on the way home about the party at Jeremy's house. Some wondered if it'd be more of a wake than a party, but all said they'd go.

Ellie had dinner at home, trying to offer comfort to her devastated brothers, but it was no use. Her father was only slightly less upset.

Jeremy's house was on the edge of town, near the river Josh's mother had died in, but further out, where the woods were thicker. Maddie pulled up outside. The street was so packed with cars that she had to park a hundred yards down. The neighbors were away—Jeremy had paid for a night in a hotel in the city with dinner thrown in. Not many seventeen-year-olds could afford that, but he'd inherited a fortune from his grandfather the year before. Jeremy's parents were progressive types who believed it was better to have their son and his friends drink in the house than in some field somewhere. He had been barred from drinking alcohol during the season on pain of being kicked off the football team. The entire squad had been, but the shackles were off now. The only players not allowed to drink now were the ones playing in college next year—Josh and four others. Ellie was determined not to be the nagging

girlfriend but had to make sure he didn't succumb to temptation. If the cops came, he could lose his offer from LSU, which
was already feeling less certain than before their crushing
defeat.

The girls were under no such pressure, however, and had a
beer from the keg in the corner as soon as they walked in. The
party was packed already. Britney Spears blasted from the
stereo in the living room. Kids were all over, drinking beer from
red Solo cups. Ellie saw one of Josh's friends from the team and
asked where he was. He directed her to the kitchen, where she
found him by the massive, granite-topped island with a few of
his friends drowning their sorrows. Ellie was disappointed to
see he was holding a plastic cup just like the rest of them.

"How are you feeling?" she said, kissing him as they turned
away from the group.

"Pretty sad." His face was pale, his movements tense and
uneven. "It's just been a tough few weeks. I honestly don't know
what happened to me today. I've been waiting for a game this
big for three years, practicing and practicing. But I blew it."

"You didn't blow anything. When are you going to give
yourself a break? None of the other players have been through
half of what you have these past few weeks in their entire lives.
And you expect to go out and perform miracles? Did you speak
to the scout from LSU?"

"Yeah. He told me not to worry about a thing. The school is
there for me. He said I'm a tiger now." He smiled, but there was
no joy behind it.

"I'm glad. You deserve it. And so much more." She paused,
looking down at his plastic cup. "Just one thing—don't go
drinking with the other boys tonight. You've been so disciplined
all season. Don't blow it now."

"That's only if I get caught. Jeremy paid off the neighbors.
They're in the city living it up. I could really use a few beers
tonight."

"At what cost?" *So much for trying not to be a nagging girl-friend*, she thought.

His face soured. "Listen, Ellie, the last thing I need right now is a lecture. Just give me a break, all right?"

Ellie knew she was in a no-win situation. If the cops didn't show, she'd have ruined Josh's night for nothing, and if they did, Josh could lose everything and fall apart. She drew in a deep breath and raised her beer to her mouth. "To your mom," she said.

He tapped her cup with his. "To my mom."

They drank back their beers.

"Just take it easy. That free ride LSU is offering is worth too much to risk on one night."

He gave her a tiny nod and put his empty cup down without filling it again.

More kids entered the kitchen, and, as usual, everyone wanted to talk to Josh. Some offered their condolences about the game, others about his mother. None mentioned his father. Ellie wondered if he'd been in the stadium that day and imagined how he would have reacted to his son's subpar performance in the biggest game of his life. Perhaps he'd never come back.

Ellie nudged him, and he turned around. "When are you going to leave?"

"The party? I don't know."

"No, when are you leaving Philly?"

His face dropped. "Soon, I guess. It's not something I like thinking about, but Maureen wants to bring me to Pittsburgh and says I should just live with them until high school ends."

"Did you ever think of just staying here?"

Josh reached out and cupped her cheek. "Of course. You think I want to leave you? I just got to this school, and now I have to move across the state."

"Is there any way you could stay?" Ellie said softly, forcing down the lump that had formed in her throat.

His voice was scratchy and weak. "I asked Maureen, but she didn't go for it. She says I can live on my own in college next year, but until then she and Carl are going to look after me."

"What if your dad comes back?"

"I have no idea. They could charge him with reckless driving, but then the brakes were cut. It wasn't his fault the car crashed. But it's his fault Mom died." He paused for a few seconds. Ellie let him continue. "Mom never should have been in that car. He put her through hell for years, and even if he didn't murder her, he's the reason she's dead. I'm done with him."

Ellie had never heard him be so forthright. She agreed with every word but kept her opinions to herself. This was for him to decide. Perhaps he'd only be a memory to her soon. It was easy to promise to love someone forever in senior year when college was looming. The reality was something different. Ellie looked at Josh's handsome face as if she'd never see it again. Her heart bled for him. The last few weeks would shape the rest of his life. Losing his mom would be a weight he'd have to bear forever. Ellie wanted to support Josh but realized that she couldn't be the stars he'd navigate home by. He would have to sail these choppy waters himself. She wasn't sure if she'd ever love anyone so hard again, but being with him had shown her another life. Ellie was a young woman now. Not a girl anymore. She'd seen what life could be, the dizzying highs as well as the lowest of the lows.

"Can we go outside for a walk?" Ellie asked.

"Sure," he answered.

The night air bit at her cheeks as they stepped outside. The trees of the forest loomed like wraiths beyond the fence, their branches reaching over like grasping arms. Josh hugged her, holding her against him as they kissed. If this was to be their last night together, she intended to make it a good one. Some other kids burst out the back door to join them, ruining the mood.

Josh smiled. "Shall we go back inside?"

"Sure."

Jeremy had organized an epic game of beer pong on the dining room table, and he soon coerced Josh into being on a team with him. Ellie went to get another drink, catching up with Maddie and Hope in the living room. The three girls talked for a while, but word about the party was out, and more and more kids came spilling in. The living room was soon so full that they barely had room to stand. An impromptu dance floor had formed in the middle, and some kids Ellie had never seen before were showing off their moves. She went back to the keg, but it was empty. One of the boys from the team brought over and tapped one of the several spares on hand, and she took another cup of beer.

Josh was still in the dining room playing beer pong with Jeremy. Ellie stood with him for a few minutes, watching him sink the balls into the waiting red cups half-full of beer at the end of the table. He was drinking quickly, but Ellie felt she couldn't stop him.

The house was so packed now that it took several minutes to get to the bathroom and longer to wait in line. She told Maddie she was going to find Josh and left her dancing with Hope and Lizzy. He was still in the dining room, but the beer pong game was over. Christina Taylor, a bleached blonde from Ellie's English class, was doing her best to drape herself over him. Ellie strolled over, unworried. Girls hit on him all the time. Ellie had already had two boys try it on with her at the party. It was just something that happened on nights out. Josh looked up at her with a smile.

"Christina, you know Ellie, don't you?"

"Yeah. For years. It must be such a hard time for you both." Her words were slurred.

"It's been awful," Ellie answered. She put her drink down on the table beside them. "Can I talk to you a minute, Josh?"

"What's going on?"

They stepped away for a few seconds. A visual flashed up in Ellie's mind—Rachel had been in her exact position with Josh at a party just before she was killed.

"Josh, what happened the night of the party?"

"What?"

"With Rachel?"

His face changed. "We've been through this a hundred times."

"Was it a party just like this?"

Josh stared back at her. His eyes were still focused, but he wasn't sober like before. "Yeah. Just like this."

A cold fear gripped Ellie. "What if whoever killed her is here tonight?"

"Don't be crazy. You being nuts is the last thing I need right now."

They walked back to the table. Josh picked up his drink and took a sip.

"Please be careful, Josh. If the cops come—"

"Jesus! I don't need you ordering me around! I'll see you later," he snapped and stormed off.

Ellie felt her eyes smarting with tears and took a deep breath to calm herself. *He's tired and grieving*, she told herself. She looked down at her beer. It seemed stronger than what she'd been drinking earlier. Her legs were tingling, and suddenly she was finding it hard to see straight. Had she drunk that much? It didn't seem to make sense.

"I have to find the girls," she mumbled to herself but found walking harder than she'd expected. She stumbled, surrounded by strangers. People seemed to be reaching out to catch her, but she slipped through their arms.

"I'm all right," Ellie said, shrugging them off.

She looked around for someone she knew, but Christina was gone. Maddie, Lizzy, and Hope were nowhere to be seen. Qadir, one of the boys from the football team, was beside her. She knew he was talking but couldn't make out the words. She could see his lips moving, but her ears didn't register the sound.

"What?"

Someone at the front of the house screamed, "The cops!"

Ellie turned and saw the flashlights. Kids scattered, sprinting for the exits.

"We gotta go," Qadir said. He took her by the hand, but she pulled back. He continued on through the back door. Dozens of kids were in the yard, scaling the fence. She only hoped Josh was one of them. She had to get out too. If her parents caught her...

She carried on, stumbling through the backyard toward the fence. Someone helped her over, and she landed on the other side with a thud. It took her some time to get up. The noise had died down, but the instinct to run drove her on. The woods enveloped her, and her movements slowed. All she wanted to do was stop and rest. She was safe. The cops were far behind. She was alone, surrounded by the dark forest, as if someone had thrown a great black blanket over her. Her legs stopped working, and she fell to the ground. Her eyelids seemed to weigh a thousand tons. Keeping them open was impossible. The last thing she felt was the cold ground against her cheek before she succumbed to a sleep unlike any she'd ever known.

FOURTEEN

THE BASEMENT

It took Ellie several minutes to calm down to the point where she could try to evaluate what was going on. The chalkboard was gone. Whoever had thrust it under the door had retracted it the same way. She'd seen nothing of who it was. No hand. Not even their feet when they stood on the other side of the door. The feeling of fear gave way to anger, and she pounded on the door again until the pain in her hand forced her to stop. She slumped to the floor. The light of day was leaking in through the windows, and she erected the same pile of books she'd stood on last night to try to peek through. When she raised herself up, she saw they were bucket windows a foot or so below ground level. All she could see through them was a patch of sky and some leaves from some bushes. Probing for weakness in the hard plastic windowpanes, she knocked and tried to dig her nails into the putty that held them in place, but their robust design barred her from any progress. She climbed back down.

Her head began to throb and breathing was difficult. She put her hand at the base of her neck and drew air in through her nostrils. The room seemed to grow darker as her vision dimmed.

The floor was cold as she sat down. She let her head drop between her knees, focusing on drawing oxygen in and out of her lungs.

It was hard to know how long she sat like that. It might have been twenty minutes or maybe an hour. A rumble in her stomach brought her back into the moment. The toast and orange juice were still on the tray her captor had slid under the door. Ellie walked over and got down on her haunches beside it. She had no idea if they were laced with something. Whoever had brought her in here had drugged her once, she was sure of it. They must have gotten into the party somehow and spiked her drink, but who could it have been? Who had been near her cup? Dozens of kids. She tried to remember the boy who'd changed out the kegs—Jacob Harman from the football team. He was always such a nice guy. It was hard to believe he'd spike an entire keg. Someone must have done it when she'd put her cup down. Maybe when she'd been with Josh in the dining room. She cursed herself for being so careless. She'd heard so many stories of girls and even some boys getting roofied. *Stupid! I just hope Josh got away*, she thought before turning her attention to the food.

She eyed the toast suspiciously. The butter had long since dried in, and the bread was cold, but it didn't look off. She picked up a piece and smelled it. It didn't seem any different than what she ate for breakfast most days. The psychopath at the door had told her to get used to being in there. She might have to eat what they gave her or starve. Ellie took a minuscule bite. It seemed fine. She ate the rest and then the other piece. The orange juice, again, seemed normal. With no way of testing it, she would have to either trust what her jailer had given her or reject it. She had no reason to trust Mr. Psychopath, the Voiceless One, but she needed sustenance to survive. Something about the juice spooked her so she drank some water from the bottle instead.

Her jeans were dirty from the forest. Maybe her kidnapper had dragged her across the ground. They must have parked just beyond the trees behind Jeremy's house and driven her to wherever this was from there. Her hands were shaking like autumn leaves in the breeze, and she had to grab them to stop.

If she could figure out who the Voiceless One was, she could talk to them and maybe get them to let her go. Rachel Kubick had never suffered this. Her tormentor had killed her there and then. Was it Gary Thomas on the other side of that door? How could he have spiked her drink at the party? She wracked her tired brain for snapshots of what she'd seen, who'd been at Jeremy Davis's house. Gary would have stuck out at a party full of teenagers like a sore thumb.

She wiped the dirt of the forest off her jeans and looked in the boxes in the middle of the room again. There didn't seem to be anything useful inside. Plenty of reading material but nothing strong enough to bash the door down.

After double-checking the shelves for anything she could use, Ellie went to the door. The black beyond it was all she could see through the keyhole. Once her eyes had adjusted to the light, she could just about make out the lines of a wooden staircase, but that was all. Nothing to see.

Her instinct to scream, curl up into a ball, and cry was hard to resist, but that was probably what her captor wanted. They might have been watching her and would probably delight in seeing her break down so quickly. She wasn't going to give the Voiceless One that kind of satisfaction. The memory of how Gary Thomas had touched her when she'd gone over for dinner sat in her memory like jagged glass. Was that what he wanted? To use her as some sort of sex slave? The shuddering from earlier overtook her again, and she had to go over to the rug in the corner to sit down.

She had to do something, but what? After taking a few moments to calm down, she checked the walls for weaknesses.

It was all solid concrete except for a section in the corner where a thick, silver-colored, paper-like substance covered a gap where the wall met the ceiling. Ellie pulled some up and saw something that looked like fiberglass insulation behind it. She was no DIY expert and knew nothing about construction but brought some books over to stand on and reached her hand a few inches into the soft material. A sound at the door made her whirl around so quickly that she almost fell. She jumped down.

The chalkboard was by the door again. Ellie ran across, ignoring the board and falling on her hands and knees. She saw nothing under the door but the rope tied to the chalkboard. They must have been standing on the step, out of sight. She couldn't even see their shoes.

"Who are you?" Ellie called out. "What do you want with me?"

The only answer she received was a tug on the rope. She picked up the board.

Shove the tray back under the door to get more food.

She let the board slip from her grasp to the floor and it disappeared through the gap into the darkness beyond.

"Mr. Thomas, is that you? Please speak to me!"

Nothing. Not even the sound of breathing. Not even something to denote the entity behind the door was human.

Ellie repeated herself, then waited. No answer. She needed to play ball. She did as the Voiceless One asked, pushing the tray back under the door. The sound of it being picked up was clearly audible.

"Can we talk? You brought me here for a reason. I'm not some lab rat to put in a cage and study. You chose me. Josh's girlfriend. That's the reason I'm here, isn't it? What is it about me? Who are you? Tell me!"

The sound of scribbling filtered through the gap, and the wooden board appeared under the door.

Ellie froze as she read the words.

Someone who loves you.

She kicked the board back under the door. "Don't you want to talk to me if you love me so much? Why would you treat me this way?"

She wasn't sure if she wanted her captor to open the door or not. This was a sick, deranged person. Perhaps it was best to humor them until she found a way to escape.

"You can let me go, you know. Anytime. I'll go home and say I stayed at a friend's house. It wouldn't be weird. We don't have to get the police involved."

The chalkboard scraped the floor on its journey under the door. A few seconds later, it came back again. The words sent a shock through Ellie's system.

You're mine now. At last.

She struggled to keep the fear from her voice. "Mr. Thomas? Gary? Is that you? I'm sorry. I didn't mean to be a distraction. I'm sorry about your wife."

A new message appeared.

Forget her. It's all about you now.

Sure that it was Gary Thomas behind the door, she began to plead once more. "I'll never talk to Josh again. I won't stand in his way. He'll be everything you want him to be."

No answer came. She pushed the board under the door again.

The sound of chalk on the board came again, along with another message.

Rachel messed with me. Don't be like her.

FIFTEEN

It had to be Gary Thomas on the other side of that door, but she couldn't be entirely sure. No one else made any sense. But if it wasn't Josh's father, then who? Appealing to him directly hadn't worked. Perhaps that wasn't what he wanted. She looked around the room for a weapon—something to defend herself with when her jailer finally came in. Because they were coming. It was only a matter of time. She got off the bed, determined to try and gain some control. She wasn't a rat in a cage. Maybe the Voiceless One thought she was, but that would be their downfall. Ellie would be ready. She lifted some old cardboard boxes off of one of the shelving units, exposing the chrome wire shelf beneath. Each shelf was supported by five long metal cylinders, which reached from one end to the other. They were held in place by a screw at the end. Ellie examined each unit's shelves, searching for a loose screw. She found one. She took off her jeans and used the metal button as a screwdriver. The screw turned. Slowly. So slowly. It took her thirty minutes to get it out, and then she had to begin on the one at the other end, which was tightly set in place.

"This'll keep me busy for a while," she said out loud as she began to work on it.

Ellie worked on unscrewing the metal cylinder from the shelving unit through the afternoon and into the night, the daylight fading which each passing hour. Her hands were screaming, begging her to stop. On fire. But she kept on fighting through the pain. The Voiceless One didn't return, and darkness eventually fell. It must have been eight or nine o'clock when the screw finally came loose. A scream of joy and relief escaped her throat. She allowed herself a moment of triumph before examining the foot-long weapon she'd freed from the shelf. The end was sharp, but she wanted it to be lethal. She might only get one chance, and she couldn't afford to waste it. The metal rod felt good in her hand. She brought it down through the air, enjoying the swishing sound it made. Using it like a sword, she stabbed the imaginary captor before her, slicing back and forth. With no way to sharpen the end, she brought it to the stone wall and pushed it against the flat surface until the edges melded together to form a spike.

"My shank."

She'd seen enough prison shows to know what inmates would have called it. It left a mark on the top of her finger. She imagined jamming it into the Voiceless One's chest and running outside to freedom. Perhaps the police were coming for her. The search must have begun by now. She had no idea where she was. If her captor was smart, she was far from Jeremy Davis's house. And the Voiceless One did seem to have put a lot of planning into her being here. The basement was clean and secure. This was no random event. For all she knew, they had done this before. Perhaps many times. The thought of that brought the latent fear in her to the surface. She gripped the weapon she'd made. It'd be nothing against a gun, but if her captor came at her unarmed, she'd be ready.

She retreated to the rug and closed her eyes, trying to

convince her exhausted body to succumb to sleep, but it was a long time coming and punctuated by dark nightmares.

She woke drenched in sweat with adrenaline coursing through her. The dull winter light was filtering in through the tiny windows. She had no idea what time it was. The shank was where she'd left it, under her pillow. The cold feel of the metal in her hand gave her comfort.

A noise at the door jolted her from her thoughts. She took the shank and shrank into the corner of the room. Three pieces of wheat toast sat on a plate, this time with what seemed like grape jelly slathered on top of the butter. The door was closed as, once again, her captor had slid the food under the door on a tray. Another carton of orange juice sat beside it.

"Are you there? Talk to me! What am I doing down here?" she yelled, her voice consumed with fear and anger.

The only answer she received was the sound of the door shutting at the top of the stairs. She collapsed onto her knees. Hunger seemed to be gnawing at her insides like an animal. It didn't seem she had any other choice but to eat the toast. The Voiceless One had her on what seemed like starvation rations. But it didn't seem poisoned, at least. She hadn't felt any detrimental effects from eating the day before. She picked up a slice and examined it for a few seconds before biting into it. Soon all three were in her stomach, but they weren't nearly enough. They seemed to awaken her hunger rather than satiate it. She drank the orange juice and then decided to try screaming for a minute or two. All she got out of that was a sore throat. There was no one around to hear her.

Ellie pushed the tray back under the door. The Voiceless One was gone, but she didn't want to give them an excuse to hold back a meal or exact some other retribution that didn't bear thinking about. Ellie tried the door again, just to attempt something. But it didn't budge.

She'd have another eight hours of daylight, and she intended to make use of it. Looking around, she spied the metallic paper covering in the corner. She brought over one of the empty shelving units and tipped it on its side. It held her weight, and she balanced on the edge as she got up to the point where her head was only an inch or two below the ceiling. The shank pierced the paper with ease, but she didn't want to mess it up too much and give herself away. She pulled it up to expose the insulation behind it. It was pink. She reached back. It seemed to go on and on. The gap it filled was about a foot high —enough space for her to crawl into, but would it lead anywhere? Stuck in there, she was dead. She drew some insulation out, using the shank she'd made to hack at it. It was stuck together in a block, shoved in tight. Moving it was hard work. She reached in as far as she could, up on her tiptoes on the shelving unit. She couldn't reach any further and wasn't able to climb up either.

She withdrew her hand and jumped down. The cardboard boxes with books wouldn't take her weight, so she tried to get another shelving unit on top of the one already on its side. It was too heavy. She took one of the larger boxes, half-full of old paperbacks and magazines, and lugged it up onto the unit she'd climbed on earlier. Then she went back to the other boxes and took everything she could find inside, and put it into the box she wanted to stand on. It was almost full when she heard footsteps at the door. *What if they come in and see this?*

Ellie ran to the door. The blackboard slid underneath.

I'm watching you all the time.

A wave of ice-cold terror washed through Ellie's body.

"What do you want from me?"

The blackboard slid back on its string. It reappeared seconds later.

For you to behave.

Ellie slowed her breathing to allow the words to come. "Please, Mr. Thomas, is that you? Just talk to me. Let me go, I'm begging you. I won't tell, I swear! I'm sorry for whatever I did. I'll never talk to Josh again."

The person on the other side of the door pulled the board back again. Ellie pressed her head to the floor to see their hands or shoes, but there was nothing. The sound of chalk scrawling came again.

I want you all to myself. If you try to escape, I'll punish you.

And then Ellie heard the whining of a drill. It was unmistakable. She screamed. Ellie was almost ashamed at showing such weakness in front of them, but she couldn't help it.

"Please!"

The board came back again.

No more begging. Just be a good girl. No more food today.

The board disappeared, and the familiar sound of footsteps up wooden stairs bled through the door.

The days wore on. Ellie used her shank to mark them off beside her makeshift bed. Six so far. Her jeans were loose around her waist now. Some days, the Voiceless One brought sandwiches or even pizza, and some days, they brought nothing. Communication slowed to a trickle. It had been two days since they'd written anything to her, and still no talking. Ellie knew the police were out there searching for her. They'd probably inter-viewed everyone at the party. If they hadn't found her by now, they likely never would. That thought haunted her. It seemed she was on her own. Her parents must have been climbing the walls, and she doubted they'd slept since she'd been taken. The thought that everyone would suspect Josh of being involved in her disappearance crossed her mind. It was like what had happened to Rachel Kubick all over again—another of Josh's girlfriends going missing at a party, except this time, Ellie was still alive. The police had probably already taken him in for questioning. But did she really know that it wasn't him behind the door? *No. Josh could never do anything like this*, she said to herself and shook the notion from her mind.

Ellie was lying on the rug, her shank in hand. She carried it with her all the time, just in case. It was her only line of defense. And one thing she'd learned from being in here was that the Voice-less One didn't care what she said or how much she pleaded. If anything, it just annoyed them more. They had withheld food twice because of it. The drill had only been a threat so far, but she couldn't put anything past someone willing to inflict this on another human being. Their motivation was still a mystery, their identity still a guess.

Ellie got up. After listening for a few seconds, she went through her now familiar routine of tipping the metal shelving unit onto its side and placing the box on top of it. Once it was filled with books, she was ready to stand up on it. The whole routine took about twenty minutes. She dreaded to think what would happen if the Voiceless One caught her doing it, but she was dying down here. She couldn't survive more than a few more weeks on these rations. She had to act before she was too weak to fight back. Maybe that was their plan, but she had no idea. Her jailer was risking life in prison for this. For what?

She reached into the gap behind the metallic paper. She'd already pulled out much of the insulation, hiding the remnants in boxes. She'd been too afraid to attempt this for several days after the incident with the drill, but she was ready again. Darkness enveloped her as she climbed into the gap between the wall and the ceiling. The insulation came off in pieces as she hacked away at it. It got in her eyes, her hair, her mouth. She kept stabbing, terrified every second she was inside. It was so dark she couldn't see anything at all. So, she closed her eyes to protect them. Breathing was hard, and after a few minutes, she backed out, gasping for air as she emerged feet first. The metallic paper slipped back over the gap. If anyone examined the spot, they'd see it was out of place right away, but if someone only gave it a cursory glance, they might not notice. She tried to convince herself as much, anyway.

Ellie looked up at the gap. It might be her only chance of getting out, but she had no idea what lay at the end of the insulation. A brick wall? She'd have to get to the end of the insulation to find out. It was awful in there. The worst place she'd ever been. But if it meant escaping, she'd go back in there again and again.

She took a break, peering at the fading light from the windows for a few minutes before climbing back up to hack away again. An hour later, Ellie made it to the end of the thick insulation. And came up against old wooden planks holding it in place; thin slivers of light illuminated the spaces between them. The planks were about two feet long and as high as the gap she was in. She could fit through! All she had to do was clear them first. She pressed her shank into the space between the two closest planks and worked it back and forth for what seemed like hours. The planks began to loosen. Her wrist ached. It felt like it was going to fall off. She used her left hand, exhausting that before changing back.

A sound from the door sent a chill down her spine. If the

Voiceless One caught her in here, she was dead. Ellie pushed off the wooden planks and crawled backward through the gap. Her legs emerged into thin air. She slid out of the hole, scraping her legs and arms, desperately trying to get out before her captor saw her. Her jeans were covered in dust, and her hair was a disgusting mess. She coughed and spluttered and fell to the floor. Pain shot through her leg, but she rose to her feet and ran to the door.

The chalkboard flew under.

What took you so long?

"I was asleep. There's not a whole lot more to do down here."

The chalkboard retreated, and a reply came back in seconds.

Don't forget that I'm watching you. You disappoint me.

How could the Voiceless One have been watching her? They would have seen her tunneling through the wall.

"What are you talking about? I was asleep."

Ellie got down on her haunches and went to the keyhole. She put her eye against it and saw the shine of an eyeball peering through. She veered backward. Ellie had the thought to push the shank through the keyhole, but when she looked again, the eyeball was gone.

Holding back your food won't do it this time. More drastic measures are required. Goodbye, Ellie.

She heard the sound of footsteps walking back up the stairs.

"What are you talking about? Where are you going?" she cried out, banging her fists against the door.

No response.

Ellie retreated to the corner, holding the shank out in front of her as she crouched. The footsteps came again.

Ellie shouted across. She knew the Voiceless One didn't respond to pleading but couldn't help herself. "You don't have to do this!"

A strange glugging sound came from the other side of the door, and then liquid poured through the gap. The smell hit Ellie like a hammer. It was gas.

"No! Please!"

Once again, her shouting elicited no response. The gas kept coming. They were going to burn her out. But maybe it was a bluff. They weren't really going to kill her like this and burn the entire house down? The gas spread like a deadly pool over the concrete, inching further toward her.

"Mr. Thomas, please don't do this! You said you were someone who loves me. You said that the first day you took me here. Please don't burn me. I don't want to die!"

The pool spread further until she heard the sound of an empty gas can being thrown and then the footsteps going back up the stairs. *Are they going to get a lighter?*

Ellie looked up at the gap under the ceiling in the corner. The box was on the ground. She ran to it, took out enough books so that she could lift it, and placed the books back in. She got up on it and climbed into the gap. *This is a bluff,* she thought to herself. But she wasn't going to take that chance. She hefted her body into the opening she'd created.

The notion that the Voiceless One was bluffing was obliterated as the room went up in flames. She crawled through the gap, the light from the fire in the basement illuminating the way. Ellie screamed as she crawled through. She could feel the heat from the flames on her back. It took a few seconds to reach the wooden planks, and she took the shank and drove it into them.

"Come on."

The planks began to weaken. It was impossible to look back, but the light behind her was growing stronger, the heat more intense. The basement was engulfed in flames. Ellie hacked at the wood in front of her with her shank. One of the planks came loose, revealing blank, dark space beyond. Ellie almost screamed but kept on at the one below it. She hit it with the heel of her hand over and over, the flames licking at her heels. The fire illuminated the crawl space, and Ellie understood she might only have seconds now. She drew her arm back as far as she could and drove the heel of her hand into the wood. It moved! She brought both hands forward and rocked the plank back and forth until it gave way, and she crawled through. She was in a lighter, dusty space she immediately recognized as being beneath a porch. The night air was clean and cold in her lungs, like a glass of water. Weak from hunger, she gathered all her strength to climb out from under it and run into the night. The house, an old, dilapidated farmhouse, was on fire behind her. Bright orange flames glowed against the inky black sky, and smoke billowed up in dark gray clouds. She looked around for anything. A car. Any sign of life, but there was nothing. She saw no other houses. No sign of anyone.

A dirt road extended from the house. Ellie crouched down beside some bushes, waiting for some sign of the Voiceless One before running out to look for help. She stayed five minutes behind that scrub but saw nothing. It seemed her captor had set the fire and left her for dead. Her legs, hands, and arms ached. She was exhausted but couldn't rest now. Ellie took another look at the old house she'd been under for a week, where she'd almost been burned alive, and ran for the road. She had no idea where she was and saw no signs.

Confident she was alone, Ellie continued on. It was freezing cold, and she rubbed her hands up and down her arms to warm herself. She looked back at the orange glow of the house then turned away for the last time. The sky above was thick with clouds, and she didn't even have the stars to comfort her. Ellie walked alone for what must have been twenty minutes before the first house came into view. The lights were off, but an old pickup truck sat outside—maybe someone was home. She trudged up the wooden steps to the front door. The mat in front of the door said "welcome." Knocking in the middle of the night would test how welcoming they were. Ellie bashed on the screen door with her fist. Nothing. She did it again, and a light went on upstairs. A few seconds later, a woman in her sixties appeared behind the screen.

"What do you want?" The woman gasped, taken aback by the sight of Ellie.

"Please, I need help. Someone took me. The house is on fire. I need to call the police," Ellie managed to croak.

The woman's eyes widened. "Are you Ellie Welsh?" she spluttered, opening the screen door. "Oh my God!"

Ellie stepped through and collapsed into the woman's arms.

SIXTEEN

TWENTY YEARS LATER

The mousy-haired new girl fidgeted in her chair, looking around as if she'd rather be anywhere else. Ellie had seen dozens like her before. If she didn't talk tonight, she'd never come back. The name tag stuck on her cheap sweater read "Tammy."

Ellie waited until Alexis, a survivor of domestic violence who'd been attending the group for two years, finished before saying, "Thank you for sharing." The twelve other women in the circle snapped their fingers to applaud. Actual clapping echoed around the hall too much. Snapping was much better.

They fell silent as Ellie glanced over at Tammy and spoke again. "We have a new member with us tonight," Ellie said. "Please welcome Tammy." The women welcomed her with kind words and smiles. Tammy nodded back and looked down. She was in her early twenties, but the lines on her face suggested someone much older. She brought deep brown eyes up to meet the rest of the group and offered a wave.

"Would you like to share with us tonight, Tammy?" Ellie asked her gently.

"I think I'll just listen," Tammy responded nervously.

Ellie knew it was now or never with this one. "We'd like to

get to know you. You already heard from Alexis and some of what she went through. I know it seems hopeless, but we're here for you."

Alexis, who was in her late forties and had two sons around the same age as Tammy, reached over and put a hand on the new girl's leg. "This group saved my life. My husband would have killed me. I know that now. I've been with Ellie two years. I never miss a week."

Ellie leaned forward. "Every woman here has a story to tell. Some of us are survivors of domestic abuse. Some have been affected by sexual assault or other violent crimes. The thing that binds us is our pain and the need we have to work through it. And this is how we do that, by talking. I know it seems safest to curl up into a ball, to shield yourself from the world by shutting it out. But that's not what we need. I can read about what happened to you online or talk to your mom like I did before the meeting, but that's never going to tell me what I really want to know—what's in your heart. So, please, tell us your name and why you're here tonight."

Tammy looked up with tentative confidence. "My name is Tammy Lockhart."

"Hi, Tammy," the rest of the group replied in unison.

The young woman hesitated a moment. Ellie was just about to prompt her again when Tammy beat her to it. "My boyfriend, Brandon stabbed me in the chest last year..."

Ellie nodded as the rest of the group settled in to listen. Tammy opening up was deeply satisfying. Ellie had been in touch with her for several weeks and had even visited her at home to persuade her to come to the group. Her words seemed like the first steps toward doing better, and that was enough for now.

.   .   .

Ellie was walking out of the gym an hour later with the rest of the group, and Tammy said goodbye with tears in her eyes. Someone standing a few yards away caught Ellie's attention. The old protective instincts kicked in and she looked away. It was only when she turned back that she saw who it was. A face she hadn't seen in years was standing before her and it felt like she had been transported back in time in a heartbeat. Josh Thomas. She felt the hairs on the back of her neck stand up and a swirling mess of emotions gripped her insides. She'd spent all this time trying to escape the past, and now here it was, in front of her eyes, with that warm, crooked smile that had stolen her heart all those years ago. The youthful sheen of his skin was gone, his hair was flecked with gray, and his eyes reflected the passage of twenty hard years, but Josh had kept his good looks.

"I hope you don't mind me coming along like this. I took the liberty of looking you up online and saw I could find you here."

He reached forward and gave her an awkward kiss on the cheek.

"I heard you were moving back to Haverford," Ellie admitted.

"Yeah, I needed a change of scene after the divorce."

"Why here? Why not Miami Beach or Malibu?"

"I like the cold," he replied, and she waited for him to continue. "The truth is, I wanted to reconnect with my past. I'm on my own now, and moving here feels like coming home."

Ellie simply nodded. Trying to hide her sheer amazement was difficult. Finding the words to respond to him was even harder.

Josh continued. "I read about the group you've been running. All the testimonies from people you've helped over the last fifteen years. It's amazing. You're an incredible person, Ellie."

"You've done some pretty unbelievable things in that time too." She looked into his eyes for a second longer than she should have and then drew them away, embarrassed. It was hard to tell if he'd noticed or not.

"Throwing a ball around a field? My achievements are nothing compared to what you've done."

She smiled. "I don't know. I'd say your bank balance might tell a different story."

He looked nervously around the parking lot outside the gym. "You want to go somewhere and get a drink?"

She hesitated. "I don't usually go out after meetings, but I think I can make an exception for you. Follow me. I know somewhere."

"Okay," he said with a smile.

"This is me," she said, pointing to her 2015 Ford Taurus.

"That's me over there." His car was a new silver Mercedes.

"I'll keep an eye out for you."

Ellie jumped out of the car and slammed the door far too loudly after she pulled up outside a little place she liked on Darby Road.

He held the door open for her. The hostess led them to the back of the almost full restaurant. It was a small place with high-top tables. The smell of fresh pizza filled her nostrils as they sat down. The clientele was mainly couples in their late forties and fifties—the type of people who didn't need babysitters anymore. A waitress in her early twenties, who definitely didn't recognize Josh, came to them and they each ordered a beer.

Ellie asked the first of about fifty questions that were swarming in her head. "So, when did you get back?"

"A few days ago. I've been looking at houses for a few weeks now. I just closed on one."

Elle remained as casual as possible while her insides churned. *He bought a house!* "Where?"

"On Maple Place."

Ellie nodded. She knew the houses there. Set back from a leafy avenue. Most were the types that came with their own pool out back.

"How long's it been?" he asked. "Must be fifteen years?"

Ellie's memory brought her back to a football game when she was nineteen. "Since you invited me to that game in sophomore year."

"Oh God, the one where I threw the interception on the first play?"

Ellie smiled. "Yeah. That one. You came back to win as far as I remember."

"It ended up being a good night."

"It was so kind of you to reach out to me like that. You didn't have to do that."

Josh's face dropped. He shifted in his chair a little. "It was the least I could do after everything that happened."

An awkward silence descended like a heavy curtain. It was strange to be in a moment she'd imagined so many times.

"It was a difficult time. For all of us," she said.

"And with everything in the papers? I'm sorry I left so soon after you... came back. My aunt didn't want to hang around. Reporters were all over me."

She looked down at her drink. "I remember."

"I wanted to be there for you."

"I know. I still have your letters."

He turned to her and smiled. "You kept them?"

"I figured they might be worth something someday. From a big NFL star?"

He took a sip of beer and placed the glass down. "Sorry that didn't work out for you."

"I won't hold it against you," she said and put her hand on his. "How's the knee these days?"

"Fine. A little creaky first thing in the morning, but we're all getting older, aren't we?"

"Yes, we are. But I didn't have three-hundred-pound defensive backs chasing me down every week for years on end."

"Didn't you?" he said with raised eyebrows. "You should really try that sometime. It gets you in touch with your vulnerable side."

"I spent enough time connecting with that part of me."

Ellie remembered the reporters who had camped on her doorstep for days after she got out. They painted her as both hero and victim. Gary Thomas was the obsessed madman, Rachel Kubick's killer. It seemed like the press had decided even before the trial had begun.

"Yeah," he said. "I can only imagine. I'm so sorry about that. If it wasn't for me, that never would have happened."

"We went over this twenty years ago. None of it was your fault. You can't be held accountable for what your dad or anyone else did."

"Yeah, whoever cut the brakes on the car is still out there. I used to have these dreams where I found them doing it, but I could never see their face. I'd wake up in a cold sweat with my heart thumping so fast I could almost see it through my skin."

"I know that feeling too well."

Ellie's mind returned to the confusion she'd felt all those years ago. Most of it was gone now. The prosecution had pieced it all together during the case. After the car crash, Josh's father had fled the scene of his wife's death in fear, convinced he'd be held responsible for it, seemingly unaware of the fact that the brakes on his car had been tampered with. He'd hidden in an apartment he kept on the outskirts of town which no one else knew about. It turned out he'd bought it in cash ten years earlier as a place to bring his women. He'd been found there after an anonymous tip-off from one of his neighbors to the police the day after the fire.

The farmhouse where Ellie was taken was south of a hamlet called Nickle Mines. It was a place Ellie had never heard of before she'd been taken there, but now could never forget. The very mention of the place sent shivers through her to this day.

Josh broke the silence between them. "It's just hard to fathom. Even still. That he'd take you like that? That he was obsessed with you?"

"I only wish he'd pled guilty and not strung things out like that," Ellie said.

"Did you believe any of what he said about the note being planted for my mom to find, and then him running because he thought he was in danger?"

The memory of Gary Thomas in the courtroom, shouting his innocence as the bailiffs dragged him out, consumed her. It was as if it had been stuck under frozen tundra and now was being freed again by the warmth of the sun. The most consequential evidence in the case was one of Gary's cell phones, which was found by the house he'd kept Ellie captive inside. He'd dropped it when he'd run. It was a burner phone with just one text message on it—sent to Rachel the night she died. It was an invitation to meet her in the woods, to give her something. The text had been sent minutes before Rachel had been killed. At the trial, the prosecution had argued that he'd intended to show it to Ellie as a warning before he'd lost his cool and attempted to murder her too.

"His story was so crazy. I don't see how anyone could have believed it, but then so much was left unexplained."

"I still don't know what to make of it all. I had to go with what the jury decided," Josh admitted.

"Me too. I wouldn't have believed you if you'd told me anything would have been as hard as being stuck in that basement—until the trial came." Ellie paused before continuing. "It's still hard to believe I went through all that. When I look back, it seems like it happened to a different person."

"I'm so sorry," he said in a low voice.

Ellie held up her glass. "Here's to new beginnings. To moving on."

Josh clinked his glass against hers. "To new beginnings. Is that why you started the survivors' group?"

"Yeah. For myself more than anyone else." She laughed. "It was a far more selfish act than people give me credit for."

"I'm sure you've saved dozens of lives over the years."

"What about you? Is that why you came back here? For a new beginning?"

"Maybe," he said, and let out a heavy breath. "But like I said, I think I just wanted to give my past another try, you know? Living in Chicago was great, but after the divorce, I started to associate it with my ex too much. She's from there. I had to get away."

"Back to the place where nothing makes sense?" she offered.

"Yeah," he said with a smile. "I'm surprised you never moved away. After everything that happened."

"I was never one to run from a fight." It was her turn to smile now, but it hurt. "My dad had his job, and Tyler and James were still in school here. We had reasons not to move."

"What about you? Are you married? Any kids?"

"Not married, no, but I have Jessica. She's seventeen."

"Same age we were when we first met! I hope she's not hanging around with anyone from the football team," Josh joked.

"She's a good girl. She's making her own mistakes, but that's what you're meant to do at that age."

"God knows I made enough of them."

"Ditto."

He took a swig from his beer and put it down. "You were my hero for a long time. I guess you still are. You know that?" he said softly.

"What are you talking about?" She could feel herself blushing.

"The way you escaped when..." He trailed off as if gathering his courage to say the next words. "When my dad set fire to the basement. You got out. You did that yourself."

Ellie shook her head. "I did what anyone else would have," she argued.

"No. You're wrong. Only an exceptional person could have done what you did. Only someone with the courage of a lioness."

"Or a real estate agent?"

"Is that what you do?"

She nodded. "I started doing it a few years back as a favor for the old boss. It's not what I'd call my ideal career, but Jess is seventeen and college costs a lot of money."

"A whole lot of money."

"Tell me about it."

"What's Jess like?"

"She's a wonderful kid. Much better than I ever was. She's a musician."

"What does she play?"

"The piano mainly but she can play anything she picks up. Drums, guitar, you name it. She wants to study music at Juilliard or at Curtis in Philly next year."

Josh's face lit up. "That's amazing. I'd love to hear her play sometime."

"You never had kids, Josh?"

"I wanted to, but Jenny had a difference of opinion. That was one of the things that drove us apart. She wanted to live a different lifestyle." She noticed him looking down at her bare ring finger. "Were you ever married?"

"Me? No. I never took the plunge," she said with a sheepish smile.

"A woman like you? I'm surprised. Is Jessica's dad still on the scene?"

"When he feels like it. I never got married, but he did, just not to me. Twice in fact! He has little kids of his own with number two. They live in South Philly."

"Not too far away."

"Sometimes I wish he did live farther away, but he's Jessica's dad." Ellie sighed. "She loves him."

"Does she look like you?"

"I'll let you be the judge of that." Ellie reached under her stool and grabbed her bag. She unlocked her phone and showed him a picture of Jess she'd taken the day before. She was standing with her friends at lacrosse practice, their arms over each other's shoulders, bright smiles in the spring sunshine.

"She's adorable. And as I imagined, she looks just like her mom." Josh handed the phone back to her. "You must be very proud."

"She's an easy girl to be a single mom to," Ellie beamed. "It's just been me and her since she was born."

"That must have been tough, raising a child alone."

"It was," she replied. "I had help from my family. I don't know what I would have done without them."

"You ever nearly get married? I don't mean to pry."

She had expected all these questions. It would have been weird if he didn't ask them. "No, it's okay. I had a couple of close shaves, but things were hard for me after what happened. I was just a kid. I suppose it took me a long time to get over it. I suppose I was protective of Jess, too, wary of letting strange men into our lives. I pushed a few away," she said with a mirthless laugh."

Josh finished the rest of his beer and put his glass to the side. "I was lucky I had football," he said in a soft, wistful tone. "The coach at LSU was so great. He even kept in touch after he moved on. The team became my family then. I needed them.

The fans too. They knew what I'd been through. I played for them."

"What were the fans in Chicago like?"

"They were great. They were just starting to trust me when it all ended. I was just finding my stride when I got injured."

"I remember. I was watching the game. It was against the Eagles."

He looked away for two seconds before he brought his chestnut brown eyes back to hers. "Yeah. Ironic that a tackle I got against the team I followed growing up ended my career, but that's football. I still love the Eagles, though. Always will." He pushed the folded napkin on the table away with two fingers and let out a deep breath.

"What are you doing now?"

"I coached high school for a while in Chicago, but I'm eager to get back into football. I miss it. Going to games isn't enough for me. I need to be a part of it. It's who I am." His eyes lit up as he talked about his passion.

"I wish I had something like that."

"You have the group you run. And your family. Are they all still around here?"

Josh's intuitiveness brought a smile to Ellie's face. "Yeah. Mom and Dad are still in the house, and Tyler and James are close by, too."

"How are the boys?"

"Not boys anymore! They're both married. They live about two blocks apart. I honestly don't know how their wives can stand it. Tyler has two boys, and James has two girls. I see them all pretty regularly, and Jess loves her baby cousins."

"Sounds great."

"It is."

They talked about old times for a while, and before Ellie realized it, the waitresses were upturning chairs on empty tables all around them. All the other patrons had gone, and the staff was standing expectantly, local hero or not.

When their waitress brought their bill over before they'd even asked for it, Josh paid it quickly, leaving a generous tip.

They walked toward the door together. The question Ellie burned to ask was on the tip of her tongue, and the words came tripping out before she realized she was saying them.

"Do you ever visit him?"

Josh turned to her. "My father?" He put his hand on the door handle and stopped. "Not for a while. I was angry at him for years. I went to him after I got injured the last time. When I was twenty-five. It was hard, but I needed to get some closure, you know? He just denied everything. He blamed Mom's death on whoever cut the brakes. Convenient that the cops never found them, of course. Some said he did it himself, that he had a death wish and wanted to take her with him, but I don't know." He opened the door. "But have I seen him lately? Not unless you consider five years ago lately. He's up for parole in two years."

"I'm well aware," she said with a sense of dread.

"I'll make sure he stays away from you. You have my word on that."

They stepped out onto the wide avenue. It was quiet.

The thought of the man she knew as "the Voiceless One" getting out after trying to burn her to death filled her with fear and rage, but she kept her feelings to herself. "What will you do when your dad gets out?"

"Make sure he never does anything like what he did to you to anyone else." Josh leaned in, his lips brushing against her cheek in a feather-light kiss. "It's been great talking to you, Ellie." He started to walk away but paused, turning back to face her. "I know it's probably not easy being around me. I must remind you of all the worst things in your life."

Ellie's heart clenched, the memories of that fateful night

rushing back in a painful flood. She swallowed hard, forcing herself to meet his gaze. "None of it was your fault," she said, her voice barely above a whisper.

Josh hesitated, his eyes searching hers. "Would it be okay if I called you sometime? We could go out and get a drink."

Ellie's mind screamed at her to say no, to slam the door shut on this dangerous path before it was too late.

"I'd like that," she heard herself say, the words slipping out before she could stop them.

Josh's face lit up, his smile genuine and warm. She put her number in his phone, her fingers brushing against his as she handed it back to him.

"Thank you, Ellie. For everything."

She watched as he walked away, his tall frame disappearing around the corner of the empty street.

SEVENTEEN

The Glock was Ellie's favorite weapon. It was compact, accurate, and packed a punch. She slid a magazine into it and closed an eye as she got into firing position. In previous years she'd imagined the paper targets to be Gary Thomas, but those imaginings had faded over time, and now she saw the targets for exactly what they were—training aids in her quest to stay safe from the evils of this world. The gun roared as she squeezed the trigger. The protective headphones she wore dulled the sound to a loud pop. Both bullets hit their mark. Taking her time, she emptied the magazine and slid in another. Satisfied, she brought back the target to check her pattern.

"Impressive, as always," Bill Winston, one of the other regulars, said to her with a smile. "How's Jess doing? Those boys come chasing her yet?"

"No. They know I have this," Ellie said and held up the Glock.

Bill laughed and took his place a few feet away from her.

. . .

She stowed her weapon in the trunk of her car beside her gym bag and walked around to the driver's side door.

Ellie couldn't help it. Her daughter was the victim of her mother's past. She'd waited until Jess was eight to tell her what had happened to her back when she was a senior in high school. It had become impossible to hide it from her any longer. Kids in school talked about it. Big brothers and sisters who'd heard it from their parents told little boys and girls who played with her daughter. It wasn't surprising. The famous case of the football star's girlfriend who got kidnapped by his father was the biggest thing to happen to Havertown in 200 years. Ellie had kept some of the newspapers at first but thrown them out weeks later.

Evening was drawing in, and the sun was slathering gold on the windshield. Jess wanted a car. Many of her friends had their own, but few of them were being raised by single parents trying to keep their heads above water. Ellie started the car and made her way toward the school. Lots of single dads had asked Ellie out over the years. She'd even said yes to a few of them. They all wanted to save her—to swoop in and rescue her from the troubles of the world. Some had even found out what had happened to her as a teenager, and rather than being put off, they'd only grown keener. She'd had no shortage of offers, but none of them had rung true somehow. Ellie had almost always been the one to break things off. She'd made all manner of excuses. Perhaps some of them had been true, but Ellie didn't really know. Maybe it was just that she and Jess had always been a team and she felt she didn't need anyone else now. It was hard to say.

Now Josh was back, and she felt like a kid again. It was impossible to see him and not feel nostalgic about the early days of their relationship, when being with him seemed like everything. She laughed when she remembered the intensity they'd shared—what only teenagers could feel. Over the years, she'd often thought of what they might have been if his father's psychosis hadn't gotten in their way. With no hurdles obstructing them now, perhaps they could find out.

As Ellie drove to Lower Merion High School, she took in the familiar surroundings. She could have drawn the pizza parlor, barber shop, library, and firehouse from memory and not missed a single detail. And as for the school itself, little had changed in the twenty years since she'd graduated. Many of the same teachers still worked there, and the building was much the same, albeit with a fresh paint job. Even the music on the radio was the same—Christina Aguilera's song came to an abrupt halt as she parked and turned off the engine.

It was a warm April evening. Jess would be graduating in less than two months. It seemed like the end of an era. Her baby, the focus of her existence, would be moving out and going to college soon. It felt like she was losing her best friend. Her own mother's tears when she'd left for college were all the more understandable now, even though at the time Ellie had been embarrassed by them. But her mother had had Ellie's brothers, and a husband. Jess was everything to Ellie, and the vacuum she'd leave in her wake would be hard to fill. Ellie was going to have to begin again. A new life beckoned at age thirty-seven.

Ellie walked past the field where Josh had played. Where his father had cursed the referees and stood cross-armed on the sideline expecting perfection. It seemed like a lifetime ago. She'd spent too much time over the years trying to understand Gary Thomas's motivation for taking her. The prosecution had argued he was obsessed with her, as he'd been with Rachel. Psychologists had taken the stand to testify to his mental state. Some had even argued that he shouldn't be held fully responsible for his crimes, but the judge had thrown that idea out. Ellie had tried to force the puzzle pieces in her mind together thousands of times, and on occasion, she'd convinced herself that it all made sense. But a lone voice in the back of her mind questioned everything. If Gary was so obsessed, why hadn't he shown himself, tried to be closer to her? Why had he tried to kill her after a week? And why had he been so sloppy as to leave the contents of his wallet and an old phone at the scene of his crime?

Ellie knew she was the type of person who questioned everything. She was born with a natural curiosity, always eager to learn and better understand the world. It was good enough for the cops who'd arrested him and the court that had convicted him. Why wasn't it good enough for her?

The football season was over, but the juniors were out practicing. Every team since Josh's had been trying to reach the standards he'd played to. None had succeeded. The run to the championship game was legend now. Old photographs of Josh still sat in the trophy case in the hallway along with a signed ball he'd sent from LSU and from when he'd been drafted to the Chicago Bears. The school's glory years were the stuff of her personal nightmares. The irony almost forced her to smile.

Lacrosse season was very much underway, however, and Ellie stopped at the sideline to watch the end of Jessica's practice. She spotted her instantly—Jess was four inches taller than Ellie, with brown hair and her father's blue eyes. Some of the girls on the team had received offers from colleges. One even got a full ride. It didn't matter. Jess loved the sport and her teammates. That was enough. Her future was in music, and Jess had already been offered a partial scholarship from several colleges. But they weren't the ones she wanted. Juilliard in New York and the Curtis Institute, only a few miles away, on Locust Street in Center City Philadelphia, were where she was aiming toward. But much would depend on the audition process, which would begin in a few weeks.

Ellie stood beside one of the coaches and made small talk as practice ended. Jess ran off the field, waving to Ellie before she picked up her bag. Lots of the other girls had cars, and Jess was never short of offers for a ride home, but Ellie enjoyed coming to pick her up. She didn't do it often but it was always the high-light of her week.

Jess was sweating as she hugged her mom. She lugged her bag over her shoulder and walked beside her.

"How was it?" Ellie asked.

"Good. I think we're ready for the game on Saturday. Coach told me I need to be more aggressive."

Ellie smiled to herself. Her daughter's gentle nature didn't mesh easily with the hard-hitting nature of the sport.

"You home tonight?" Jess asked as they got into the car.

"I thought we might watch a movie after you finish your homework."

"Yeah, sure. I'll try and get it finished as soon as I can. Can we get takeout tonight? Chinese?"

Ellie thought of her bank account. "We have food at home. I was going to make tacos."

Jessica moaned in protest and changed the radio station as Ellie started the car.

Jess's phone buzzed, and she reached into her bag for it. She turned up the volume of the radio without asking before returning to the screen in her hand. A bright smile lit up her face.

Ellie knew she shouldn't ask but didn't care. "Who's texting you?"

Jess replied without hesitation. "Cooper Elliot."

Ellie nodded as she tried to be the cool mom but broke after about five seconds. "What's going on with you two?"

"Nothing. We went out a couple of times, but it's nothing big," she said in a bored, dismissive tone.

"So, the same as Owen Burkett and Chase Shapiro?"

"Pretty much. He wants to take me to a Phillies game next week."

"With anyone else?"

"I don't think so."

Ellie's heart twinged, but she kept her mouth shut.

"I was thinking about applying to be a ball girl for the Phillies after school gets out for summer."

Ellie smiled. "Sounds fun. You won't make your fortune there, but you do love that ballpark. As long as it doesn't get in the way of your piano practice."

Jess let the phone drop into her lap for a second and stared at her mother. "Mom, do you really think I'm going to let anything get in the way of practicing?"

Ellie shook her head. "No. I don't."

For a few days she had toyed with the idea of telling Jess about Josh coming home. It was time to take the plunge. "I met someone I hadn't seen in a long time a few nights ago."

"Who?"

"Josh Thomas. He was waiting for me after my meeting ended, and we sat down and had a drink together."

Jess's mouth dropped open. "What?"

"It's not a big deal."

Her daughter seemed incredulous. "Your teenage boyfriend who played in the NFL came back to ask you out? I'd say it's a big deal!"

It was hard to tell if she was excited or fearful. Either way, she was shocked. "I heard he was moving back to the area. He divorced that actress too."

Ellie nodded. "Yeah, he said he wanted to come home. I think he's trying to cleanse himself of the past."

"By coming here?" Jess laughed. "Where the worst things happened?"

Ellie gripped the steering wheel, her knuckles turning white. "That was a long time ago. His father's in jail."

"I know. It's just weird," she asserted.

"He's a good person. He said he wants to meet you."

Jess smiled and arched her head to look at Ellie. "Mom?"

"What?"

"You're not getting some of the old feelings back for him, are you?"

"Of course not. It's been twenty years since we were together. We're just old friends now, bonded by what happened."

"Oh yeah, sure," Jess said, her voice dripping with sarcasm. "I believe you."

"Come on, Jess. What would he want with me?"

"The same thing he did twenty years ago? Except now, you don't have his psycho dad in the way to mess things up for you."

Ellie laughed. It was so ridiculous. The notion that Josh Thomas would be interested in her...

"Okay, you know what, we can get Chinese tonight and eat it while we watch the movie."

Her daughter cheered the decision.

"But get your homework done first. And your keyboard practice."

"When do I ever not finish my homework or not do my practice?"

"I'm just saying it out loud. There are certain things I have to verbalize every so often as your mother."

Ellie smiled as she drove on.

The chicken fried rice and beef with black bean sauce were in place. The trays were laid out, and the silly romantic movie that she had allowed Jess to pick was about to begin when Ellie's phone buzzed. She didn't pay any attention at first, preferring to keep her focus on the food and on the opening credits of the movie. She'd promised herself months ago to cherish every moment she had left with Jess before she left for college—when everything would change.

"Can you check that before we get into the movie?" Jessica asked.

Ellie glanced at her phone on the coffee table and reached for it. The message was from Josh. She almost blushed in front of her daughter.

> I was wondering if you wanted to go out for dinner sometime.

Ellie put the phone back down without responding.

Jessica was chewing her food and eyed her mother suspiciously.

"What's going on? Who was that?" she asked.

"Nothing. No one important," Ellie muttered, feeling her cheeks color.

Ellie needed some time to think. Could she see him again after everything they'd been through? She'd always thought he'd suffered more than her. He'd lost his mother and then his father went to jail, but he'd had his talent to fall back on and had fulfilled his potential as a college star, even if he hadn't made it in the NFL to the degree some had predicted. But she was still reeling from her time in that basement. No one thought she'd become the person she was today.

Would they drag each other into the mire as they had twenty years before, or could they rebuild together and fulfill the potential they'd had?

Jessica pressed pause on the remote control. "Come on, Mom. I know that face. You're about as hard to read as a kindergarten book."

"I got an interesting text."

"From who?"

"Josh Thomas."

Jess jumped to her feet in a way only a teenager could. "I knew it!"

"What did you know?"

"That he came back for you."

"He didn't even know I was single."

"It's not hard to find out these things."

"How? He's not on social media either."

Jess dismissed the triviality. "I don't know, but whatever. Are you going to text him back?"

Ellie reached forward and picked up her phone. "I'm still weighing that up."

"It'd be rude not to. You don't want him to think you're rude, do you?" she joked. But her daughter's mood changed as the reality hit her. "Wait, actually—are you sure about this? I'm sure he's a nice guy, but with everything that happened between you..."

"That was a long time ago. His father is in jail. He can't hurt me now."

"So are you going to text him back? What are you gonna say?"

Ellie forced a smile. She wanted her daughter to think she was in control. "Just give me a few minutes to let him sweat a little."

Jess threw her arms up in faux annoyance. "I'm not going to be able to concentrate on the movie now."

"It's not exactly a complicated plot."

Jessica pointed at the phone in her mother's hand.

"Okay, okay," Ellie said. "I'm doing it, but we're not staring at the phone, waiting for him to respond."

She typed out a message then showed it to Jess.

> Sounds good. When were you thinking?

"There! I did it. Can we watch the movie now?"

"Oh my God! My mom's going to be one of the Real Housewives of Philadelphia!"

"That show doesn't exist."

"Not yet!"

EIGHTEEN

Date night had come around, and Ellie hid her nerves in front of her daughter. The truth was she didn't know if she should be going or not. Jess had insisted on helping to choose her mom's outfit, and she dug into her closet and held up various dresses Ellie hadn't worn in months or even years.

Jess pulled out a short black wrap dress. "What about this one?"

"Yeah." Ellie nodded. "I like it. Not too suggestive."

"But just suggestive enough. Good thinking." Jess winked at her.

Ellie slipped into the dress, and her daughter helped with the zipper. Ellie went to the mirror, running her hands along the smooth sides.

Jess appeared over her shoulder. "You look amazing. You're going to knock him out."

"We'll see. I don't even know what tonight is yet. It's probably just meeting an old friend."

"Sure, Mom, sure. Put it this way—I won't be waiting up for you tonight!"

"It's not like that."

"We'll see."

Forty-five minutes later, Jess was driving her to the restaurant—
Del Frisco's Steakhouse in Center City. It was somewhere Ellie
could never afford.

Jess beamed as they pulled up outside. "Best of luck, Mom.
He'd have to be blind or stupid or both not to love you!"

Ellie turned around and kissed her. This felt like something, but Ellie was conflicted. Getting together with Josh had
precipitated the worst things to happen in both their lives
before, but maybe this was their chance to set things straight.
Still, the naysaying voices in the back of her mind were
screaming at her to turn around and walk away. She'd been
fine all these years without Josh Thomas in her life. Most of
her friends were married with kids much younger than Jess.
She'd been unprepared for motherhood and for what life had
thrown at her, but she'd adapted. She wasn't jealous of
anyone but did sometimes wonder how her life would have
turned out if Gary Thomas hadn't imprisoned her in that
basement.

With one last look at Jess, Ellie took a deep breath and
stepped out of the car.

Josh was waiting for her at the host's lectern. He was
dressed in a gray suit and white shirt with no tie. He smiled as
he saw her.

"You look incredible," he said. "You haven't aged a day."

"And you still know how to say all the right things."

The hostess, a pretty, college-aged girl with blonde hair,
showed them to their seat. The table was covered in a white
cloth, and the silver knives and forks shone in the candlelight.
Lounge music drifted across the room from the singer playing
the piano in the corner.

"This makes a change from the diner," Josh remarked and

then seemed to realize what he'd said as Ellie laughed. "I was talking about when we went out as kids."

"I got it. We couldn't afford somewhere like this," Ellie said. "I still can't, but don't tell anyone."

Josh leaned forward. The candlelight danced across the surface of his eyes. "I dug into the couch and fished out a few nickels and dimes. Don't worry, I have it covered."

When the waiter came to take their order, Josh ordered the filet rare. Ellie opted for a medium-rare sirloin. She tried not to balk at the prices. The sides were outrageous.

"What was it like?" she asked when the waiter left.

"What was what like?"

"Playing in the NFL."

Josh smiled and sat back in his seat. His dimples had always driven her crazy. She was a kid again. "Nuts. It was the culmination of a dream, but it was a job. I was an employee. There was no doubt about that. Tens of thousands of players tried to make it the year I was drafted, but only about two hundred and twenty got onto NFL teams. It was humbling."

"How hard was it on your body?"

Josh looked away as if reaching into the past. "We got used to playing hurt but not injured. It was an old adage I learned. I got to know my body well enough to know the difference between an ache and something serious."

"So, you knew when you got that hit against the Eagles?" she asked sensitively, taking a sip of wine.

Josh nodded. "Yeah, I knew right away. I didn't know it was the end, but it was clear something serious had happened. I was lucky enough to have signed my first full contract, so I got paid. If it had happened the year before when I was still on my rookie contract..."

"We'd be eating in the diner again?"

Josh laughed. "Exactly."

An older couple beside them looked over at Josh. The

husband leaned forward to tell his wife who they were look-ing at.

Josh paid them no mind.

"I saw the game. I got into football more over the years. It helped knowing one of the players," Ellie said.

"Another thing we have in common."

"It was funny watching you from afar after knowing you so well." Ellie smiled as she stared across the table at him. She real-ized she was leaning toward him and sat back.

"I think when you know someone as well as we knew each other..." He trailed off for a second before beginning again. "Those bonds endure."

Her heart leaped in her chest, but she hid it, or at least she hoped she did. "I don't know. You went in such a different direction than I did."

"That doesn't make me a different person than the kid you knew," he declared.

Ellie sighed. "I'd love to say I haven't changed, but with everything that happened... it was hard not to."

"How would you say you're different?" he asked. Now he was the one leaning toward her, staring into her eyes.

"I don't know. I didn't think I'd be doing this at age thirty-seven."

"Doing what?"

"Struggling. Still reeling from something that happened twenty years ago."

Josh nodded. "Life has a habit of making a joke of the plans we make as kids. I never said it out loud, but I was sure I'd be an NFL MVP Hall of Fame quarterback with so many Super Bowl rings I'd hardly be able to lift my fingers."

"You might have been if it wasn't for your injury."

Josh shrugged as if there was no answer to what she'd said. "What did you want to be?"

Ellie smiled and shook her head. "I'm not sure I even remember."

"I think I recall you said a teacher back when we were dating."

She laughed. "It might have been. I retreated into myself a little after what happened. I didn't thrive in college like you did. It was hard to imagine myself in front of a bunch of kids. Then I got pregnant with Jess."

"You can still do whatever you want. You're a smart, confident, beautiful woman."

The waiter returned just as she was about to answer. Ellie marveled at the presentation of the food on their plates. The steaks looked like works of art. It seemed wrong to eat them. They tasted just as good, and the wine Josh had ordered for the table was the perfect complement.

Ellie waited until they'd finished their meal to continue on the theme of their conversation. It seemed cathartic. Important.

"I wondered about meeting you. I thought it might dredge up too many bad memories. None of what happened was your fault, but those were the hardest times I've ever had."

He finished his wine and put the glass back on the table. "We thought the same thing, then."

"So, why did you come find me?"

"I've met a lot of people in the last twenty years. Everyone wants to shake your hand when you're the starting quarterback for LSU or even the backup quarterback for the Bears."

"You were a starter when you got injured."

"Yeah, for about a season altogether. But I met a lot of people back then. Some of them were famous, others were trying to get something out of me. Few compared to you. I know we lost touch for years, but who you are and what you did in escaping that basement and saving your own life never left me. I was married for years, and my ex wouldn't have appreciated me looking up my ex-girlfriend from high school too much."

"But here we are."

Josh shook his head with a handsome grin. "I'm not married anymore."

Neither of them wanted dessert, but Josh insisted they get coffee. Ellie wondered what she was getting into here. It seemed like Josh had some specific intentions in mind for coming back.

"What's your new house like?" she asked as her espresso arrived. The aroma drifted up from the cup.

"It's big and empty."

"No furniture yet?"

"I have some, but it's four bedrooms, six bathrooms. It was the house I figured I should get, but I'm all alone in there. You and Jess should come and see it sometime."

"You'll have to catch her soon. She'll be off to college in the fall."

Josh was holding his coffee in front of him but hadn't taken a sip yet. "How do you feel about that?"

"I'm excited for her but struggling to conceal my inner devastation. It's the next step in her life and she can't wait. It's something she's earned, but I feel like I'm losing my best friend. She picked out my dress for tonight. She's always been there for the past seventeen years."

"She'll still be your daughter."

"I know, and I have to get used to the idea that she's not going to live with me anymore, but it's not easy."

"You'll be free to do whatever you want."

Ellie smirked. "Yeah. What about you?"

"What am I doing? I want to set up a business here, set down some roots."

"What kind of business?"

"I bought a share in the Toyota dealership on Lancaster Avenue. I also want to go into the inner city and set up some football programs there—give the kids something to focus on to set themselves on the straight and narrow."

"Sounds noble."

"It did in my head. What about your noble pursuit—your survivors' support group? It's incredible. I'm sure you've saved a lot of lives."

Ellie's face tightened a little. "It's funny. People gush with admiration for what I do with those ladies, but a lot of the motivations behind it are selfish."

"What are you talking about? You're actively helping survivors of domestic violence, aren't you?"

"And women dealing with the aftereffects of other crimes too."

Josh was perplexed. "I don't understand how it could possibly be selfish."

"I set up the group as a place where women could talk and deal with pain, but I'm not sure anyone's got as much out of it as I have. I wouldn't have started it if I didn't need help myself."

Josh laughed. "Oh, if only more people were selfish like you are!"

Ellie couldn't help the smile that spread across her face. "I just wanted to set a good example for Jess more than anything else."

"I'd love to meet her. Maybe we could all go to a Phillies game sometime or something."

"You'll have to get in line behind the boys taking her," Ellie joked.

"Oh!" Josh exclaimed. "But she doesn't have a boyfriend?"

"Not yet. I don't know which would be worse. At least if she had a boyfriend, I'd know who I'm dealing with."

"Some things you can't fight."

"Don't I know it? After she came, I just focused my energies on her. Her dad, Pete, didn't stick around long."

"Where were you living at the time?"

"With my parents. We were there until Jess was seven."

"Are you still close?"

"We see them all the time."

Silence dropped like an anvil. His mother's grave was a few miles away. His father's jail cell was a couple hours' drive.

"You still think about her much?" Ellie asked and immediately regretted it. "I'm sorry, of course you do."

"I kept her photograph on the inside of my locker when I played. For a while she was on my mind all the time. But time erodes everything, doesn't it? I still think about her most days, but then that brings up thoughts of my father too."

"I'm so sorry for what you went through."

"Poor little rich NFL quarterback, eh?" He smiled.

"There's more to you than just that side. That wasn't the reason I was with you when we were kids."

"I know, and that's why I asked you out. No one else has seen me as anything more since I was fifteen years old."

Josh held up his hand and got the check.

"I can pay my half," Ellie said.

He reached into his pocket and drew out his wallet. "Absolutely no chance."

They left the restaurant together. Most tables were empty now. It was after eleven o'clock. They'd been at dinner for almost three hours. Ellie had the inkling to call Jess but dismissed it.

"How did you get here?"

"Jessica gave me a ride. Fringe benefit of having a kid."

"I took a taxi, figured I'd have a glass of wine or two. You want to get a drink somewhere?"

"I could go to a bar for a little. We never had the chance when we were seventeen. We may as well take advantage of getting old."

Josh laughed and agreed. They walked a few blocks to an Irish pub, where they took seats by the bar. Josh ordered beers for them both.

The bartender handed them the drinks and they just had

time to clink them together when a voice came from behind them.

"Josh Thomas, is that you, man?"

They both turned around to see Jeremy Davis, the former center on the football team, and the boy who'd hosted the party from which she'd been taken. He'd been huge as a teenager, but time hadn't been kind. Muscle had turned to fat and Josh could hardly get his arms around to hug his old friend. Ellie felt like she was in the schoolyard again. Whispers all around her. Her heart dropped at the prospect of their night ending like this.

"What are you doing here?" Jeremy said before bringing his eyes over to her. "And Ellie Welsh." He pointed at her and then him. "Are you two guys...?"

"Having a drink together?" Josh said with a smile. "Yes. We are."

"Good to see you out together. It's just like old times. I'm here with a few of the old crew. You should come over."

Josh looked at Ellie. "We were just going to get a quiet drink. I'll tell you what, send me a text and we'll go out next week. I'm going to keep it low-key tonight."

"Have it your way," Jeremy said, and he and Josh exchanged numbers.

"I suppose we'd better get used to that kind of treatment if we're going to be stepping out around here," Ellie said once Jeremy had returned to his table.

"We have nothing to hide."

"Of course not, but most of the kids we grew up with are still living in the area, and they haven't stopped talking about twenty years ago. You being back here is only going to stoke those fires."

"They'll burn out soon enough."

Ellie wasn't so sure, but she didn't want to go down that road. "Maybe."

Jeremy's interruption had brought her back to reality and

muted the energy between them. Perhaps their past was too much to overcome.

They sat for a few minutes, sipping their beers and chatting about old times, but a sudden wave of exhaustion hit her. "You want to share a taxi home?"

"Sure," Josh replied.

"Good, because I ordered it already. It'll be here in a minute."

They went back out on the sidewalk to wait. Ellie crossed her arms. She looked over at him in silence, not knowing what to do next.

The car pulled up to rescue them and they got inside. Josh sat a respectable distance from her.

"I hope seeing Jeremy didn't bring back too many bad memories," Josh said, at last breaking the silence between them.

Ellie was looking out the window but turned back to face him. "I don't know. It seems we have more to deal with than most. Maybe seeing him brought that back into focus."

"That doesn't take away from the time we had together," he protested.

She looked out the window again. "It's just a lot to take on board all at once. I'm sure I'll get used to it in time."

The truth was that seeing Jeremy had brought her right back to his house on the night she'd been taken. She didn't want to admit that her chest was tight, and she was finding it hard to breathe.

Josh made conversation about the good times in the past and his feelings on how Havertown had changed in the last twenty years, but she didn't talk much and was relieved when the taxi arrived at her house.

She kissed him on the cheek and said goodnight.

Ellie didn't know what to say so blurted, "Call me," and shut the taxi door behind her.

The light in the living room was on when she walked inside

the house. Jessica was on the couch practicing her fingerwork on her keyboard. She pushed it aside and jumped up. "So, how did it go?" she asked anxiously.

Ellie smiled. "It went great. He's a really nice guy."

"You want to see him again?"

"Can we talk about this tomorrow? It's almost one in the morning. You should be in bed."

"Can you answer the question?"

"I might see him again, yes. We'll see if he calls. He's a busy man."

Jessica smiled and kissed her mother on the cheek before bounding upstairs to bed. Ellie switched off the lights and locked the front door before following her up a few minutes later.

The yearbook from senior year was at the bottom of her closet. She took it out and flicked to the pages about the football team. The first picture was of Josh throwing a pass. Pain burned through her at what should have been.

"We were only kids," she said quietly to herself.

NINETEEN

Ellie's clients came early and had little interest in the house she was showing. They were a couple whose kids had flown the coop and were looking for something smaller, more fitting for their new life as parents to grown-up children. Ellie left them with an offer to show them a three-bed twin that had just come on the market. They seemed happy and left after promising to call her. Ellie didn't take them at their word, of course, and made a note to follow up with them the next day. Trusting customers to call you back was a surefire way to go out of business. People had to be guided toward what they wanted. Sales was about showing people their best options and letting them realize they should take them, not talking them into buying something they didn't want or need. It had taken Ellie a while to learn that, but it had made all the difference.

The house she was showing was in Narberth, and Ellie stopped at a coffee shop she knew in Suburban Square in Ardmore for lunch. Her phone buzzed as she parked her car on the street outside. It was Jess. She was in school but apparently excited about Ellie's date with Josh later that evening.

> What are you going to wear tonight?

Ellie chuckled, her mind drifting to the couple she had just shown the house to. What would her life look like next year, with Jess no longer by her side? Ellie's entire world had revolved around her daughter since the day she was born, and in a few short months, she would be moving out. A profound, hollow ache filled her chest. There was a life beyond Jess, she knew that, and she wasn't going to hold her only daughter back because she couldn't bear to let her go. She reached for her phone, a mix of emotions swirling within her.

> I was thinking about my navy dress.

The text came back seconds later. Jess promised to help her pick out tonight's outfit. Ellie smiled and got out of the car. It was a fine, sunny day, and she was reaching into her bag for her sunglasses when she saw a familiar face on the pavement outside the café. It was Tammy, from the survivors' group she ran. The young woman tried to look away and folded her arms as Ellie approached her. She had a fresh bruise on the side of her face.

"Tammy," Ellie said. "You weren't at the meeting this week. What happened?"

Tammy looked Ellie in the eyes for a brief second before averting her gaze again. "I was busy. I don't think I need it as much as I thought."

Ellie's heart dropped. She knew what was coming next. "You should try and come along next time. You mean more to the rest of the group than you realize. We all missed you the other night."

Tammy jawline was tense. She nodded but didn't answer. Just then, the door of the café opened, and a man about

Tammy's age walked out carrying two to-go cups. She turned to him.

"Let's get out of here," he murmured.

Ellie held her emotions in. "Is this Brandon?" she asked.

The man who'd stabbed Tammy in the chest the year before, took her by the arm, ignoring Ellie, and led her to a pickup truck parked on the side of the road. Tammy looked back at Ellie before she got in, a strange mix of sorrow and defiance painted across her pretty face.

"Don't forget about the meeting next week," Ellie repeated. "I'll see you there, okay?"

Her abuser started the truck and they drove off. Ellie couldn't help the brokenhearted feeling that overcame her as she walked into the café.

Ellie was still doing her makeup when the doorbell rang. She put down her mascara and shouted out her bedroom door.

"Jess, can you get that? It's probably Josh."

Three weeks had passed since their first date in twenty years, and they'd been out three times since. Ellie had been wary of going out again, but with much cajoling from her daughter, she'd agreed. They were taking things very slowly, and she was enjoying getting to know him again.

A few strangers had recognized him when they were out, mainly hardcore football fans who wanted to talk to him about the game rather than his dead mother or incarcerated father. And no one recognized her. She was the girl on the football hero's arm, just as she had been all those years ago. He was still funny and charming. Still determined and driven. Still suffering from what had happened. Who else could understand how she felt other than someone still nursing the wounds of that horrible time? He was the only other person she knew whose adulthood had been molded by the same cruel hands as hers.

Jess brought Josh inside and they sat down in the living room together—they'd met the week before when he'd come by to pick Ellie up.

Ellie had dreamed up every scenario over the last week or two. It wasn't crazy to think she and Josh might end up together. He could be Jess's stepfather. Josh wanted children of his own. Was she ready for that? She shook the thought from her mind. It was ridiculous to think like that. She had to take things one day at a time, despite her instinct to look into the future.

Jess was sitting on the armchair opposite Josh when Ellie walked into the living room.

"Can you play me something?" Josh asked Jess.

After a few seconds of cajoling, he convinced her. She took the keyboard from the table and set it on her lap. "Are you a Beethoven fan?" she asked.

"Probably without realizing it," he replied.

Josh and Ellie sat down as Jess played the first two minutes of "Moonlight Sonata."

"That was incredible," Josh said as she finished. "You have an incredible talent."

Jess smiled but didn't respond.

"Talent and hard work will get you places," Ellie said.

"That's the key," Josh said. "You can have all the natural ability in the world, but if you don't put the work in, you'll never get better."

"When are you going to stay here for dinner?" Jess asked, deliberately changing the subject.

Josh smiled and looked up at Ellie. "Whenever your mom invites me."

Ellie squirmed a little. "I'll rustle up something one of these days."

"I'd love to sit down with you and Jess soon," Josh said.

Jess was loving every second of this. "I need to see if you're fit to date my mom."

"I welcome the challenge."

"Shouldn't we be leaving?" Ellie said. "What time is our reservation?"

Josh stood up. "Your mom's right, but I'll continue this conversation anytime."

"I'll jot down a few questions," Jess said before hugging her mother goodbye. "I won't wait up!"

Ellie smiled. "You do what you have to!"

Jess leaned in and whispered in her ear, "Good luck, Mom."

Ellie looked at her beautiful daughter and saw her as a little girl again. "I love you so much, my sweet girl."

"I love you too."

"She's a character," Josh said as they walked out to his car.

"That she is."

She felt the familiar hesitancy once again as she climbed into his car. Being with Josh was what had caused all the trouble in her life.

"How do your parents feel about us seeing each other again?"

Ellie fiddled unconsciously with the hem of her dress. "They're understandably wary, but they don't hold what happened in the past against you. It's just... difficult."

He nodded with a tight smile on his face. "I understand. I wrestled with guilt about what my dad did to you for years. And Rachel too. I just wish her family would talk to me—I've tried over the years to contact them."

"It must be so hard for them."

"I hoped they'd get some comfort from my dad's conviction and that I could get some closure, but that's not their job. I understood their reluctance."

Unsure what to say in response, Ellie buckled her seat belt and looked back at her house. Jess was at the window with a

wide smile on her face. Ellie waved to her daughter as Josh
started the engine.

It was close to midnight when they arrived back at Ellie's house.
She was a little drunk and felt warm and happy.

"You want to come inside for a little?" she asked.

"Sure."

The words had the desired effect, and seconds later, they
were walking toward her front door hand in hand. Her street
was quiet. The small home her parents had helped her buy
when Jess was a baby was dark. Ellie hoped her daughter was
asleep. That would prevent certain awkward conversations. She
put the key into the lock and turned it. The foyer was unlit, and
Ellie reached over to the lamp.

"Jess must be in bed," she whispered.

Josh smiled. "This is a little different. We used to sneak
around to avoid our parents. Now it's your kid!"

Ellie laughed. It was unusual for Jess to turn in early. Ellie
gestured for Josh to follow her into the kitchen. The light was
on in there—the only one on in the house.

Ellie walked over to the cupboard and picked out two
glasses. "You want some wine?"

"I'd love some."

She poured them each a glass of red, and they took a seat at
the kitchen table. She was facing him, with the glass door to the
small backyard behind her.

"Here's to another great night," he said. They clinked
glasses, but before he took a drink, a strange look crossed his
face and he peered around her at the back door. "Did you know
your door was broken?"

Ellie turned around, unsure what he meant, and could
immediately see the pane of glass beside the door handle was
missing. Ellie felt her pulse quicken and she got out of her seat

to take a closer look. "No. This happened while we were out." She got down on her haunches to examine the void where the pane had been a few hours before. It was clean. No jagged shards were left behind.

"Maybe Jess took the pieces out after she smashed it?" Ellie said, but she could feel something was off. She stood up. The clock on the wall said it was nearly twelve thirty. "I'll go check on Jess." She climbed the stairs quickly, her body now screaming at her that something was horrible wrong. Jessica's door was open, the bed perfectly made as it had been that morning. Panic coursed through Ellie's body.

"Jess?" she shouted.

Josh ran up the stairs, and Ellie turned to him. "She isn't here." Ellie pushed past him and checked the bathroom.

"And she didn't tell you she was going out?" he asked. "She didn't text you?"

"No, she didn't," Ellie snapped.

"I'll look through the rest of the house," Josh replied anxiously.

The small house had few places to search. She wasn't there. Ellie met Josh in the foyer.

"You're sure she didn't mention she might go out?" he asked, somehow hoping for a different response.

The pressure in her chest was almost unbearable. "No. She was meant to stay in tonight. She has a game tomorrow morning." Ellie ran to the kitchen and picked her phone out of her bag. She texted several of Jess's friends, trying to tone down the manic energy rushing through her veins. She sent ten messages and put the phone down.

"Did she go for a walk around the block?" Josh asked. "Is that something she does?"

"At night? Never."

Josh ran back to the front of the house and went outside.

Ellie once again examined the glass door to the backyard. A

debilitating black terror fell over Ellie like a cloak as the reality hit her. Someone had smashed the glass to get inside. She walked into the backyard, lit silver by the moon. It was only a few yards long with a wall at the end. A row of houses sat behind it, separated from theirs by an alley.

"Someone broke the glass and got in the door. I think they took her," she said as soon as Josh found her in the backyard. She didn't wait to hear his reply. An urge to collapse into a ball on the ground and cry reared up inside her, but she knew she didn't have time for that. Suddenly, she was in the basement again. The flames were licking her heels, and no one else was coming to save her. Ellie climbed over the wall, hoping to see something. An old ladder lay discarded. She went to move it, but the horrible thought that the police might need to dust it for fingerprints stopped her. Josh didn't seem to know what to do but followed her over the wall.

"The ladder," Ellie said.

"Was that there before?" he asked urgently, locking eyes with hers.

"I haven't been back here in years. I have no idea," she gasped.

"How could someone carry Jess over the back wall without anyone noticing?"

Ellie ignored him and ran around the houses to the block beyond. It was quiet and most of the small houses were dark. Only a few random lights broke the blanket of night. She looked up and down the street, desperate for some sign of her daughter.

"There's nothing here," Josh said.

"Maybe they took her out the front door," Ellie replied.

Josh put his hands on her shoulders. "I understand why you're feeling this way, but it's much more likely she's out with a secret boyfriend or drinking with her friends."

Ellie shrugged him off and jogged back to the wall behind her house. She scaled it in seconds and ran to check her phone. She cursed herself for having left it on the kitchen table. Two of Jessica's friends had replied. Neither knew where she was.

Ellie dialed 911.

"What are you doing?" Josh asked.

"Calling the police," she responded breathlessly.

He was trying to control his nerves, but she could hear them flaring in his voice. "We don't know how long she's been gone. Jess could walk back into the house any second for all we know."

Ellie could feel panic begin to take over. "Something's wrong. I can feel it."

"They're not going to be able to do anything. It's way too soon. We've only known she was missing for a few minutes. There's no sign of a struggle—"

"What about the broken glass in the back door?"

"For all anyone knows, she cracked that herself and tried to cover it up."

Ellie dismissed Josh as the emergency dispatcher answered. Josh might have been right, but that didn't mean she was about to sit here and do nothing.

"There's been a break-in at my house. My daughter is missing," Ellie gasped.

The dispatcher took her details and promised to send a car out in the next few minutes. Ellie hung up the phone to continue the search while she waited.

She felt the urge to go upstairs to the safe in her closet and get her gun, but what good would that do now? It had only been a few minutes since she'd sent the texts to Jess's friends, but she'd already waited long enough. She called Hadley first, but she had no idea where Jess was. Two of her other friends answered too, but both thought Jess was staying in. Ellie's frustration almost boiled over as she hung up.

Josh searched the house for clues. "Her bed's still made. She wasn't asleep. There's no sign of a struggle up there. But come with me."

They walked into the small living room together. The TV was off and an empty bowl of breakfast cereal sat on the coffee table by Jess's favorite chair. The flakes were still soggy and stuck to the sides. Her keyboard was on the table where she'd left it earlier.

"Look at this." Josh got down on his knees. "Feel the floor."

It was wet to the touch. "Did someone clean this up?" Ellie asked. "Did someone disturb her here and then come back to clean their tracks after?"

"Or else Jess spilled it herself and just went out for a walk. The simplest explanation is usually the most likely."

Ellie got up, trying to slow her breathing. "So, what are you saying? What do you suggest we do?"

"I'm not dismissing the notion that something... bad happened, but it's best you stay here in case she comes home. The cops should be here any minute, too. I'll go out in the car and look for her. Maybe she's out walking."

Ellie nodded. The thought of being alone wasn't one she relished but his idea made sense. "Okay."

The light-heartedness she'd felt upon coming home was gone, replaced by anxiety and fear. Josh kissed her. "We'll find Jess. I promise you."

He hurried out the front door and got into his car. She stood at the window and watched him pull out. The house was quiet as the grave. Ellie sat down on the couch, consumed by terror, battered by horrific thoughts of her daughter frightened and alone. Memories of her own kidnapping she'd thought were long gone were rising to the surface.

TWENTY

Josh was asleep on the couch beside her as Ellie picked up her phone. It was nearly seven in the morning. Jess had been missing for at least six and a half hours, and Ellie was waiting with the phone in her hand to call the rest of her daughter's friends. Seven seemed like an acceptable time. Jess was due to play lacrosse in a few hours. She never missed a game. Even when she'd sprained her ankle the year before, she went to the field on crutches to cheer on her teammates. The policeman who'd come the night before was polite but not terribly helpful. He'd repeated much of what Josh had said about her daughter being a teenage girl and that she was probably out with one of her friends. He wondered if Jess had broken the glass in the back door herself and said that because nothing else was missing, it was hard to treat it as a break-in. After arguing with him for a while, Ellie had agreed to wait until morning to call again. But she would try Jess's friends first.

Ellie got up and went to the bathroom. The woman staring back at her in the mirror was so far removed from the person who'd gone on a date with Josh last night. Her eyes were red and puffy, her skin sickly and pale. She walked back to the couch and called the first of her daughter's friends. She didn't receive an answer until the fifth call to Alexandra, who had no idea where Jessica might have been. Ellie threw the phone down in helpless frustration and thought about what Josh had said about a secret boyfriend. Jess had always been so open with Ellie. She would have noticed her daughter behaving differently, sneaking out at night, or the glow of a seventeen-year-old who thought they'd found love.

After thirty minutes of calls and texts, the grim realization that none of Jess's friends had any idea where she was settled over Ellie's consciousness like a noxious fog. Ellie rubbed her eyes, trying to ease the pain behind them, but it was no use. This was how her parents must have felt twenty years ago. Ellie stood up and went to the front door, staring at it as if she could will her daughter to walk through it, before returning to the living room and collapsing onto the couch. It was time to call the police again.

Debilitating anxiety gripped every cell in her body. She looked over at Josh with jealous eyes as he lay asleep. She longed for sleep that wouldn't come.

Days passed. She wandered through them like a ghost, sleeping little. The anxiety became part of her being, almost like a second skin. Jess was still missing. Ellie had heard nothing in 105 long hours. The police had recognized what she'd known since she'd arrived home from her date with Josh the previous Saturday night: this was a missing persons case. A kidnapping. But with no ransom note and no demands, the detectives in charge were beginning to think the worst. It wasn't hard to read the looks on their faces as they spoke to each other, or the earnest kindness in their eyes when they addressed her. No one wanted to say it out loud. The search parties were out for Jess, covering every inch of ground for miles. The volunteers looked in places where they could only find a corpse, just as Ellie had heard they'd done when she'd gone missing twenty years ago.

Josh had been helping where he could, leading several search parties in the woods, and had indulged Ellie too when she'd asked him to take her back to the house where she'd escaped the Voiceless One. But it was still a wreck. The old Farrington farm, as the locals called it, was as it had been when the fire had finally died down all those years before. Jess wasn't there. The man who'd taken Ellie was behind bars. The police insisted this was something different, but a voice inside Ellie told her something else.

It was a dull spring morning. Ellie went to the window and pushed open the blinds with her thumb and forefinger. The TV trucks were still outside, the reporters milling around. Yesterday's newspaper had been full of stories of the copycat kidnapper, or murderer, who'd targeted the same poor girl who'd escaped twenty years ago. This time was different. The national news was here. The story of the quarterback's girlfriend, drugged and taken by his father, was something, but this was five times bigger. Dozens of reporters from all over the country and beyond had descended on her house, hoping for a glimpse of Josh Thomas's ex-girlfriend, whose beloved daughter had been snatched from her house in the night with none of the neighbors seeing anything. None of it seemed real. It was like some deranged joke, some nightmare she couldn't wake up from.

One of the reporters noticed some movement from the window and pointed over, and Ellie released the blinds. Her phone buzzed, making her jump. Every text, every call filled her with hope and then immediately dashed it. But Jess could call any time. The first thing she felt every single time her phone vibrated was the hope that it was her daughter. But once again, she had to dispel that hope. The message was from Josh.

> Can I come get you? I want to be there when
> you make the statement.

The police agreed with his sentiment. Having the former starting quarterback for the Bears with her in the press conference could only help to raise awareness, and that's what the cops wanted. The thought of the world watching her implode was the last thing she wanted, but the detectives in charge of finding Jess reasoned that the more people who saw it, the higher the chance of someone coming forward. This wasn't about her feelings, though the cops were sensitive to her plight. This was about getting a wife to come forward who'd noticed her husband acting suspiciously, or jogging a passing driver's memory of seeing Jess in the back of someone's car the night she disappeared.

Right now, it was clear the cops had nothing. Someone had climbed over Ellie's back wall and into her yard. They'd broken the glass so quietly Jess hadn't noticed. The police suspected the assailant might even have cut it. Then, once inside, they'd taken Jessica without much of a scuffle. None of the neighbors had seen anyone carry her out or even a strange car in front of or behind the house. Nobody had seen a thing. Nothing could have been more maddening.

Ellie texted Josh back.

> Can you be here in 20 minutes? Watch out for
> the gaggle of reporters outside. There must be
> 10 of them.

The reply came back in seconds.

> Nothing I haven't dealt with before. I'll be there.

Ellie went upstairs. She was already dressed in her best suit, a gray outfit she normally used to meet prospective buyers outside vacant properties, but work was the furthest thing from her mind now. She hadn't worked since Jess had been taken. It was the longest she'd taken off in years. Her survivors' group meetings were a different matter. She needed the other women more than ever now.

A little lip gloss finished the look. The cops had urged her to look good but not too glamorous. She didn't think that either was possible the way she felt, but she walked away from the mirror satisfied that she'd done as they'd instructed.

She sat on the bed, gathering herself for what was to come. Waiting. The doorbell made her jump, but she stood up, checked herself in the mirror again, and descended the stairs to the front door. Josh stood stony-faced in an expensive-looking suit. Reporters swarmed them, taking pictures and jabbing microphones in their faces. Josh took her by the hand and led them through the scrum.

"I'll be making a statement at the police station in a matter of minutes," Ellie said as they reached the car. But her words didn't satisfy the insatiable appetite of the press in her front yard, and they roared questions at her as she climbed into Josh's car.

Josh edged past the pack of journalists and photographers to get in on the other side.

"If you'd told me a week ago I'd be under siege by the members of our esteemed press..." Ellie put her head in her hands. Every waking moment was a living hell. Josh reached over and put his hand on her leg. It felt good, but only as a few drops of water on the flames raging within her.

They arrived at the police station a few minutes later. Detective Amelia Manning met them at the door. She was in her thirties, perhaps a few years younger than Ellie, with long brown hair and piercing blue eyes.

The room was already set up, with at least twenty-five reporters waiting, when Ellie and Josh walked in. A poster-size picture of Jess in her lacrosse uniform, with a bright smile on her face, almost brought Ellie to tears. Her parents, her brothers, and their children were all in the front row for support. Detective Manning showed her to her seat in front of the large poster of Jess and another with the details for anyone to call if they remembered anything. The television cameras were front and center. Josh sat down beside her and reached across to take her hand. The prepared statement was on the table, and Ellie picked it up as Manning addressed the crowd.

"Ms. Welsh will make a statement first. After that time, we can take questions. Please make sure to respect the family during this difficult time."

She nodded to Ellie. The time had come.

"Last Saturday, April 22, my daughter Jessica, the light of our lives, went missing. She was at home preparing for a lacrosse game the next morning. I was out with my friend, Josh Thomas. We arrived home just after midnight. I expected to find my beautiful daughter in bed, but someone had broken into the house we've shared since my little girl was a toddler, and that person took her. Jess is a good girl, a straight-A student, and a talented musician who's popular with her classmates and always conscientious and attentive to the needs of others. She doesn't have a boyfriend, preferring to focus on her studies and enjoying the company of her friends. None of her friends have any idea where she is. The police and search volunteers have been conducting a thorough investigation, which so far has turned up nothing. I need your help. If anyone out there was in the vicinity of Dunmore Street, where Ellie was taken from our house on the night of April 22, and saw anything, please come forward. No matter how inconsequential you think the information might be. If you know anyone who was out that night and has acted strangely since, please think of my sweet, beautiful daughter. She needs help."

Detective Manning stepped forward and went over the details to call once more. "We can take some questions now."

A dozen hands flew up. She chose one. A man in his forties wearing glasses stood up. "Jamie Sweeney, *New York Post*. Question for Josh Thomas. What is your relationship to Ms. Welsh, and what is your reaction to the same thing your father put her through happening to her daughter twenty years later."

Josh considered the question for a few seconds before answering. "Ms. Welsh is a friend. An old, cherished friend. I'm deeply saddened by her daughter's disappearance and am praying for her safe return."

"And what about the copycat nature of the crime?" the reporter asked. "Your own father is sitting in jail as we speak for abducting Ms. Welsh."

Josh looked down at Ellie's family sitting in the front row. "The anguish this family has been through over the years is tragic. They're such good people—"

Another reporter cut him off. "Josh, have you been in contact with your father? Has he acknowledged the copycat?"

Detective Manning spoke up. "We haven't confirmed that this is a copycat case yet. We're not working on rumor or conjecture, just facts, and that's why we're here today—to gather as many as we can."

Every hand in the crowd of reporters was up. The policewoman chose one, a man with a potbelly and a black beard. "Josh, do you think your father might have anything to do with Jessica's disappearance?"

"He's in jail, sir," Josh said with admirable self-restraint.

The crowd of reporters was like a pack of wild dogs. Ellie felt herself filling up with revulsion as she looked down at them.

"Do you think he could have orchestrated this from inside his jail cell?" the potbellied reporter asked.

Josh remained composed. "I don't see how that would be

possible. The police have already questioned my father. He doesn't know anything."

A female reporter stood up without having been called on. "Josh, do you think the girl's disappearance has to do with your high profile in the local area? Do you expect a ransom note?"

"Her name is Jessica, and I think we need to focus on the facts of the case rather than hypothesizing what this might have to do with me or my father."

Ellie felt like she was on a bucking bronco. It was vital the cameras kept rolling. The more publicity the better, but she didn't know how much longer she could take this.

Another journalist stood up, this time directing her question to Ellie. "Ms. Welsh, do you think it's a coincidence that as soon as Josh Thomas came back into your life, you suffered this terrible experience?"

Ellie looked at Josh. "Josh has nothing to do—"

Detective Manning stood up. "Okay, enough questions for today. Make sure to call the number on your screen if you have even the smallest tidbit of information to share. Remember, what you think is inconsequential might make all the difference in a case like this."

The reporters rose to their feet as one and continued shouting questions. Ellie could still hear them screaming after her and Josh as they walked out.

Manning took them into a private room. "I'm sorry," she said. "I know that must have been hard for you, but the media scrum was necessary. Millions of people will see that, and who knows what we might get out of it?"

Josh put his hand on her arm. "I'm so sorry, Ellie. I shouldn't have come. The entire focus shifted because of me."

Ellie shook her head. "No. You being here will make all the difference. It'll get eyes on TV screens. We need all the help we can get."

Ellie's family entered the room. Her parents were both in tears. She hugged them each in turn. Josh stood back, watching. Helpless.

TWENTY-ONE

The house was horrifically quiet. Ellie's mother had stayed the first few nights but had returned home, and now Ellie was alone once more. She sat in the armchair, frozen, transfixed on a clock on the mantelpiece Jess had given her for her thirty-fifth birthday two years before. It was cheap and had stopped working three times in the two years she'd owned it, but nothing could have been more precious now. A framed photo of her and Jess at the shore the summer before sat on the coffee table, and she reached forward to pick it up. Ellie didn't need to suppress the tears as she beheld her daughter's beautiful, smiling face. She was all cried out. Sitting here blubbing wasn't going to do her any good.

She tried to move but seemed stuck to the cushions. It was night outside, two days after the press conference. Nothing had changed. The police were still sifting through the thousands of calls and tips they'd received since the telecast. The cops weren't prepared for the flood of calls they'd received. They hadn't counted on Josh's celebrity being such a magnet for every crazy out there. The expectation was that more than ninety-nine percent of them were cranks. And Detective Manning had been frank in alerting her to the real possibility that none of them would lead to anything.

Ellie tried to hold on to hope. Her daughter was out there. Still alive. She could feel it. The media was treating this as a murder case, but they were wrong. She and Jess had a bond. It was hard to explain. Only Ellie's mother understood, but their hearts were connected. Their spirits overlapped. Ellie could feel Jess's aura. They were a part of each other and always would be. She would feel it if that were broken. It was impossible to put a finger on how, but she believed it with her entire being. That belief was the chewing gum holding her life together.

Ellie closed her eyes and saw Gary Thomas. He'd been under her skin again since this had begun. It had taken years to flush him out, but she had achieved it. Days and even weeks went by now without the specter of the Voiceless One invading her dreams, but Jessica's disappearance had revived those latent memories. They were alive within her again. The police had questioned him, and, of course, he'd protested his innocence and claimed he knew nothing about it. But he was lying. She knew it in her soul. He knew something. He would open up to Josh. The only question was would Josh see him again?

Ellie picked up her phone. Josh answered almost immediately.

"Everything all right? Did you hear anything?" he asked breathlessly.

"No. Nothing new. It'll take the cops weeks to wade through all the crap thrown at them since the press conference."

"Something good will happen."

Ellie wasn't so sure. "Jess might not have the time it'll take to find out if the cops are onto something."

"You don't know that."

A dark cloud came over her. It was always hovering now. "She's been gone a week. When your... When I was taken, my captor grew sick of the game after a few days. It was only sheer luck that I got out of there."

"It wasn't luck, Ellie, and Jess has the same steely spirit as her mother."

Ellie knew Josh was trying to be supportive, but she didn't have time for niceties.

"The cops talked to your dad, but he didn't tell them anything."

"So Detective Manning said."

"Do you think he knows anything?"

"I have no idea. I don't even know who my father is, or ever was."

Ellie took a few seconds to pause and take in what Josh had said before continuing. The thought of his father made her feel ill, but she had to put that aside now. "Do you think he'd open up to you?"

"I haven't spoken to him in five years."

Ellie felt herself bristle with anger. "But you're his son. He still says he's innocent, doesn't he?"

"As far as I know."

"Maybe if you go along with that story, he'll tell you what he knows about Jess."

"Does he even know she exists?"

"It's too much of a coincidence. Maybe the copycat wrote to him or visited him. It could be an old friend of his, trying to get revenge. We won't know until we talk to him."

"We?" The incredulity in Josh's voice wasn't disguised. "You want to come along and see him too?"

"Want to? No. I can't think of anyone I'd like to see less, but if it'll get me one step closer to bringing my daughter home, I'd be prepared to do it. My comfort zone isn't important." Josh didn't answer. Ellie spoke again. "But I need you with me. If he sees the two of us in front of him, maybe he'll open up. He said he loved me twenty years ago—maybe he still has some twisted sense of affection for me."

Josh breathed down the phone. "Okay. If you think it'll help. I don't see how he'd know anything about any of this, but I'll pick you up tomorrow morning."

"That'll give me some time to get my head together. To pluck up the courage to see him."

"That's something you never wanted for."

Ellie wasn't so sure. She was still terrified at the thought of seeing him after all this time. She was about to hang up the phone when she blurted, "Can you come over? It's so quiet here. I thought I could be alone, but..."

"Of course. I'll be there in an hour."

She hung up and felt silence envelop her once more. The facts of the case were stark. Something needed to change. She opened up the browser on her phone, and a search for a private investigator yielded hundreds of results in seconds. Any one of them would jump at the chance to take on such a high-profile case. She scrolled through, looking for someone to catch her eye. Settling on one, she clicked through and read: *Have a problem you need help with? An ex-cop who sees things differently. An expert in what others miss.* That was what she needed because heaven knew the police didn't have any solid leads. It was up to her.

Ellie was awake with the dawn, but she hadn't gotten more than a few hours' sleep in a row since Jess had disappeared. Lying in bed, she reached for her phone. Josh was asleep beside her. They'd done little other than hold one another the night before. It was what she needed. It was the only comfort she felt in the dark cavern of her soul. Seeing her daughter again was all she desired. Nothing else could soothe the agony inside her. Only Jess could do that. She pushed herself out of bed, not making any effort to be quiet, but Josh didn't wake up. Ellie threw a dressing gown over her pajamas and trudged downstairs. She made herself a coffee and stared out as the morning sun filled the backyard with gold, waiting until she could call the private investigator.

She waited until eight thirty. He picked up on the third ring and agreed to see her immediately. An hour later Ellie was sitting in his office about fifteen minutes away from her house. Josh was beside her, but her entire focus was on the man behind the desk. He was in his mid-fifties with a graying mustache. His thinning gray hair was cut tight. He had a thin, wiry build and a scar that extended along the side of his face. The nameplate on his desk was set in silver. It read: *Pete Rivers P.I.*

Ellie didn't waste any time with niceties. "I assume you've read about my case in the newspapers?"

"Of course," Rivers said. "You're not happy with the police investigation?"

"They're busy sifting through every tiny lead from every crazy that called in after my appeal. I think they're treating it as a murder case now."

Rivers clasped his hands together, pausing a few seconds before what he said next. "And you're not?"

"Whoever did this is trying to re-enact what happened to me."

Rivers glanced over at Josh. "What his father did to you?"

Ellie nodded. "I'm glad you're aware of the facts of the case."

"I'd have to be living under a rock not to be."

"My daughter's missing. Someone is trying to torture me and Josh."

"Why would they take your daughter if they're trying to torture him?"

Josh coughed before he began. "I don't have children, and

Ellie is precious to me. I'm with her every step of the way. I see the pain she's in, and it kills me."

"You think someone is trying to toy with you? To use your daughter to deliberately hurt you?"

"I do," Ellie said.

"Is there anyone from your past that you suspect?"

"The person who cut the brakes on my father's car. They were never found." Josh took a moment to explain what had happened the night his father and mother had crashed into the river.

"Do you have any idea who that might be? Someone who hated your father enough to try to kill him?"

A morose look spread over Josh's face. "I don't. I didn't know then, and I don't know now. My father didn't share much with us."

"Your father was the target twenty years ago, not you. That was before you were taken, Ellie?"

She nodded in reply.

"Okay. We've got to figure out who hated him enough to cut his brakes. He mistreated your mother?"

"Yes," Josh said.

"Okay. Does she have family?"

"A sister. I moved to Pittsburgh with her after the funeral. But she'd never do that."

"You're sure?"

"As sure as I can be without knowing a hundred percent."

Rivers picked up a pen and started scribbling down notes. "We can never be sure about what other people are capable of, can we? Josh, can you think of anyone with an axe to grind against you or your family? Anyone I can look for?"

"I already went over this with the cops," he answered.

"Well then, why are you here?"

"I can't think of anyone."

"No one hated you or your father in high school? No one was jealous of the star quarterback?"

"I had a few people."

"That girl who warned me about you wasn't a fan," Ellie piped up.

"Julia Leonard? She was crazy. Or was it Tina Morris? Maggie Fitzgerald? A few of Rachel's friends had it in for me."

"Rachel Kubick was the girl your father killed, your girl-friend he was seeing behind your back?" Rivers asked.

"Yeah."

He shoved the pad across the table. "Write down the names of everyone you just mentioned, and of Rachel's family too. I'll look into their backgrounds and see what they're doing. The answer to Jessica's disappearance is more than likely right under our noses. We just can't see it yet. First thing you need to do is go and see your father."

The weight of what they were about to do brought itself to bear on Ellie. Up until that moment it hadn't seemed real. But they were going to do it.

"We're on our way after we leave your office," Josh said.

"Good. Try to appeal to him. Either he knows who took Jessica, or he knows the person who took her. He's the key to unraveling this."

Josh picked up the pad and looked at it. "The cops already questioned him. He didn't tell them anything."

"You're still his son. Appeal to him. He might just open up to you."

Josh spent a few minutes jotting down the names of people who might have had a vendetta against him or his father. Ellie's breath quickened. She tried to remain engaged in the conversation, but it was difficult.

"I'll look into these names. It might take a day or two," Rivers said.

"My daughter might not have that long," Ellie blurted.

"I'll move as quickly as I can, but I can't perform miracles," he replied.

Josh took Ellie's hand as they left together. "Are you up for this?"

She nodded without speaking. Her body tensed with each step, and she leaned on Josh for support as they walked.

Josh stopped her at the car door. "I can do this myself."

Ellie took a deep breath, regaining some clarity. "No." She shook her head. "I can do this. I have to be there. For Jess."

She got into the car and steeled herself to meet the man who'd haunted her nightmares for the last twenty years.

TWENTY-TWO

Ellie stayed quiet for the journey west. The fear within her grew with every mile, and as they neared the prison, it almost overtook her. The prison was less than thirty minutes from the now burned-out hulk where Gary had kept her. Just being near it was enough to raise Ellie's heart rate and send her into a cold sweat. The Voiceless One hadn't gone far.

Her hands were shaking as she pulled the mirror down and almost gasped at the pallor of her skin. Josh didn't push her to talk. He turned up the radio, playing classic rock that her father had blasted on the record player in the basement when she was growing up. The familiarity of the music took her back to happier times, and almost distracted her from what she was about to do. But the relief was temporary.

Josh pulled up in the visitor parking lot and reached over to her. "Are you ready for this?"

"Are you?"

Josh smirked and shook his head. "I don't think either of us is ever going to be ready."

"Let's go."

The reception looked more like a modern high school than a

prison, with large black windows and manicured shrubs outside.

Ellie walked alongside Josh, though neither of them spoke. It felt like a nightmare. It was one she'd had dozens of times. But she cast her fears aside. Nothing was more important than finding Jess. Her own comfort was trivial in the face of the prospect of seeing her daughter again, of wrapping her arms around her. Ellie kept Jessica in the forefront of her mind as she and Josh presented their IDs. The guard behind the counter eyed Josh as if he knew who he was but didn't say anything. A female guard met them at the desk. She was about the same age as they were with dyed blonde hair that seemed at odds with her dark eyes. Her pretty oval-shaped face seemed out of place here. There was something familiar about her.

The guard nodded. "You here to see Gary Thomas?"

Ellie stepped forward. The guard knew who she and Josh were. They probably all did. "Yeah. You know him?"

"I've been working here seventeen years. I've run into all of 'em at one time or another." Her voice was deep and raspy.

"What's Gary like?"

"Not the worst. Keeps to himself mainly. I see him in the yard lifting weights. He stays away from the drama in here."

"You talk to him much?"

"A little. Seems pretty straight up, but you get to know the liars in here quickly. He always seems to be hiding something to me," she casually asserted, and then eyed Josh. "Not every day we get an NFL quarterback in here."

Josh smiled tightly before asking, "Does my dad talk about me much?"

"Back in your playing days, he did, but after you got injured, he stopped. I hadn't heard him mention your name in years, until what happened with Jessica."

"What did he say about it?"

"Same as everyone else—how crazy it all is. Some of the

other cons say he's pulling the strings—orchestrating the whole thing from in here, but I honestly have no idea about that."

"Have you known anything like that to happen before?"

"Guys to organize crimes outside from in here? Yeah. Time enough goes by in here, and you see everything. But we have no reason to suspect him."

"Has he had any visitors lately?"

The guard shook her head. "Just a few women. Desperate types. No one unusual. Other than the cops and a few reporters that is."

"Was that a big deal in here?"

"The cops and the journalists coming in? No. We let them take Gary into a private room. The warden figured it was best to keep them away from the rest of the prisoners." She paused for a second to take Josh in before continuing. "Look, I wish I could help you more, but I don't know much. My name's Fletcher if you come looking for me later."

"Thanks," Josh answered.

"I can lead you down to the visiting room if you'd like," Fletcher said.

Josh's nod of approval was more than enough for the guard, and she turned to show them the way. Ellie felt like she was walking to her own execution. The tension within her built with every step, and as they reached the visiting room she almost couldn't walk inside. The thought of Jess, in some basement somewhere, as she had been herself, drove her forward. It was the only thing that could have.

The large visiting room was painted white, with round tables dotted throughout. Several prisoners were sitting with visitors already. They passed a man covered in tattoos holding up a baby girl with a bright smile on his face. The light of the sun flooded in through the open windows, lending the space an ethereal quality Ellie hadn't expected. Several visitors and prisoners raised their heads to stare at her and Josh as they walked past. They found a spare table and sat down.

"I'll get your father," Fletcher said reassuringly.

"Thanks," Josh replied.

The guard strode out of the room. Ellie's body went stiff. She looked at Josh, who took her hand. He was trying to whisper reassuring words to her but she couldn't hear him. The room seemed to be closing in around her. Two long minutes later a door at the end of the room opened, and Gary Thomas strode through. Ellie's heart almost exploded in her chest. She was back in the basement and saw the board under the door. The smell of gasoline burning and the heat from the fire. Unable to look at him at first, she finally brought her eyes to meet his as he neared the table. He was gray now but still had a full head of hair. His broad shoulders bulged through his orange jumpsuit. His face was lined and tanned. His skin reminded her of old leather. Fletcher brought him to the table and then stood back with her hands folded in front of her, well within earshot. Few of the other prisoners had guards standing with them. Ellie supposed it was because of the case. The guard was probably trying to pick up some juicy tidbits for the press.

Gary sat down and clasped his hands in front of him. A few seconds passed but it felt like longer before he began to speak. "I was wondering when you'd be here."

"You knew I'd come?" Josh answered.

"I had an inkling." Gary's voice was scratchy and raw as if he'd been shouting too much the day before. "You brought her?"

"We want answers," Ellie managed to say. She held her hands under the table to hide how much they were shaking. It was hard to know what she'd expected. Not an apology, but more than this. He was barely acknowledging her.

Gary Thomas shifted his eyes back to his son. "How long's it been, Josh?"

"Years and years," Josh said through gritted teeth.

"Yeah. You've been out living your life while I've been stuck in this hole."

He shifted in his seat. "I didn't come here to sit around the campfire and sing songs, Dad—"

"I didn't kill your mother or Rachel Kubick. And I certainly didn't kidnap her!" he exclaimed and jutted a finger toward Ellie. "Surely the fact that this is happening all over again while I'm in here is proof enough of that."

"What do you know about what happened to Ellie's daughter?"

"I've already talked to the cops about this."

"And now I'm asking you," Josh said. His voice wavered as he spoke, his brave expression cracking. Other than their undeniable resemblance, no one ever would have known that the man sitting across the table was his father. They hadn't touched each other yet. It was hard to believe they could be so different.

"I've been talking to a lawyer about getting out of here," Mr. Thomas said. "He seems to think I have a good case. That evidence at the house was planted. I didn't even know where that farm was." He turned to Ellie with a stern look in his eyes. "I have no idea who took you, but whoever it was framed me, and they're still out there. They took your daughter. Their sick little game isn't over, and they're not going to stop. Who knows who'll be next? Have you heard from them yet?"

"No," Ellie responded angrily. "But you know that already, don't you?"

"Girly, you must have me confused with someone else. I'm just sitting in here doing my time, waiting to get out of here. I'm no criminal mastermind. I'm following along with the news stories about your daughter's disappearance like everyone else."

He seemed convincing. For some reason, Ellie found herself believing him.

"Have you had any different visitors lately?" Josh asked.

"We spoke to one of the guards, who said you'd had some women in to see you."

"I can't help who comes in here to visit me. I have women who write to me. Lonely ladies who believe the truth that I tell them. They know I'm innocent and come see me to give me some of the comfort I deserve. I'll be out of here in two years, and they'll be waiting for me. I have a lot of life left in me, kid."

"Did any of these women talk to you about the case?" Josh asked.

"They're all true-crime nuts. That's all they want to talk about. I'm a freak in a cage to amuse them, but I'll take any attention I can get in here."

Ellie looked over at Josh. He had no idea how to handle seeing his father, and the hurt he was feeling was visible in every movement he made and audible in every word he said.

"Have you had anyone reach out to you about what happened to Jess?" Josh pressed.

"Listen, son, I didn't kidnap Ellie, and I don't want to see anything happen to her daughter either." He turned to face Ellie. "I know what you heard during the trial, but I didn't do it."

Ellie looked away. This was going nowhere. The prison guard was still standing a few feet from the table, her arms folded. She was probably enjoying the show. Ellie had no idea what the protocol was, but surely they deserved some privacy?

"So, there's nothing you can tell us to help with the case?" Josh asked.

Ellie reached into her pocket and pulled out a photograph of Jess from her junior prom. She was beautiful in her red dress, and her date was smiling at her. "Look at her," Ellie said. "You say you didn't take me, that you didn't kill Rachel? Well then, show us this inner goodness you've hidden away all these years." She stood up, jabbing her finger at the photo. "Look at her!"

Fletcher stepped forward. "Please stay calm. No shouting."

Gary glanced up at the guard and twisted his head back as if the sight of her burned his eyes.

"There is something else," he said. "Something I kept to myself."

"What?" Ellie shouted.

Fletcher stepped forward. "Keep your voice down! I will be forced to end the visit."

Gary Thomas reached forward and took Josh's hands. The words flowed from his mouth like water. "I'm sorry for what I did to your mother, but I've served my time. I didn't kill anyone. I swear." His knuckles were white as he grasped his son's hands.

"What were you going to tell us, Dad?"

Fletcher stepped in. "This is going too far." She put her hand on Gary's shoulder, but he reared back with his elbow like a wounded animal lashing out.

"No more," he said. "Leave me alone."

The guard stumbled back and drew a baton from her belt. "This visit is over."

"Please," Ellie begged. "Just a few more seconds!"

Two other guards ran across and grabbed Gary by the arms to drag him away.

"What were you about to say?" Josh asked desperately.

"There's something I never told you, Josh, about my past," Gary uttered quietly.

"Visiting privileges have been revoked for the day," Fletcher said.

"Come tomorrow," Gary said. "I should have told you years ago, but it's time now."

Ellie looked at Fletcher. The guard scowled back at her as she and the two others dragged Gary away.

"Please!" Ellie pleaded. "My daughter! This is my daughter's life!"

"Get your hands off me!" Gary said as they dragged him

back through the door he'd walked through. It shut behind him, and Ellie and Josh were alone once more. They looked at each other for a few seconds, not knowing what to say.

Ellie was the one to break the silence. "I'm not comfortable here."

They strode out of the visiting room and through reception, not stopping until they reached Josh's car in the parking lot.

He gripped the steering wheel with white-knuckle fury. "He was just about to tell me something. We just needed a few more seconds." He hit the wheel with an open palm and clutched it again.

"Do you have any idea what it could have been?"

He released his hands and turned to her, his breath thundering in and out of his lungs.

"None," he said. "He waits until now to get an attack of conscience? I don't get it."

"You haven't seen him in years. Maybe he's trying to make up for the past."

Josh took her hand. "I can't forgive him for what he did to you, and my mom."

Ellie didn't have the time or the inclination to get into a conversation about forgiveness. "Okay. Assuming they don't put your father into solitary for elbowing that guard, we'll come back tomorrow and find out what he was going to tell us."

"Yeah," Josh replied.

Ellie drew her phone from her bag and held it to her ear. "I'll let the P.I. know what happened."

"Not the cops?"

"Maybe when we have something more solid."

Josh started the car, and Ellie dialed Pete's number. He picked up and asked her to wait for a few seconds while he took out a pen and paper to make notes.

"And who was this guard, Fletcher?" he asked. "Did she and your father seem to know one another?"

"She seemed interested in our conversation. She stood so close I could almost hear her breathing. I swear she reminds me of someone."

"That's not normal. Maybe she's trying to sell the story to the press."

That seemed the logical explanation. Ellie had hardly had time to think of Fletcher with everything that had happened.

"See what happens when you go back tomorrow," the private investigator said. "Watch the guards, particularly this Fletcher. You never know what's going on behind the scenes. The answer's somewhere we're not looking."

"Any progress on those names Josh gave you?"

"Nothing yet. Just some now grown women who had a crush on him when they were sixteen. But it'll take a day or two for anything to show up."

Ellie promised to call him as soon as they found out what Gary Thomas had to tell them and hung up.

Comforted by her conversation with Rivers, Ellie settled down to stare out the window, but thoughts of her daughter interceded once more.

"How are you doing?" Josh asked.

"Every time I stop doing something, my mind returns to her and the torture begins again."

He reached over and took her hand. They sped back toward Philadelphia in silence.

Ellie couldn't stand to be alone but didn't want to leave her house either. She missed her survivors' group meeting that night and offered curt responses to the concerned text messages she received from the other women, who went ahead without her for the first time. Her gun was in her nightstand, but it didn't offer her the comfort she thought it might. Josh suggested she stay with him, but she didn't want to leave the house. Part of her desperately wanted to believe that Jess might come home. So, Josh stayed over. They slept in the same bed, but only to hold one another. Sleep came in patches for Ellie. Her body was wracked with exhaustion, but the grisly images she saw when she closed her eyes prevented her from getting the rest she needed.

It was just after seven in the morning when Josh's phone buzzed on the nightstand beside him. He was still asleep. Ellie propped herself up on her elbows to look over his body. It was an unknown number. She shook him awake.

"Your phone's ringing. It could be important."

It took him a second or two to emerge from sleep. He reached over for the phone.

"Yes, I'm Gary Thomas's next of kin."

It was bizarre to hear him say those words, but the look that transformed his face was even more so. Ellie inched closer.

"What happened?" Josh said.

He listened for a minute or two, only replying a few times, before hanging up. A strange, vacant sheen washed over his eyes, and he let his hand drop to the mattress.

"He's dead."

"What?"

Josh turned to her. "My father was murdered in prison last night."

TWENTY-THREE

Ellie put her arms around Josh, as puzzled as he was about how to react to his father's death. Her instinct to say how sorry she was didn't seem appropriate here. Her first thought was that they'd never know what he wanted to tell them now. A dagger of pain hacked at her, not for Gary Thomas. The truth was that she'd never mourn someone who could inflict that level of suffering on others. The pain she felt was for Josh.

"What happened?" she asked.

"Somebody stabbed him. His body's in the prison morgue now."

"Are you okay?" she asked.

He nodded. "Yeah. It's weird, but I'll be fine."

A thousand thoughts flooded Ellie's mind, but she kept them to herself. No matter what Gary Thomas had done, or who he had been, he was still Josh's father.

Josh got out of bed and walked to the window. He opened the curtains to let the dull morning light through. He turned to her a few seconds later.

"What was he going to tell us? Was it so important that someone was willing to kill him for it?"

Ellie shook her head, and Josh headed for the bathroom. When he emerged, he said, "I have to go out to the prison to sign some papers."

"Do they have the person who did it at least?"

"No. His body was found somewhere they didn't have cameras. They have no idea. It could have been anyone."

Ellie stood up and went to him. "I'm sorry. I know you hadn't seen him in years, but..." She trailed off, unsure of how to finish the sentence.

His voice was lifeless and dull. "Yeah. I don't know how to feel. Whatever happened, we can't let this distract us from finding Jess."

Ellie nodded. "You go to the prison. I'll see Rivers. He'll be in his office in about an hour. Maybe he'll know what to make of this."

"I love you, you know," he said. "I don't suppose I ever stopped. Even when I was married."

She took a few seconds to digest his words before responding. "I love you too. Now, go and see about your father."

He pulled on his pants. "I'm gonna go home before I head to the prison. I'll be in touch in a few hours. Let me know what happens with Rivers." And with that, he walked out the door.

Ellie was alone again. She got into the shower, wondering who had ordered Gary Thomas's death and what the female guard knew about it. She'd seemed more interested in their conversation than most, and had she really been justified in ending their visit so abruptly?

Ellie got into her car more determined than ever. She called Rivers on the way. He told her he'd be in his office when she arrived.

He was wearing a blue blazer over a gray shirt. A picture of his wife and three grown children sat in front of him on the desk beside his wallet and car keys. The room smelled of cigarettes, and Ellie could see the smoke in the air as she sat down.

"Nasty habit," he said. "Just don't tell the wife, okay?"

Ellie nodded, unable to respond to his quip. "Gary Thomas was found dead in prison last night."

The private detective nodded. His face changed little, but his eyes showed his surprise. "So, someone wanted to shut him up for good, eh?"

"I don't know any details," Ellie responded.

"Okay. I know someone who works in the prison. Jim Peters. Good guy. Used to be on the force with me. Let me give him a call."

Ellie thought he meant at a later time, but the private investigator picked up his phone and pressed it to his ear.

"Jim!" he said a few seconds later. "How are you? Wife treating you good? No? Join the club. How are the kids?" He listened to the response before asking the questions Ellie wanted to hear answers to.

"What d'you know about this murder last night? Gary Thomas? Did he have any enemies?"

Rivers listened for a few minutes, only interceding to ask questions. He wrote a name down on a pad on his desk, and hung up.

"He doesn't know much," he said. "But he gave me the name and address of Gary's old cellmate. They bunked together for twelve years until our friend, Lorenzo Rivera, got out six months ago. If anyone knows what was on Gary's mind, it's this guy."

"Where is he?"

"I have an address for him in West Philly. His mom's house."

Ellie stood up. "Ten minutes away. Let's go see him."

"You wanna come along?"

"Jess is out there somewhere. I know she's alive. I'm in for whatever I can do to get her back."

"Okay. A pretty face like yours might make him open up a little more too."

Ellie ignored his comment. "I'll drive."

Rivers agreed and reached for his wallet.

Ellie decided not to call Josh as she drove to West Philadelphia with Pete Rivers. He would call her when he needed to. In the meantime, she had an ex-convict to meet.

Lorenzo's mother's house sat in the middle of a sad line of row homes. The acidic smell of trash filled the air as they got out of the car. The ground was littered with old newspapers and food containers. Some of the houses looked vacant, with doors hanging off the hinges and blacked-out windows. They passed a group of men sitting on the steps of a house with wooden planks nailed over the door.

"Any of you Lorenzo Rivera?" Rivers asked.

"Who wants to know?" One of the men cocked his head at them.

"A friend. Someone who wants to make his day."

None of the men replied. Rivers drew out a twenty-dollar bill, and the nearest man took it. "He should be home now. I saw him get in from his shift a few hours ago."

"Thanks."

They continued to the address Jim had given them, and Rivers stepped forward and tapped on the screen door. A man in his late thirties answered.

"Lorenzo?"

The man nodded, and Rivers showed his credentials. "I'm Peter Rivers. You been watching the news lately? Did you see the story about the missing girl?"

"I've seen it," Lorenzo replied. "I know who you are too," he said to Ellie.

"Can we come in and talk?" Rivers asked.

Lorenzo nodded and stood back. He gestured for them to sit down on an old couch. The room was simply furnished but clean. Several pictures of the Virgin Mary sat among framed family portraits on the wall.

Lorenzo sat down across from them. He offered them coffee, but they declined. He left them in the living room alone while he got himself a cup. The aroma from the mug in his hand came with him as he sat opposite them.

"We don't want to put you to any trouble," Rivers said.

Ellie wasn't in the mood for small talk. "You knew Gary Thomas, the man who took me?" Ellie asked.

"You could say that. I shared a cell with the man for twelve years."

Rivers took a notepad out of his pocket and drew a pencil from a holder inside it. "We want to ask you a few questions about him, in connection with Ellie's daughter's disappearance. I should tell you that Gary was found dead last night."

Lorenzo looked shocked. "I hadn't heard." They talked about the details of his death for a few minutes, though she and Rivers knew few of them.

"Ellie went to see him yesterday with Josh," Rivers said and looked over at Ellie.

"He seemed different than the man I knew years ago," Ellie said. "He apologized about what happened to his wife. That was the first time I ever heard him say anything like that."

Lorenzo didn't seem surprised. "I saw the change in him too. He was all fire and brimstone those first couple of years, always shouting about how he'd been framed and whatnot, but he mellowed over time. Took responsibility for his wife's death if nothing else."

"He said he killed her?" Rivers asked.

"No. He never admitted to cutting the brake lines. Why would he if he was driving the car? But he said he beat her, and that he put her in the position to die, but there was someone else."

Rivers scribbled some notes. "Who?"

"Some woman, Kate Downing. He said he drove her to kill herself. Gary said he deserved his time in jail for what he did to her, even if he was innocent of the crimes he was convicted of. He said he abused her over the years. It wasn't something he was proud of."

"He never admitted to taking Ellie?"

Lorenzo shook his head. "No. The opposite. He denied it until the end—and Rachel's murder. He was adamant about that too. I'm sure he died thinking someone set him up."

"What about this other woman, Kate? Do you know where she was from? Or anything about her?"

"He talked about her from time to time, but I wouldn't want to mention a lot of what he said in front of a lady. She lived in Media for years but wasn't from there. She was from out in the sticks somewhere. Nickle Mines or somewhere like that."

"Where?" Ellie exclaimed. The mention of the area she'd been held in sent a chill down her spine. She stood up. "Are you sure?" Rivers motioned for her to sit back down.

"Near Lancaster, out in Amish country," Lorenzo answered. "But she wasn't one of them. They moved, though. Her parents live in the town of Intercourse now." He smiled. "That's not the type of name you forget."

"That's where I was held," Ellie whispered. "Where the farmhouse is."

The mention of Nickle Mines threw Ellie off her stride. She thought for a moment she might need to step outside for some fresh air.

"Can I get a glass of water?" she asked.

Lorenzo nodded with a smile. "Sure thing."

Rivers turned to her when Lorenzo was gone. "Are you okay?"

Ellie took a deep breath in through her nose—something she'd learned was useful in regulating her fears. "Yeah, I'll be fine. It's just the mention of that place."

"Gary must have gotten to know it when he was visiting Kate and scoped out the house," Rivers reasoned.

Lorenzo arrived back and handed Ellie a glass of water. She felt the benefit of it in seconds.

Rivers started again. "Do you have any idea who hated Gary enough to want him dead? Anyone on the inside?"

"We all had enemies in there, but that one guard, she had it in for him from the start. Seemed to take pleasure in watching him suffer for a while."

"Fletcher?" Ellie asked.

"Yeah, that's her. She controlled him, who he saw, what he did. It was weird. I always wondered what she got out of it. She didn't seem to care about the other inmates but was always right there when Gary fell down."

Ellie looked at Rivers, who remained stoic and asked, "Did he ever talk about her?"

"All the time," Lorenzo said. "He couldn't figure out what she had against him. He tried reasoning with her, but she wouldn't say a word."

"What did she do to him?" Ellie asked.

Stupid little things like pushing over his lunch tray and making him clean it up. But big things too. She reported a couple of assaults that he denied and had him thrown in the hole and his parole put back. Rumor was that she's rich too. Married some old dude fifteen years ago and got all the money when he croaked a couple of years later."

"How did the old man die?" Rivers asked.

"In his sleep. A lot of guys said she had a hand in it, but the cops disagreed."

The adrenaline shooting through Ellie's veins made sitting hard. "Who is she? Where's she from?"

Lorenzo smirked. "We never had sat down to sing Kumbaya together."

Rivers was still an island of calm. "Who do you think might have killed Gary?"

"No idea, man. Could've been any one of a dozen psychopaths. And if someone on the outside wanted to hit him, all they'd have to do is contact one of those psychopaths' families and pay them off. I've seen it happen."

"Who sent them is the real question," Ellie said.

Lorenzo shook his head. "Of that, I have no idea. But it could have been a fight or some stupid vendetta."

"I saw him yesterday," Ellie said. "He didn't have any visible bruises and didn't mention feeling threatened."

"I don't know about that. Your girl's still missing?" Lorenzo asked, and Ellie nodded. "I hope you find her. Let me know if there's anything else I can do to help." He stood up. "But I gotta get to work now."

"I thought you just got back from the night shift a few hours ago," Ellie said as she stood up.

"Day shift is starting in an hour. I gotta get out of my mom's house."

Ellie shook his hand, and Rivers did the same.

"Thank you," she said.

"No problem."

Ellie stayed silent until they were in the car. "How quickly can you look into the guard, Fletcher?"

"I'll make a call right now and do some more digging when we get back to the office." He searched his contacts list, and a number appeared on his screen. It rang a few times before a tired-sounding man picked up.

"Pete! To what do I owe this pleasure?"

"Eddie, how's the wife and kids?"

"Still there every time I go home."

They chatted briefly before Pete asked the question. "Can you run a background check for me on a Kate Fletcher? She's a prison guard."

"Do I want to know why?" Eddie answered with a question.

"Not if you want to live a quiet life. Thank you, my friend. Rest assured, I'll return the favor soon."

"Okay," Eddie said. "I'll talk to you later." He hung up.

Ellie started the car.

"How long is that going to take?" she asked.

Rivers looked at her as if he was about to berate her for being so impatient before catching himself. "A few hours, maybe longer. I know what you're thinking, but we're getting closer. Killing Gary was a mistake. Whoever ordered the hit is going to pay for that mistake."

"Do we go to the cops with this?"

"Not until we have something more solid. All we're working with at the moment is a bunch of theories and hearsay. But if I think we can find Jess, I'm not hanging around. I'll go straight to where I think she is. In the meantime, drop me back to the office."

Ellie nodded in agreement. "I think I'll take a trip out to Lancaster to see Kate Downing's mother."

"Alone? I have to go back to the office."

"Josh is at the prison. I'll meet him."

"Good luck, and be careful," Rivers said. "I'll find an address for Kate Downing's mother and text it to you."

"How?" Ellie asked.

"I have her daughter's name, it shouldn't be too hard," the PI replied with a grin.

After dropping Rivers off, Ellie drove home, retrieved her gun, stowed it in the trunk of her car, and hit the road.

TWENTY-FOUR

Ellie tried to do the private investigator's work for him. The Google searches for Kate Downing turned up nothing. Ellie wasn't surprised nothing showed up for Kate as she'd been dead for more than twenty years. She'd expected more from her searches for Fletcher, but they hadn't resulted in more than a few photos of her in uniform at various outreach events and a record of her service as a prison guard. Her history was strange in so far as it didn't exist. She didn't seem to have a life prior to becoming a guard. Ellie found no mention of her marriage to the older man Lorenzo had referred to, and no address or list of assets for her. But the more Ellie thought about her, the more she seemed familiar. The essence of her was in Ellie's memory somewhere. Not as something solid, but like a mist, something Ellie couldn't grasp.

The text from Rivers with Kate Downing's mother's address came as she was beginning to doubt him. Ellie thanked him and kept driving.

She called Josh on the way and arranged to meet him at a diner just outside Lancaster.

Josh was leaning on his car, waiting for her, as she pulled up to the Rising Sun Diner. Its silver exterior shone in the after-noon light.

She parked beside him and gave him a hug. "How are you doing?"

He had bags under his eyes, and his skin was paler than she'd ever seen. "I'm okay. I just got back from the prison. They still have no idea who did it."

Ellie didn't know what to say next. It was hard to feel sorry for a man like his father, and Josh hadn't wanted him in his life all these years.

He beat her to the punch. "What did you find out on your trip with Rivers earlier?"

Ellie gulped back the words on the tip of her tongue. She had been dreading telling him all the way here.

"He's doing a background check on that guard."

He got off the car. "Fletcher? I saw her today. She offered her condolences."

"Did she say anything else?"

"Yeah, she said she's sick of all the violence. She quit today."

"How long did you speak to her for?"

"A few minutes. She came down to the warden's office and waited outside for me."

"Did you ask around about her?"

"No. Why the sudden interest in her?"

Ellie explained what they'd found out about her grudge against his father.

His jawline tensed and he turned his head. "You think she had something to do with his death?" he asked.

"I have no evidence of that right now. Was she working when you left?"

"No, I noticed her getting into her car as I left—a blue BMW. Not what I'd expect from a prison guard."

"I think she's got something to do with Jessica's disappear-ance," Ellie stated. It felt good to verbalize her thoughts.

Josh was puzzled. "Why on earth would she want to take Jess? I don't understand."

"It's just a hunch, but someone ordered the hit on your father."

"And you think it was her? I understand she had a grudge against my dad, but is that rare in prison? I wouldn't think so."

"We'll see. Rivers is doing some digging."

"There's something about Fletcher," Josh mused with his thumb and forefinger on either side of his chin. "I can't quite place her but I swear I know her from somewhere."

"Me too," Ellie answered.

"There's something else." Josh took out his wallet and threw it on the hood of his car. "My driver's license is missing. I don't remember taking it out, and I only noticed it was gone when I stopped off to buy lunch on the way home. I couldn't find my hairbrush either. I always leave it in the same place. It's weird."

Josh was meticulously clean, as his mother had been. "You think you got burgled?"

"I don't know. I haven't got the alarm installed yet. With everything going on, I didn't have the chance. I also didn't have the chance to check what was missing. I noticed the brush because I wasn't able to use it when I went home this morning and only realized the license was gone when I got here. I have no idea what else they took or when they were taken. But who would break in and steal a hairbrush and a driver's license?"

"Did you ever think your dad might have been telling the truth? That he didn't kill Rachel or kidnap me?"

Josh flashed an incredulous smile. "What?"

Ellie looked around to make sure no one was listening and stepped closer. "Did you ever doubt his conviction?"

"They found evidence. A text to Rachel on his burner phone asking to meet her in the woods, his wallet at the Farrington farm after you escaped. You testified yourself. You said how inappropriate he was with you from the start."

"I never saw who took me, or even heard their voice. I always wondered how he could have gotten into that party and spiked my drink. The district attorney never had an answer for that."

"You think he was working with someone else? You think they killed him to shut him up?"

Ellie brought her hands to her face and rubbed her eyes with her fingertips. "I don't know. I have no idea anymore. I just need to find my daughter, before it's too late."

"You think someone framed my dad, and are trying to do the same to me?"

"Why would he admit to beating your mom and being indirectly responsible for her death, but not the crimes he'd been convicted for?"

"Because he was a liar."

"Josh, there's something else I haven't told you—something I heard this morning. It might be what he was trying to tell you before the visit ended yesterday. I wanted to tell you in person."

"What?"

"Lorenzo said your father had an affair with a woman called Kate Downing. He also said..." Ellie had to dig deep to continue. She knew her next words could devastate Josh. "He also said he drove her to suicide. Abused her until he drove her over the edge."

Josh looked around in silence for two seconds before bringing his eyes back to hers. "Are you sure?"

Thoughts were swirling around Ellie's mind. The pieces weren't quite connecting, but she was close.

"That's what he said. Rivers is looking into it, trying to find out the truth."

"Lorenzo also said your dad insisted he never took me or killed Rachel all to the end."

Josh nodded. He balled his fists, perhaps to prevent his hands from shaking. He looked away and then back at her. "My dad had an affair for years, and this Kate Downing killed herself because of him?"

"Her mother lives about twenty minutes from here. I think we should go see her."

Josh nodded. "Yeah, you're right. Maybe she knows something about my dad."

Ellie took his hand. "I know this is hard for you."

He accepted the comfort she offered but drew back quickly. "We have to find Jess. Nothing else matters now."

"Will you be okay to do this?"

He nodded. The strength was returning to his eyes. His tone was unequivocal. "Yeah. I'll follow you in my car."

Ellie knew better than to ask him again and got into her car.

The address was on the outskirts of town, and the GPS stopped working as Ellie reached the end of a long country road shaded by leafy trees. The road gave way to a dirt track as she searched for the house. A rusty truck with four flat tires sat outside a dilapidated wooden bungalow with a couch on the porch. The lawn was overgrown with wildflowers. An old caramel-colored Toyota Camry sat in the driveway. Josh pulled up behind her and got out.

He gestured toward the Camry. "Looks like they're home."

Ellie took his hand, and they walked up toward the house together. Josh knocked on the screen door. It was rendered opaque by the layer of dirt that covered it. A woman in her seventies with curly silver hair opened the door. Smoke from the cigarette in her hand curled up around her as she poked her head through.

"Can I help you?" she asked, eying them both suspiciously.

"I'm Josh, and this is Ellie. I don't know if you've seen us on the news, but Ellie's daughter is missing."

The woman shook her head. The look on her face changed from curiosity to defensiveness. "I don't know anything about that."

Josh smiled. "We both know that. We'd just like to ask you some questions about your daughter, if that's okay. You're Mrs. Downing, right?"

"That's me," she said in a cautious tone. "I suppose you'd better come in."

"Thank you," Josh said.

They followed her inside. The house was shabby and worn but clean. Mrs. Downing led them to the living room, where they sat down on a couch opposite her armchair. She didn't offer them anything, so Ellie began. "I hope you don't mind if we ask you some questions about your daughter Kate."

Mrs. Downing took a drag on her cigarette. The end burned red-hot, then faded to gray. "She was a wild one. Always was. Right from the time she was a baby. Not like her sisters. They live in Pittsburgh but still visit all the time."

"It must have come as a terrible shock to you when she passed," Ellie stated.

"Not to me. I'd hardly seen her in years." Mrs. Downing stared out the window as if looking into the past.

"You were estranged?" Josh asked.

"It was hard keeping up with her and her crazy ways, particularly when she moved to the city."

Ellie sat forward. "Did you ever meet Gary Thomas?"

"I remember him being around in the early days, before everything that happened. He's behind bars now for the last how long?"

"About twenty years," Ellie supplied.

Mrs. Downing stubbed out her cigarette. "Yeah, he was around more in the early days—when Julia was little."

Ellie's heart froze. "Julia?"

"Yeah, their daughter," Mrs. Downing said casually.

"Gary had a child with your daughter?" Josh said.

"You didn't know?" Her casual demeanor barely changed.

Ellie looked at Josh in disbelief. "Her name was Julia Downing?"

"No. Kate loved my mother more than anyone. More than me, anyway. When she passed, Kate started going off the rails. She gave Julia the same name as her—Leonard. I suppose it was her way of trying to keep my mom's memory alive."

"Gary and Kate's daughter's name was Julia Leonard?" Ellie asked.

"Yeah. I didn't see her much for most of her life, but when her mom..." Mrs. Downing stopped herself and took a breath before continuing. "When Kate died, Julia went to live with her aunt first, but they didn't get along, so after that, she came to us for a while, just before she moved to the West Coast. I couldn't say we were ever close. She was an angry, bitter girl. Mad at the world for what happened to her mother. I wasn't sorry to see her go, if I'm honest."

Josh sat back. He seemed to be struggling to find words.

Ellie took over. "Do you have a picture of Julia?"

"Not many," Mrs. Downing said and raised herself off the threadbare armchair. "But I have one from when she was about twelve. One of the few times I saw her in those years." She took a framed photograph off the mantelpiece and handed it to them.

Ellie's hand was shaking as she took it. She felt her body freeze in disbelief. The girl in the picture was young, but it was unmistakably Julia Leonard—the girl who'd tried to warn her off Josh in high school and who'd always hated him.

"She got married in Los Angeles years ago. That was the last I heard of her. She found some rich old guy. I hardly recognized her in the photo with all the surgery she'd had done."

Josh looked at Ellie with blazing eyes. "Do you happen to have a wedding photo?" he asked the older woman.

Mrs. Downing nodded and walked into the kitchen. Josh and Ellie remained silent while she was gone. She came back a few seconds later and handed them another photograph. It was

Kate Fletcher, the prison guard, in a white wedding dress. The man on her arm was fifty years older and about four inches shorter than her. Ellie's entire body was cold.

"It's her," Josh said to her.

"Do you know where Julia is now?" Ellie asked. Her heart was thumping in her chest.

Mrs. Downing didn't seem to pick up on how frenzied Ellie and Josh had become. "I have no idea, and to be quite honest, I don't care. I have enough crazy in my life without her. I never heard from her again after she sent me this. I think she wanted to rub it in that she married a rich man, while I was still stuck here." Mrs. Downing shook her head.

Josh coughed into his hand before speaking. "How long have you lived here?"

"More than twenty years. We didn't move far. Our old house was down in Georgetown—just a few miles away."

"Is that near Nickle Mines? By the Farrington farm?" Josh continued.

Mrs. Downing stopped for a second as if she realized why he was asking her. Her words came with hesitation. "It's right there. Less than a mile away. Julia used to play there all the time as a little girl before her mother stopped visiting... Is she... Is she in trouble?"

Josh had his head in his hands. "I saw her a few hours ago."

Ellie stood up. Adrenaline was pumping through her veins. "Thank you, Mrs. Downing. I think we've taken up enough of your time."

Mrs. Downing nodded. "She was happy once, but something in her changed."

"We need to leave," Ellie said and pulled Josh out of his seat.

Mrs. Downing didn't move. "Maybe I could have done more," she lamented.

"It's not your fault," Ellie assured her, but her mind was already somewhere else.

Josh followed her back out to their cars.

"Kate Fletcher has Jess, I'm sure of it," Ellie said to him once they were out of earshot of the house.

"Yeah, but how do we find her? Julia quit the prison, and they won't give out the addresses of their guards."

"Follow me back to the diner. We'll get that address. My daughter's life depends on it."

TWENTY-FIVE

Josh pulled up beside Ellie's car at the diner. He was pale as he got out. His lips had taken on a bluish tinge, and his movements were languid and slow.

"My sister?" he whispered. "She's my sister, and she did all this to destroy me?"

"And your father," Ellie reasoned. She took him in her arms. His body was cold. "She took Jess to finish the job she began twenty years ago. I guess she couldn't stand to see you happy."

"But why your daughter? Why not come for me?"

"Because this is all part of the game she's been playing since Rachel and her mother died."

"My father didn't take you, and he didn't kill Rachel either."

Ellie shook her head. "We have to find Jess now. She might not be as lucky as I was."

Stepping back from Josh, Ellie reached into her bag for her phone. She called Rivers for the third time in the last five minutes. Finally, he picked up. She put him on speaker so Josh could join in.

"Ellie, I have news. I saw you called. I was on the phone to my source checking on Kate Fletcher."

"We were doing some digging too. What did you find out?"

"Turns out Lorenzo was telling the truth about her," he said. "She's rich. Has two houses in her name. One in Pottsville and a lake house up in the Poconos. She married Terence Fletcher about fifteen years ago. He died in mysterious circumstances a couple of years later, but the cops weren't able to make anything stick. He was seventy-five. She was twenty-four. So, what did she do next when she had all that money? She became a prison guard. Then, according to Lorenzo, she proceeded to make Gary Thomas's life hell until he died."

Ellie explained to him what they'd just learned from Mrs. Downing. "She took her mother's name."

Rivers was stunned. "So, Kate Fletcher and this girl Julia, who hated Josh in high school, are the same person?"

"Yes, and I'll bet everything I have that she's holding Jess somewhere. We're in Lancaster."

"You didn't recognize her?"

Josh spoke next. "She looks so different now. I hadn't thought about Julia in years. I never thought I'd see her again."

"She came to me when we were teenagers to warn me to stay away from Josh. Why would she become a guard and victimize his father?" Ellie said.

"I don't know yet," Rivers replied. "But we're onto something here. I think it's worth checking out her houses tonight. We're against the clock here. I'll stake out the house in Pottsville, and I'll text you the address for the lake house in the Poconos. But don't do anything stupid. Call me or the cops if you see anything, and don't go alone. Only together."

"Should we call the cops now?" Josh asked.

"Not yet," Rivers reasoned. "We don't have anything solid. Just keep an eye out."

"Got it. One more thing, Pete," she replied. "Josh thinks someone broke into his house. His license is gone, and some other things."

"Sounds a lot like the stuff they found at the Farrington farm after you escaped," Rivers said. "No better way to plant DNA at a crime scene than with an old hairbrush."

"Text me that address."

"As soon as I get off the phone. It'll take me a little less than two hours to get to Pottsville from my place. The Poconos house will take you about the same. Get going, and remember to call me if you see anything unusual."

"We will, but you too, though," Josh asserted.

"Roger that," he said and hung up the phone.

"Julia Leonard?" Josh said as she turned to him. "She despised me in high school, but this?"

Ellie stared at him.

"She went to live with Mrs. Downing near Nickle Mines, after..."

Ellie finished the sentence for him. "She left Lower Merion High School. Just before I was taken."

"Let's get going! My car's faster."

"Give me a minute."

Ellie ran to the trunk of her car and reached in. The pistol was loaded. She put it in her pocket. "Just in case." She ran back to Josh.

They were in his car speeding toward the Pocono Mountains moments later.

"So, Julia Leonard is my sister? All those years we were in school together?" He hesitated for a few seconds, stunned. "I remember playing with her when I was little. When did she find out?"

Ellie didn't have an answer to his question and remained quiet.

They were on the highway in minutes, and Josh was driving at ninety miles per hour, slaloming in and out of traffic.

"That makes more sense as far as taking you—she could

have gotten into that party and spiked your drink pretty much unnoticed, but what did she have to do with Rachel's death?"

"I don't know yet," Ellie replied. "But I have a feeling we're going to find out soon."

Her palms were so wet she had to wipe them off with a tissue from her bag. Every second, every mile they drove, seemed to get them closer to finding Jess. The silver barrel of the handgun in her bag glinted as they drove under a streetlight. She hadn't told Josh about it yet. She just hoped she wouldn't have to use it.

"You think Julia—or 'Kate'—would be dumb enough to keep Jess at her house? She's been so careful about everything so far."

"I have no clue. She might not even be at the lake house."

Ellie picked up her phone and called Rivers, but he was still en route too. She reached over to Josh and took his hand. He drove on.

The blanket of night had fallen by the time they reached the lake in the mountains. Unlike many lakes that dotted the state, it was natural and had been a tourist destination for many years. The houses they passed ranged from functional to opulent, with the latter ones being those that ringed the water.

"This is it," Josh said. He pulled up at the side of the road and killed the engine. The house was dark, about fifty yards away, and barely visible through the trees. The water shone silver beyond it. "Let me dump the car somewhere, and we can get out and take a look. Chances are she's not even here."

He started the car again and parked it in a layby a hundred yards down the road. They got out. The air was cool and thick, and the sound of insects filled their ears.

"Let's check it out," Josh said.

Ellie couldn't speak. Trying to stifle her fear, she felt for the gun in her bag, her hands shaking. She would do whatever it took to get her daughter back. They moved through the shadows toward the house. It was two stories with a large wooden deck.

A jetty stretched out to a boathouse, and Ellie was able to make out the covered speedboat parked there. The only sound was of their breathing and the night itself. The house was dark. No light shone through the windows, and the driveway was empty.

Josh turned to her. "Doesn't look like anybody's home."

"Is there a basement? Somewhere Jess might be?"

"Let's take a look."

They crept up to the house. Ellie was wary of being disturbed, paranoid about every sound, every stick that broke under her feet as she walked. Her heart was thundering in her chest. But the house was silent. Nothing around them was moving. A few places across the lake had lights on but nowhere nearby. They tried the doors, but each was locked. Before she could think twice, Ellie picked up a rock and broke a window— no alarm sounded. They crawled through, but found nothing inside. The house was spotless. It didn't exhibit any sign that anyone had been there in months. The basement was empty except for a few boxes and some fishing equipment.

"Nothing," Josh stated.

They were just about to leave when Ellie noticed some photographs on the wall in the living room. "Wait."

Josh followed her to the wall. She turned on the flashlight on her phone. None of them were recent pictures. They were all of a woman and a little girl.

"Julia and her mother," Ellie whispered.

"None of her late husband."

Ellie almost smiled. "Are you surprised?"

She spent a few more minutes searching the empty house until Josh urged her to come outside with him. "There's nothing here, Ellie. Just a few old photographs on the wall."

She almost cried. She wanted to scream. They seemed no closer to finding Jess. Her daughter could have been dead for all they knew. Frustration gripped her like a vise. She pulled her phone out of her bag to call Rivers.

The private investigator picked up.

"We're at Kate Fletcher's lake house. Nothing here. It doesn't look like anyone's been inside in a while other than the maid service. I thought this was it. Where is she?" Ellie felt her frustrations tearing her apart and struggled to contain her emotions.

His voice was calm. "Her main house is empty too. Sit tight and watch the place for a few hours. You never know what you might see. I'm going to do the same. Let me know if anything changes."

Ellie agreed and hung up.

They walked back to the car. The house and the driveway were visible from their parking spot in the layby. They sat and waited, speaking little as they watched the house.

Midnight came, and Josh turned to her. "Maybe it's time we thought about going home. I don't see anything."

But just as he spoke, lights appeared on the road. They'd seen several cars pass, but this one turned into Julia's driveway and drove down to the house. Ellie nudged Josh on the shoulder. The BMW stopped, and they could just about see her climb out.

"What do we do?" Josh whispered.

Ellie was already calling Rivers. "She's here!" she said when he answered.

"Okay. Watch her. Don't charge in there. You're already sure Jessica's not in the house."

"I thought I was."

"Make sure Julia doesn't see you. Let me know what happens next. If she doesn't come out in an hour, call me and I'll come up and watch the place."

"Okay, okay." Ellie hung up again.

"What if she's going to bed?" Josh asked.

"She's not!"

Ellie could make out the figure of someone coming out of

the house and getting into the car. The lights went on as Julia started the engine. She turned the car around and came back up the driveway.

"Where's she going?" Josh whispered.

"Start the engine," Ellie said. "But kill the lights. We're going to find out."

Josh waited until Julia drove past and followed her. The road was pitch black, but Josh was able to keep her lights in his sights as he drove. The BMW kept on for half a mile before pulling off the road again, down toward another house.

"That's where she's keeping Jess!" Ellie said. Her intuition was screaming at her, pointing toward the house. "Be careful she doesn't see you."

Josh turned off the engine on the road outside. They watched as Julia came to a stop outside the house. It was at the end of the lake, out on its own. Ellie could see in the dull light that the paint was coming off and the windows upstairs were cracked and dusty.

Ellie balled her fist and gritted her teeth. "Come on, I'm going to get my daughter."

"Wait. We don't want to disturb her and make her do something stupid. Let's give her a minute. We need to call the cops."

"And tell them what? That we followed someone here? We have no evidence. We have to get inside the house," Ellie said as she drew the gun from her bag. She took a few seconds to check it before placing it back in.

Josh looked surprised but nodded, and they set off into the darkness. Ellie took a few seconds to text Rivers what they were doing before continuing on. They kept to the trees, inching toward the old house. The BMW was outside the front door. Ellie almost jumped when she saw Julia emerging alone—she'd only been inside a few minutes. She got back into her car, and the lights went on. Ellie and Josh hid under a bush as the car turned around and drove back up to the road. In a matter of seconds, Julia was gone.

"Let's get inside that house," Ellie said.

Ellie ran down the hill toward the door. The waters of the lake were lapping against the shore a few yards away. She took a rock and smashed the glass above the door handle.

"She's going to know we were here if she comes back."

"She probably knows we were in the other house. We might only have a few minutes before she returns."

"Or this could be a trap," Josh said.

Ellie reached through and unlocked the door before pushing it open. "I have to find my daughter."

Josh followed her inside. The lights were off, and they both used the flashlights on their phones to guide them. After a few seconds of silent searching, Ellie couldn't stand it any longer.

"Jessica!" she roared. No reply came. She screamed her daughter's name again, frantically searching the ground floor of the old house. They popped into a bedroom, then a laundry room with two ancient machines rusting away.

"Jess!" Ellie screamed.

And the reply came. "Mom?"

The voice was muffled and distant.

Jess. She was alive.

Ellie felt her legs almost give way beneath her.

"Jess? Jess?" No reply came. "Where's that voice coming from?" Ellie roared. She shone her flashlight around the walls frantically before Josh turned a light on.

"Check out the steps over here," he said. A white door was ajar, leading to some steps down to a basement dug into the lakeside dirt. Another door lay at the bottom of the stairs. Ellie sprinted down them.

"Jess! Are you in there? I'm here with Josh!" she called out.

"Get me out of here!" her daughter called out frantically.

They heard the thumping on the other side of the locked door, and saw the space cut out at the bottom.

"Stand back!" Josh said and kicked the lock. It gave way on the third try, and the door flew open. Ellie ran through and grabbed her daughter. She held her in her arms, kissing her cheek. Both were crying.

"Mom!" Jess said.

She was thinner, and her clothes were dirty, but otherwise seemed okay.

"We need to get out of here," Josh said.

Ellie drew back from Jess, kissing her cheek one last time before nodding her head. She had never felt relief like it. It was almost too much to take. Ellie hugged Jess again.

A voice from behind them interrupted her.

"Touching," Julia said. "So good to see you all back together."

She was at the door behind them in her prison guard uniform. She flicked off the safety on the Glock 17 she was holding. Ellie looked down at the jerrican of gas in her other hand. The fumes drifted through the air, and Ellie was transported back twenty years. Ellie grabbed her daughter and felt the old familiar fear flush through her. "Let my daughter go."

"Julia, don't do anything you'll regret," Josh said. "Let us walk out of here, and we won't say a word to anyone."

A cruel half-smile spread across her face. "Don't do anything I'll regret? Like your father did to my mom?"

Josh stepped forward. "Our father, Julia. I never knew. I'm so sorry."

"So, you worked it out?" Her eyes were on fire. "I tried to warn you years ago, Ellie, but you didn't listen. Neither did Rachel Kubick. She tried to fight me. I didn't mean what happened to her. I texted her to talk. I just wanted to warn her about you. Like father, like son. But when I confronted her about seeing Gary, the crazy bitch came at me. Can you believe your girlfriend was sleeping with him behind your back? I had to defend myself. I suppose I lost my temper."

Josh corrected her. "But you were wearing gloves. You cleaned the scene afterward and lured her there. She thought she was meeting my dad."

"That was the test. I knew she was seeing him when she showed up. And the gloves? I like to come prepared for anything."

Ellie stepped in front of Jess. "Just leave my daughter out of this."

They had to keep her talking. Rivers was on his way.

"I never planned on taking you, you know," Julia said with a devilish smile. "I just wanted to kill Gary. I learned all about cars and how the brake lines work, but that psychopath assaulted his wife and dragged her into the car with him. I never thought she'd be the one to die, and I certainly didn't think he'd go AWOL like that. What could a girl do then? I figured taking you was the next best way to torture Gary's golden goose."

"Why did you try to burn me?" Ellie hissed angrily.

"Boredom. I don't know. It had gone on long enough."

"Why Jess? Why my daughter?"

"I had some fun torturing Gary over the years. Much more than if I'd just killed him, but when the quarterback jock came back to town, I figured what better way to get revenge for my mother than by torturing the one he loves? He never had any kids of his own, and he treated that ex-wife of his like something he found on the underside of his shoe. The thought of doing it again amused me."

"You don't have to do this," Josh said with his hands out. "My father's dead. Your revenge for your mother is complete. I'm sorry for what my dad did, but he's gone now."

Julia pointed the gun at Josh. "And now my focus is on you, brother. You always had it so easy. Worshipped everywhere you went, while I went to bed hungry. You had everything!" Her face was red, and the words came as a torrent of vitriol. Hate contorted her face into an ugly mask.

"We're both scarred by him," Josh reasoned. He took a step forward. So did Julia. He stopped, and so did she. "He destroyed all of our lives."

Julia took a deep breath in and tightened her finger around the trigger. She seemed to ignore Josh's words. "I've been dreaming about this moment."

"Julia, you have so much now," Josh blurted. "All the money you could ever need. Things have changed," he said.

"Thanks," Julia sneered with wide eyes. "I had your license and your DNA all ready to pin her murder on you. It would have been fun to watch. But now, you all get to die together. Just like the happy little family you are. I'll be in Canada before the cops even realize what happened."

Ellie stepped forward. The gun was in her bag, but Julia would shoot her before she had a chance to pull it out. Jess clung to Ellie's side like she had done when she was a little girl.

"So, that was the plan? Burn the house to the ground, like you tried to twenty years ago?" Ellie said.

"You don't think I knew about the gap in the wall at the Farrington farm? I spent days readying that space. I knew it inside out. It was more amusing for me to give you a fighting chance. And you surprised me, Ellie."

"And we're together again. Surely that's got to be worth something," Josh said. "Julia, you're the only family I have left."

"It's Kate," she said and pulled the trigger. Ellie jumped at the sudden sound of the bang in the enclosed space. Josh crumpled to the floor, clutching his right thigh. Blood poured out between his fingers. "That's to make sure you can't run."

Ellie went to him. Josh looked up at Julia, speaking between gritted teeth. "Stop this. I never hurt you."

"You were everything I could have been." She kept the gun trained on Ellie as she bent down to screw the cap off the jerrican. "Everything I should have been. I had to watch the world fall at your feet while it spit in my face. I should have done this a long time ago." She kicked over the gas can, and a puddle spread across the floor to where they were gathered a few feet from her.

Ellie looked around the room for something to jump behind and fire at her. But there was nothing.

"Let Jessica go. She has nothing to do with any of this. She never even knew who you were."

Julia smirked. "My hands are tied now. It's too late to turn back."

Ellie tried to stall. "What about your houses and everything else you'll leave behind?"

"That's what offshore accounts are for."

Julia reached into her pocket and took out a lighter. Jess screamed.

"Don't burn us. Ellie and Jess never hurt anybody. I'm your brother," Josh said, grimacing through the pain.

"And you're so concerned about me now, aren't you? Now that you're drenched in gasoline, and I'm holding the lighter. I've been in a pool of gas my entire life!"

"I never threw the match," Josh said.

"The police are on their way," Ellie said. "You'll never get away."

"You called someone?" Julia pursed her lips. She seemed to reconsider her plan. "You're right. The girl never did anything. Come over here, Jessica."

Jess didn't move. "What?"

Julia gestured with the gun again. "I could use a hostage until I get across the border. Get over here!"

"No," Jess said.

Ellie pushed her daughter forward. Better to go with her than to be burned alive in here. "Do as she says, Jess. She'll let you go at the border."

"That's it," Julia said. "Listen to your mom, just like I always did."

Julia's eyes left Josh and Ellie. She was watching Jess walk to her through the puddle of gasoline. Ellie reached into her bag and drew out the pistol in one swift movement. She pointed it at Julia, who noticed just as Jess reached her.

"Oh, no!" she shouted and dropped the unlit lighter on the ground to reach an arm around Jessica's collarbone.

"Put the gun down!" Ellie said. "It's over, Julia."

Julia laughed. She pressed the gun against the girl's temple, using her as a shield. "Nothing's over. I have your daughter, and she and I are going to walk out the door."

Ellie brought her finger to the trigger. She didn't have a clear shot. Josh tried to struggle to his feet but fell down again in seconds. The blood from his leg wound was mixing with the gasoline. He needed medical attention.

"Please let her go. Don't do this," Ellie pleaded with tears in her eyes.

Julia looked down at the lighter, out of her reach. "We're leaving now."

She put a foot behind her on the bottom step. Ellie walked forward, the gun still trained on Julia. Josh was helpless. Julia kept a hold of Jessica as she backed up the stairs. Ellie walked to the door and saw them at the top of the steps, entering the house. She kept following them, the gun pointed at Julia. They disappeared from her view, and she ran up the stairs. The light was on in the kitchen. Julia was still backing away. She was smiling. The twisted psychopath was enjoying this. She reached the balcony, which overlooked the lake. It was on stilts. The ground was maybe thirty feet below—a sheer fall onto rocks.

"I'm taking her again," Julia said. "And there's nothing you can do about it."

"I'm not letting you do that," Ellie said, searching for an opening.

They were on the balcony now. The lights were streaking yellow across Julia's black eyes. Still using Jess as a human shield, Julia inched backward. Ellie knew that if they reached Julia's car, she'd never see her daughter again.

"It'll be okay, Mom," Jess said. "I'll go with her. You stay here."

"Yes, she's right," Julia said. "You stay here." She took the gun from the girl's head and pointed it at Ellie.

"You know what we always say, Jess," Ellie said. "There comes a time in life when we have to fight!"

Her daughter understood. She leaned forward and elbowed Julia in the ribs. Taken completely by surprise, Julia yelled in pain and let go of Jess, who ducked to the ground. Time slowed as Ellie took aim. She'd been preparing for this moment for years. She squeezed the trigger. The first bullet hit Julia in the shoulder, driving her back. The gun was still in her hand.

Jess scuttled away like a crab. Ellie stepped forward and fired again, this time hitting Julia square in the center of her chest. She fell back but, after releasing a guttural roar, got back to her feet again, trying to level the gun to fire back. Ellie wasn't going to give her that chance. She fired again, and again. Julia stumbled backward and hit the railing over the balcony. One more shot sent her body over. And she disappeared into the void beyond. Her body collided with the rocks below with a sickening thud. Ellie ran to the edge and looked over. Julia's lifeless body lay still.

Jess ran to her, and Ellie took her in her arms.

"Are you okay, my love?" Ellie asked her as she kissed her sweaty forehead.

"You came for me!" Jess cried. "You saved me."

The joy at having her daughter again was tempered by thoughts of Josh in the basement.

Ellie frantically took her phone out of her pocket to call an ambulance. She ran back to Josh with Jess.

He was white, weak from loss of blood.

"I knew she was no match for you," he said between shivering lips. His skin was cold and clammy. The floor was painted ugly crimson.

Ellie sat him up. "The ambulance is coming. Please hang in. Don't leave me. We're finally free."

"I'm sorry." His voice was so weak she had to put her ear to his lips to hear it. "I brought all this on you. You never would have..."

"Stop talking like that. None of this is your fault. It never was."

"Where's the ambulance?" Jess roared.

"Let's get him up the stairs."

They tried to lift him, but he was too big, too heavy. He couldn't move and collapsed at the bottom of the stairs.

"Stay with me!" Ellie said between tears. "Don't go. Not now!"

"I'm sorry," Josh whispered and closed his eyes.

EPILOGUE

NINE MONTHS LATER

Ellie took a deep breath to steady her nerves. The echo of the nightmare she'd woken up from was still reverberating through her. The house was quiet. The morning sun, obscured by gray clouds, leaked through gaps between the blinds, but it wasn't enough. She flicked on the light in the bathroom and looked at her reflection. As she took in her tired eyes and pale complexion, flashes of Julia's dying moments appeared before her. They came less often now. Some days she barely thought of her at all. But those days were few and far between, and it was the night-time she feared most. That was when Julia came for her and those Ellie loved. She brushed her teeth and had a shower to wake herself up. As she emerged from the bathroom in her robe, with her hair in a towel, her phone buzzed beside her bed. It was Jess. Ellie's heart bloomed as she read the text.

> Guess what? I'm getting a ride down from New York today with Sloane. You want to meet for lunch in the city and I'll come home for the weekend?

Ellie couldn't type back fast enough.

> Sure! Can't wait. I have a showing this morning, but I can be in for about 1.30. Where do you want to go?

The answer came back within a few seconds.

> Let's treat ourselves. How about Parc on Rittenhouse?

> Those rich kids at Juilliard must be rubbing off on you. Can't wait!

Ellie put down the phone with a bright smile on her face. Jessica wasn't too far away but losing her to college was like having a part of her body amputated. She felt like half a person without her, but Jess wasn't a child anymore. Holding her close for her own selfish needs wasn't real love. Real love was letting her go.

Ellie went to her showing, an overpriced four-bed in Narberth that was selling for about ten times what the owner had paid for it thirty-five years earlier. Ellie tried not to look at her watch as the young clients talked about the house, but Jess was on her mind the entire conversation.

She drove into the city afterward and was sitting at the table in the bright French restaurant overlooking opulent Rittenhouse Square ten minutes early. Her daughter walked in wearing a white dress and a radiant smile. She'd never looked more beautiful. Something about her was different. Her little girl was gone, replaced by this brave, incredible young woman. The damage she'd suffered in her captivity was still there in her eyes, but her therapist was amazed by the progress she'd made in the short time they'd spent together so far, and the fact that she'd moved out to pursue her dreams as a musician amazed Ellie every day. Jess's recovery was progressing much like her own. It was taking some time, but her daughter was determined not to let what had happened hold her back.

Ellie greeted her as if she hadn't seen her in a year. It had been three weeks.

"You look gorgeous," Jess said.

"So do you! How's New York? Are you keeping up with your practice?"

"Yeah, you know me, I don't go out much, but I'm getting better."

Ellie reached over and took her daughter's hand as they sat down. "You were at that party on Thursday night. You're doing great!"

Jess laughed. "Not many moms I know encourage their kids to go out."

"I know I don't have to worry about the other things."

They were in the corner, just beside an old grand piano.

"You mind if I have a go? I play," Jess said to a passing waitress.

Ellie was puzzled. "What are you—?"

"Go right ahead," the waitress said with a sly smile.

Jess stood up without another word and sat at the piano. Ellie was shocked. Jess had never done anything like this before. She brought her fingers to the keys and began to play. Ellie felt tears welling in her eyes as her daughter began her favorite piece—Debussy's "Clair de Lune." Ellie settled back, letting the music wash over her, cherishing this precious time with her daughter.

She closed her eyes briefly and couldn't help seeing the scene from that night which invaded her mind. Pete Rivers had arrived at the lake house before the ambulance and helped lift Josh's unconscious body to his car. She'd held Josh's cold hand as Pete sped through the tiny roads to the hospital. Ellie had thought he'd slipped away several times, but the tourniquet they'd applied stopped just enough of his precious blood to keep him alive until they'd reached the hospital.

Ellie had expected the doctors to come out with grim faces to deliver the news, but Josh had had other ideas. The newspapers wrote about the miracle of his survival, but Ellie knew better. He wouldn't accept death.

She barely noticed him walk in, handsome as she'd ever seen him in a gray suit and tie. He was holding flowers in one hand with the other behind his back.

"What are you doing here?" Ellie asked.

Josh didn't answer. Jess gave her mom a knowing smile. Everything seemed to stop but the music. Josh handed her the flowers. She kissed him. He got down on one knee. The waitresses gasped. He reached for the box behind his back and opened it up to reveal a diamond ring.

"Ellie, I love you. I have from the moment I saw you, and I never stopped. I know now, I never will. Make me the happiest man in the world, and marry me."

Ellie turned to her daughter; both had tears running down their faces. "You knew about this!"

Jess and the waitresses laughed. The music built to a crescendo as Ellie turned to face Josh again. She nodded her head. "Yes!" was all she could manage before embracing him. The crowd in the packed restaurant erupted into applause. Jess ran over and threw her arms around them both. Nothing had ever felt so wonderful, so complete.

Another waitress came over. Ellie's heart constricted as she read her name tag—Julia. Josh squeezed Ellie's hand. Ellie took a deep breath and blew away the memories. She smiled, looked up at the puzzled young woman, and ordered champagne.

A LETTER FROM THE AUTHOR

Dear Reader,

I hope you enjoyed my book. If you'd like to hear about my new releases from Storm Publishing, you can sign up for my mailing list here.

www.stormpublishing.co/eoin-dempsey

Head over to my website to learn more and to sign up for my readers' club. It's free and always will be. If you want to get in touch with me send an email to eoin@eoindempseybooks.com. I love hearing from readers, so don't be a stranger! You can also follow me on Facebook and get to know me a little.

Reviews are the lifeblood of authors these days. If you enjoyed the book and can spare a minute, please leave a review on Amazon and/or Goodreads. My loyal and committed readers have put me where I am today, and their honest reviews have brought my books to the attention of other readers. I'd be eternally grateful if you could leave a review. It can be as short as you like.

This was my first ever psychological thriller, and I loved writing it! Get ready for a lot more!

Eoin

KEEP IN TOUCH WITH THE AUTHOR

www.eoindempseybooks.com

 facebook.com/eoindempseybooks

ACKNOWLEDGMENTS

A massive thank you to my technical advisors for this novel—Matt Coppa, Eric Kvelums, Cory Zarra, DJ Frimmer, and the irrepressible Jeff Slanina. Thank you to my wonderful editor, Claire Bord, without whom you wouldn't be reading these words! And thanks to all the team at Storm. Thanks to my family for their support. Extra special thanks to my gorgeous wife, Jill, who was the perfect sounding board for the ideas for this novel and who convinced me to change the original ending. It wouldn't have been half as good without her.

And lastly, thank you to my three sons, Robbie, Sam, and Jack, who, despite being the biggest disruptors to my writing process, remain my ultimate inspiration.

Made in the USA
Las Vegas, NV
21 July 2024